A VERSION OF THE TRUTH

A VERSION OF THE TRUTH

JENNIFER KAUFMAN
and KAREN MACK

DELACORTE PRESS

A VERSION OF THE TRUTH
A Delacorte Press Book / January 2008

Published by Bantam Dell
A Division of Random House, Inc.
New York, New York

This is a work of fiction. Names, characters, places, and incidents
either are the product of the authors' imagination or are used
fictitiously. Any resemblance to actual persons, living or dead, events,
or locales is entirely coincidental.

2|08

Book design by Jill Weber

Delacorte Press is a registered trademark of Random House, Inc.,
and the colophon is a trademark of Random House, Inc.

Library of Congress Cataloging-in-Publication Data
Kaufman, Jennifer.
A version of the truth / Jennifer Kaufman and Karen Mack.
p. cm.
ISBN-13: 978-0-385-34019-9
1. Women naturalists—Fiction. 2. Truthfulness and falsehood—
Fiction. I. Mack, Karen. II. Title.
PS3611.A837V47 2008
813'.6—dc22   2007026698

Printed in the United States of America
Published simultaneously in Canada

www.bantamdell.com

BVG   10   9   8   7   6   5   4   3   2   1

ACKNOWLEDGMENTS

A Version of the Truth is a work of fiction, but it is written with a belief in the mysterious and spiritual nature of our ever-shrinking wilderness. Like the narrator in Dante's *The Divine Comedy*, our heroine Cassandra finds herself lost in the wilderness—a wilderness of old-growth forests, threatened species, and a myriad of mythical characters. In an effort to create Cassie's strange and secret world, we turned to the classic nature writers and transcendentalists, including Ralph Waldo Emerson, Walt Whitman, Henry David Thoreau, and John Muir, all of whom had a visceral and passionate vision of the miracles in the wild and who ultimately found the truth of nature.

Regarding Cassie's odd and amazing sightings, we would like to acknowledge the works of several veteran birding experts who extensively researched and recorded the story of the "now-you-see-it-now-you-don't" ivory-billed woodpecker. Thanks to Tim Gallagher (*The Grail Bird*), who is credited with being one of the first people to see the iconic bird, Phillip Hoose (*The Race to Save the Lord God Bird*) and Jack Hitt (*13 Ways of Looking at an Ivory-Billed Woodpecker*).

As for the character "Sam," Cassie's quirky and lovable African gray, we would like to thank Sandi Shapiro and her parrot named Seymour, Joanna Burger for her informative, bittersweet *The Parrot Who Owns Me*, and Ruth Hanessian for her delightful guide, *Bird on the Couch*. Both of these authors owned and wrote about parrots that were strikingly similar to Jennifer's beloved and now departed Sara. We would also like to thank Sharman Russell (*An Obsession with Butterflies*) for her descriptions of Polygonia-C-albom and other wonders with wings.

Special thanks to the fine work and tireless dedication of the volunteers and staff of Malibu's California Wildlife Center in the Santa Monica Mountains. Their program of rescue, rehabilitation, and release saves thousands of native animals every year.

Our shy professor of geology, Hank, morphed into a bawdy-mouthed limerist thanks to Robert Nachman, who kindly allowed us to reprint several selections from his work. Also appreciation to Franck Verhagen, an artist and a gentleman.

Heartfelt thanks to Kim Dower, whose energy, ingenuity, and unflagging optimism never cease to amaze us. And to the brainy and talented Frances Jalet-Miller, the only person we know who could rewrite *War and Peace* and make it better.

Finally, we are grateful to the excellent people at Bantam Dell, especially our esteemed editor Danielle Perez for her keen intelligence, encouragement, and always astute guidance. And to our legendary literary agent and champion, Molly Friedrich, thanks for her integrity, humor, and sage advice.

And last and most important, to our families with gratitude and love.

A VERSION OF THE TRUTH

PART ONE

"You are what you pretend to be."

KURT VONNEGUT JR.

Prologue

I flunked the second, third, and ninth grades. In my heart, I knew I was dumb. No one actually said it. In fact, everyone went to great lengths to avoid the issue altogether. I wasn't dumb, I was simply the opposite of smart—which, at the time, meant slow, unfocused, undisciplined, and uncooperative. My mother used to insist that I had faulty wiring. As if I were some kind of dud appliance. I can't tell you how many times I wanted to quit. I finally did when I was sixteen. Instead of driving lessons, my mother agreed to let me get my high-school equivalency. The fact of the matter is we were both worn out.

Like the way I felt when Frank, drunk as a skunk, flew off the highway in his F150 Supercharged Lightning and got himself killed. A witness described my husband's truck as skidding off the cliff into the ocean like a set of dishes sliding off a tray. I imagined him speeding toward home at midnight in his usual state of bonhomie, his Johnny Cash CD blasting away, his Hawaiian shirt whipping in the wind, and then—*boom!* All that hotshot charisma and sex appeal smashed to smithereens.

It was rotten weather the next morning when the cops drove up to break the news. The rains came freakishly late in the early spring and then just hung around—wet, sloppy streets, dead leaves, the sky the color of dirty dishwater. They must have thought I was a pretty tough cookie as they handed me the baggie with his personal items, his blood-stained address book, his wallet, his watch, and the change that had jangled in his pocket. I think they worried I'd gone into shock. But I'd already done that a few years back when the poison in our marriage lurked under the surface like a jellyfish. He was dead and I wasn't mourning.

I'm not a bad person. Really. It's just that I'm not the grieving widow. And that's not acceptable in our society unless maybe you've murdered the son of a bitch, which I didn't. But, as the therapist told me in our community center shortly after the funeral, when I confessed my lack of feelings, I was the epitome of freeway fantasy for divorcees and unhappy housewives. Here's how it goes. Your partner walks out of the house one morning and shortly thereafter you get *the* call, the one you've been hoping for all those lousy years. It's clean. It's final. You're free. A life cut short by a happy coincidence.

The worst part was the week after the funeral. My mother and I sat, side by side, on Frank's shiny leather sofa, like two crows on a telegraph wire, as the procession of people with sympathetic faces and hushed voices paraded by. The silences were long and awkward. There's no way anyone can start a halfway interesting conversation at a time like this. You can't exactly talk about something fun you've done the weekend before or anything good that's going on in your life—parties, business successes, vacations, or big purchases. And you dare not refer to the growing pile of grief-counseling books stacked on the coffee table. *When God Doesn't Make Sense, The Grief Recovery Handbook*, four copies of *Why Bad Things Happen to Good People*, and a paperback version of *Living Through Personal Crisis* (this one might actually be of some use).

No. You are limited to a very narrow range of topics. Like the food, the memorial service, recapping the accident (at what exact angle did the truck career off the cliff), and by the way, where do you keep the scotch? Most of the time, people end up drinking too much and telling unfunny vignettes about the deceased.

"Remember the time Frank got totally blasted and cannonballed naked into the pool at that wedding and got all the bridesmaids' dresses soaked?" Ha ha ha. "Cassie, is there anything I can do?" Everybody asks me that as they plunge their raw carrots into the sour cream dip.

Wouldn't they like to know. How about paying off Frank's credit cards, getting rid of the ugly football trophies from his high school days, dumping his drug paraphernalia hidden in his smelly sock drawer. Oh, and how about picking up his ashes, selecting the urn, and delivering it to his family in Florida who couldn't bother to come out but assured me they would be having their own memorial service as soon as they get the remains and by the way, could I send them his computer, his junky macho furnishings, his country western collection, and yes, even his truck, which I'd be only too happy to ship if it weren't flattened like a coin on a railroad track. They also asked about his life insurance policy, which he cashed in several years ago to buy the fucking truck.

I know it's not good to speak ill of the dead. But is dishonesty any better? Most of the people who come here mean well. Even if they have it all wrong. They're coming here to pay their respects to someone who didn't much like them and to offer their sympathy to someone who doesn't want it. Okay. He did have a few friends who will miss him. And, despite his disloyalty to me, he was a good friend to them. My mother has always believed there is good and bad in everyone. I should remember that.

But still, I'm not grieving. I do, however, suffer from guilt, festering anger, frustration, and, oh yes, did I mention that I'm broke? It *is* a kind of grief, let me assure you. I didn't always feel this way. There was a time when I just wanted him to love me. Not in a passionate way. I didn't hope for that. I wanted him to love me in the way one goes about an ordinary life—doing the same mundane things, following the same uneventful routines, knowing what comes next, day after day, until you lie in bed beside him at night and listen to the familiar sounds of traffic way off in the distance. I wanted him to call me when he got there, or when he was on his way home or if he was late or stuck in traffic and wanted to just hear the sound of my voice the way I wanted to hear his. I wanted him to leave me money for groceries, fix the DVD player, tell me to drive carefully, complain about the business, leave wet towels on the bathroom floor, admire my dress but add that it might be too low or too tight.

In the last few months he was barely there at all. Mornings, he was out the door before I even had my coffee, and we rarely talked all day. When I called him, his voice sounded gruff, like he was in the middle of something, but he never called me back. We didn't have a set dinner hour or anything like that, and pretty soon I stopped asking what he'd like to eat because he always said he didn't care. The last time I fixed him dinner he complained that the chicken was half-cooked and shoved the plate so hard across the table, it fell into my lap and then crashed to the floor. Even before he admitted he was seeing someone else, I figured it out. I'm not that dumb.

When I told him to get rid of her or I was leaving, he did what most men do. He lied. In my experience, men would rather commit hara-kiri than tell you to your face they prefer someone else. But then he told me he'd change, resenting me for it, and zeroed in on the one thing that brought me to my knees. He made me feel dumb. You shouldn't tell people your darkest secrets. It always comes back to bite you.

In the end, he broke my heart. Even a louse can break your heart. The progression of it all was swift and constant, like the onset of rain in November and then freezing winds in winter. I couldn't swallow, I couldn't sit down, I couldn't concentrate. It was like a cold, hard sentence. I could tell when he used a false tone or eyed me with stony resentment. I learned the routine, the mechanical switching of the mouth, that nervous thing he did with his fingers when he lied. So there I sat in an empty house, the mail piled up in a dump heap by the door, unread soggy newspapers littering the lawn. Me, lying in bed all afternoon, drapes drawn, lights dimmed, overdue DVDs scattered around like unwanted possessions put out with the trash.

"Hi, honey, how're you doing?"

"Great, Mom. Frank and I are on our way out. Going to a dinner party."

"That's nice, dear. Is it fancy?"

"Sort of. I'm wearing my new cocktail dress."

"Don't forget the hostess gift." Oh yes. A lovely little grenade would be perfect.

"Absolutely."

"You two have a good time now."

I felt ashamed, the way I did in school when I'd study all week and still blow the test.

Eventually, I just wore myself out. I got sick of struggling, immune to failure, and, finally, felt nothing at all. I quit. I simply didn't love him anymore.

No one ever plans for this to happen. I remember the first time I met him, four years ago. He was tall and lean with high cheekbones and sleek black hair pulled back in a ponytail, like a samurai. A mixture of brute force and grace. Who knew he had the heart of a cockroach. He was holding a wounded red-tailed hawk that he jokingly called roadkill. When he walked into the Topanga Wildlife Center, where I worked with my mother, he looked around like a warrior, his black, penetrating eyes fixed on my face. He reminded me of a falcon. Predatory and dangerous. I should have known better. Biologist Konrad Lorenz has proven that baby chicks run for cover when they see a silhouette of a falcon—even a plywood model.

We talked a bit. Later he called. He was cool, aloof, with a sexy languor about him. Trouble. Like the devil himself. Handsome and terrific in bed. He liked my long legs, he said, my dark water-green eyes, my wide mouth, and the fact that I didn't chatter on and on like other women. I've always thought I was plain, but he made me feel pretty. He swooped me up. Came on strong. Decided it was time for him to get married. All his friends were married off. Lucky me. The timing was perfect. He proposed after two months. I felt grateful to have him.

After we got married, I started helping him part-time in his business, a towing company located on Pacific Coast Highway. Every day, surfers, stoners, and tourists would park their cars illegally along the highway and come back wet and tired to an empty space. His lot was behind the Mobil station across the street from the most expensive shopping area in Malibu, and he stacked up so many cars on beautiful sunny weekends that it looked like a parking lot for a rock festival or a giant swap meet. I worked in a cramped, air-conditioned office/trailer that sat at the top of a stony, dusty road leading to the lot. Anxious people in everything from wet suits to bikinis and flip-flops would show up there at all hours, sometimes in cabs or on foot, staring numbly at a handwritten sign which informed them that they owed Frank's Towing $240.00 (no checks!), plus $65.00 a day for storage, plus whatever the city parking ticket was for leaving their cars in a tow-away zone.

Often, they'd leave their wallets or purses in the vehicle and I'd have to accompany them like convicts to their car, unlock it, and stand there while they grabbed their stuff then lock it back up again.

"Don't you give them the keys," Frank would warn me. "They'll split if they get the chance."

"How can they split? You've got them stacked in. Give the kids a break," I'd always say, looking at their sandy bare feet and sweaty, stressed-out faces.

"Who told them to park there? Did I tell them to park there? I just do what the cops tell me to do. Don't be such a bleeding heart," he'd say contemptuously, flashing a hostile smile.

In one afternoon, Frank would go through an assortment of moods. From "fuck you" indifference to moody sulks to chattering, hustle-like rants. He survived on his wits and scared me out of mine. I could always tell when he was about to blow—he'd get the fixed eye of a man with a serious grievance—bullying eyebrows, and those muscles around the mouth would tense up and sort of pop. I'd sit there rigid, waiting for the unpleasantness that filled the air to disperse, then I'd get on with my day.

Working in the lot, I always felt like a crumb, especially with the kids who didn't have any money. I'd sit at my desk, avoiding their gazes as they called their parents. Then I'd listen to their sad, sad stories, feeling their embarrassment. One kid had to wait for about six hours until his mother got off work in the city and then drove all the way to the beach to bail him out. In rush hour. That may have been the day I'd added up the bill wrong, messing up the numbers, and Frank got so steamed he scrawled "BIRDBRAIN" like graffiti across the back of my chair.

Then, in a voice barely above a whisper, but with the force of a shout, he announced in front of everybody that this was a place of business, not "The House of Dumbness," and that I was a freak of nature—a flunky with no future. I walked right out on my job that day. Quit. Indeed I did. I told him I preferred working at the wildlife center. In retrospect, I should have walked out on him.

It doesn't really matter anymore. Seems Frank had mortgaged the business to the hilt and cross-collateralized it with our house. I've now moved back in with my mother, to my childhood home on the crest of Topanga Canyon, a small community thirty minutes from LA, with one traffic light and one turtle-crossing sign. It's the kind of neighborhood where people are slightly vague about how many dogs or cats they own, so they simply leave out giant bowls of kibble by the back door. You see mangy, one-eared cats lazing around people's porches, elaborate wind chimes, and hand-carved birdhouses. My mother calls it rustic (as opposed to seedy) and I tend to agree with her.

My backyard is part of the Santa Monica Mountains Conservancy, almost six hundred miles of hiking trails, forests, and valleys. It's a wild, uninhabitable mountainous area with dark forests, lakes, waterfalls, mysterious caverns, and lush green canopies filled with the songs of hundreds of birds.

As a child I was free to roam the hills with no thoughts of my shortcomings or deficiencies. I'd spend whole weekends in the outdoors in a dreamlike state of opulent imaginings, making up stories of my accomplishments and amazing feats. I'd see bobcats, wolves, coyotes, foxes, and red-tailed hawks who torpedoed down like missiles to impale their prey. I was at home in this world, never afraid of animals. Even the dangerous ones.

❡ ❡ ❡

So now I've done my bit, sitting in the living room with acquaintances and distant relatives like my great-aunt Stella who tried to buck me up with depressing clichés from her grief counseling sessions, such as "closure" and "circle of caring." Thankfully, no one drops by anymore. My mother and I have finished wrapping the hardened, half-eaten casseroles and cakes and storing them in the freezer. I walk into my cramped bedroom that didn't seem this small when I was a child and look out the narrow window toward the mountains.

This used to be my favorite time of year. Soon the Monarch butterflies will make their spectacular migration along the California coast on their way to Mexico. They arrive here every year in the same spot, brilliant blotches of yellow and black, dripping from the trees like fall foliage. They litter the driveways and cover the windshields of the cars. I'm always so careful not to crush their delicate wings as I gently sweep them from the steps of our house.

I always tell people, you don't need to go to the Amazon or New Guinea to be wonderstruck by nature—you can just walk out my front door any day in the fall and you'll see those glorious beings, flitting and darting in the air—a rush of iridescent color—like fairies or angels in disguise. It doesn't matter what kind of mood you're in, or even if you're in no mood at all and just carrying on, like a robot, trying to get through the day. There they are—swirling in

the air like escaping bits of fragmented color from a kaleido-
scope.

My mother says that watching Monarchs is solace for the
pain of living. I guess I wouldn't go that far but they're a
miracle just the same. They follow the sun—fly as far as fifty
miles a day and as high as a hundred feet. Then they end up
in Mexico right on schedule, around November 2, the Day
of the Dead. Legend says they are the souls of dead relatives
returning home. Lord, I hope not.

CHAPTER 1

I didn't intend to lie on my resume. It just happened. It was after the icy reception I received at the last two employment agencies. The first time, a man with a rodent-like profile, eyes too close together, and a gnawing slash of a mouth suggested I try getting a job at a pet store. The next agent walked me to the door of her office after a quick glance at my resume and said the only thing she could possibly think of was telemarketing from my home—check the classifieds.

As you can imagine, I was feeling pretty deflated as I headed for yet another employment agency. This one had a bulletin board near the entrance, cluttered with notices such as "Accent Elimination" (as if it's some kind of disease). "Speak American, Free Consultation." I noticed no one had torn off the fringed bottom with scrawled vertical telephone numbers. I sat in a cracked vinyl armchair still warm from the last sweaty bottom, filling out forms, but even in this dump, the agent couldn't get rid of me fast enough.

So here's my situation. Considering my educational background (a graduate of the University of Nowheresville) and my age (thirty), I am now virtually unemployable. My years at the wildlife center didn't seem to matter to anyone, especially the employment agencies. They just whizzed right by it and focused on my education or lack of it. "Tell us again why you left high school?" As if I had no business even being there.

My mother was always trying to reassure me, her optimism unflinching. "They'll be sorry they didn't hire you. All the studies say that slow starters are more likely to become billionaires."

"What study was that, Mom?"

"I read it in the dentist's office."

It feels like I'm back in elementary school, where I had failure written all over me. What seemed to come effortlessly for everyone else was torture for me.

"Cassie, try not to hold your pencil like a spike," the teacher would urge, breathing down my neck like a truant officer and wincing at my abominable handwriting. "And stop sucking on your lip so hard. Lord, you'll tear it to pieces. Why don't you just take a deep breath and start over later."

That was the signal I eventually waited for—she gave up and so did I. You'd think she'd put a stop to my misery but the fact was she just didn't get it and neither did anyone else. The rest of the year I was either "sick" or late on Fridays, very late. It didn't make any difference, I was the dunce in the corner with a scarlet *D* on my chest.

Sometimes I'd hear a friend of my mother's talking about her child, little Stacy or darling Susie. "My daughter is amazing. She just woke up one morning and could read everything."

"Is that so?" my mother would reply in a monotone. "What a marvel."

I kept thinking, "Why didn't that happen to me?" When would I "just wake up" and be able to read? And then later, with each mounting failure, "What's so great about reading anyway?"

My mother would sit with me for hours reading things she thought I'd like. Her favorite was an illustrated anthology of Greek myths. We read about gods and heroes like Athena, Diana, Aphrodite, Zeus. The stories I liked the most were the ones where humans changed into birds or beasts or flowers. But my mother liked the stories where the gods bestowed special powers on mortals. I guess that's why she named me Cassandra. After the beautiful goddess who could see the future. She loved the magic—that's what she was hoping for me when she'd hand me the book—but I still couldn't read a word.

In junior high, I made up the plots of the books I read based on the first and last chapters. As a result, my test scores on comprehension were all over the place. Sometimes I guessed right. Sometimes I didn't. I was a whiz at basic algebra, but if I had to solve how far Mr. Smith traveled on a train from his home in Phoenix to his regional office in Albuquerque and at what velocity it collided with a freight train carrying textiles to Tucson—well, you get the picture. All through school, kids whispered "dim" or "dense" or "dumbbell." Not my friends, though. We never talked about my "problem." Mostly, they were oblivious. They'd always get rewarded with As and I'd get my usual Ds.

"God, Cassie, that test was so easy," they'd say incredulously.

"I didn't study." I'd laugh, like it meant nothing. *Heathers* became my favorite movie.

Eventually, I figured out the way to survive. Most kids do. I hid my tests and assignments like they were pornography. When my mother asked how I did on my spelling test, I'd say, "Great," and if she questioned me about my homework, I'd tell her, "I did it at school." "Doing it at school" meant shoving it in my desk along with a half dozen other worksheets I found impossible to complete. I'd always get found out, of course. The teacher would call my mother, who'd ask, "What's the matter with you?" We'd spend holiday weekends completing all the work that everyone else had finished during school. The threat of "special ed" loomed over me like a death sentence.

So the masquerade went on. I made small strides. But mostly I feigned boredom or talked to my neighbor. In the meantime, my imagination soared. I made up words. I invented spelling. I created wild fantasies in my mind that were ever so much more entertaining than anything I tried to read at school.

"Once upon a time, a bunch of mean, foulmouthed bullies wandered into the woods to gather berries . . ."

It was about this time my burnt-out mother hired a beautiful silver-haired tutor named Janet Monroe. She lived in a lovely little cottage with a view of the ocean. The plan was for me to go to her house once a week over the summer. But, after an initial evaluation, she recommended two-hour sessions three times a week. In the beginning, I felt like a rich kid, although I was well aware that this was a serious financial burden on my mother.

Every afternoon, Mrs. Monroe would lead me through her house to an airy, sun-drenched porch filled with leafy palms, overstuffed furniture, and faded Persian rugs. You had to take your shoes off when you walked in and then say hello to her parrot—a magnificent African gray named Sam who imitated her voice and learned my name pronto. He gave me my first whistle and screeched a flirtatious "Hi, gorgeous!"

All through that summer I struggled with the process of decoding—learning how a written word represents a sound. It's something most kids take for granted, like swimming or riding a bike. But for me, it was hard work.

"This just happens sometimes to smart kids," Mrs. Monroe told my mother in a breathy smoker's voice that trailed off into nothingness. "You have a reading disorder called dyslexia." I was trying to digest all this when she asked Sam to tell her who, besides me, had a similar problem in their youth. That bird was so damn brilliant. He shot back, "Einstein, Rockefeller, Edison, Picasso, Walt Disney, and John Lennon."

"There," she'd say when he was done. "You're in fine company."

We did a lot of workbook exercises and read out loud. Sam would imitate my labored, choppy voice when I read, memorize passages, and give me a beaky kiss when I was done. I got so I couldn't wait to see him. Then it was September and I went back to school. I never saw Mrs. Monroe again.

Sometime in the fall, she called to tell us that she was ill. A month later, my mother came home with Sam. Mrs. Monroe had died and left him to me. The note on the cage read, "Dear Cassie, next to me, you are Mrs. Monroe's favorite student."

Parrots mate for life, but somehow Sam accepted me. The South American tribes believe parrots have human souls. And I'd have to agree. He'd sidle up my arm after school and kiss me all over my mouth and ears. Sometimes he'd say, "Love you. Miss you. Did you pass?" Okay, so he was repeating my mother, but still, he meant it. Other times he'd repeat my depressing downers.

"I'm just a dumbfuck!" I'd shout.

And he'd repeat with glee, "Dumbfuck! Dumbfuck! Dumbfuck!"

"Shut up!" I'd yell.

"No!" he'd squawk back, flapping his wings and bobbing his head. Sam loved to get me all riled up. It was just a game to him, my deficiencies.

When Sam and I first moved in with Frank, they took an immediate dislike to each other. When we'd argue, that parrot would fasten his small beady eyes on Frank, morph into his aggressive pose, crouch low on his perch with his wings outspread, and peck furiously at Frank's face and hands. Maybe it was Frank's tone of voice.

"Close the fucking door!" Frank would yell at me as he retreated from Sam's sharp-hooked beak.

"Close the fucking door! Close the fucking door!" Sam would shriek back in Frank's exact same voice as if he were mocking him. Parrots do not grow meek in the face of anger.

The two of them never did make peace, even though I tried to reason with Sam. He continued to bedevil Frank in sly little ways. He could imitate the telephone and the doorbell so perfectly that at least once a night Frank would go running to the door and Sam would cackle and scream, "Dumbfuck!"

More than once, Frank told me to give Sam away or he was going to "kill that fucking bird." It got so bad that at one point I told my mother she'd have to take him for a while till things cooled down. Sam's not mourning either.

I get back in my car and head to a small employment

agency across from the university that came highly recommended . . . from the Yellow Pages. As I walk in the door, I overhear the agent tell a woman, "Sorry. That's all I have. You know, these days a BA is no better than high school. You really need an advanced degree to get yourself out of the assistant pool."

So what pool am I swimming in? Maybe the cesspool. I watch the woman leave. Sleek is the word I'd use to describe her. I pull on the elastic waist of my khaki pants. I'll never look like that. What does it take, anyway, to look put together like that?

No, I'm not sleek, I'm ordinary—sort of like a generic brand of human being. I don't naturally stand out like some women I know. Although my mother would disagree. She tells me I have "good bones" like one of those characters in her classic myths and that all her friends think I'm beautiful. But I certainly don't feel that way, especially when I walk into a room. Frank used to call it the "wow" factor, something that makes people notice you. Maybe it's my hair. I wear it pulled back in a long ponytail with Peter Pan bangs in the front. I don't know, I've always done it that way. Frank liked it that way too. Every time I wore it down, he'd ask me why.

"You look better with it off your face," he'd say. But after we got married, he never did say I looked good. Come to think of it, whenever I got dressed up he'd tell me I looked like I tried too hard.

I take the application form and slowly start to fill it out. Name: Cassie Shaw.

Education: There it is. I remember watching the Rose Bowl one year with Frank. Who played? Wasn't it one of those big schools in the Midwest? Michigan or Wisconsin. An arena filled with thousands of cheering students. Who'd ever know? A place where when asked what it was like I could just laugh and say, "Cold as hell." Okay. I'm doing it. Michigan. I know about Michigan. They make cars there. Shit. Major: Now what? My hands are shaking. Well, I'm turning into a psychopath, so how about psychology? Sounds good. Everyone knows about psychology.

I fill out the rest—driver's license, Social Security number, address (my mother's post office box, we haven't had mail delivered in two years), age, etc. When you really think about it, most of the application is true. Anyway, doesn't everyone lie on these things?

"So how'd you like Michigan?" the agent asks. I focus on a hairy plant in a too-small plastic pot on the windowsill with roots trailing out the bottom like worms.

"Cold as hell," I reply. She laughs.

"Well, I see why you're here. Psychology. What can you do with that?"

"Right." I laugh conspiratorially.

"It says here, after the wildlife center, you worked at your husband's towing business."

"Yes, I did. He recently died." Okay. So I played the widow card. Sue me.

She immediately softens. I hate that look. Pity. Surprise. I can hear her thinking, "And so young too."

"Well, we don't have much right now, but we do have an entry-level job at the university. And it is in behavioral sciences, so you have some background."

I am oddly pleased by the compliment—even though it's based on a total lie.

"Look, I'm not going to kid you. Basically, it's answering phones, typing, delivering mail, filing, you know, front-office stuff." Better than the back-office stuff I haven't been offered. I casually agree to go on an interview. I'm elated. That is, until I hit the street, at which point I start to get nervous about my lies. But this wasn't just a lie. It was a Category 2, maybe Category 3 lie. Oh, come on. Frank was a lying piece of shit and God didn't strike him down. Well . . . I carefully look both ways before crossing the street.

CHAPTER 2

The campus looms in front of me, high on a hill, like Oz. Red brick buildings, landscaped lawns, grassy areas with footpaths and sculptures. I pass under a canopy of leaves through the Van Dorman Gates, black ornate wrought iron supported by two imposing pillars, one of which is inscribed with the words of Cicero.

"The first duty of a man is the seeking after and the investigation of Truth." I continue walking, gripping my resume. I'm not going to think about the consequences.

Liar. Liar. Pants on fire.

When I was a kid, Sunday school was all about God and Satan, the Twelve Apostles, the Ten Commandments, and the Seven Deadly Sins. The world as we knew it was ordered and manageable, with hundreds of laws and punishments methodically arranged according to the gravity of the transgression. There seemed to be no gray

area when it came to sin—just a cold, stark landscape of excruciatingly painful punishments or heavenly rewards de-
pending on the path you took.

I remember the teacher stabbing the blackboard with a
piece of chalk as she repeated a bunch of *thou shalt not*s.
Thou shalt not kill. Stab. Thou shalt not steal. Stab. Stab.
Thou shalt not commit adultery. Negative, negative. Life is
so much more complicated than that. And frankly, even as a
shy and earnest kindergartner, I never related that much to
the subject matter.

I believed in God in a general way but not in eternal
damnation. If you did commit a sin, sure, there were consequences, but I knew in my heart, even when I was six, that
God would never stand by and watch someone get boiled in
cauldrons of oil or smothered in fire and brimstone like
they were saying on that religious channel one Sunday
morning when I was sick and couldn't go to church.

When you come right down to it, I guess I believe that
being a good person is all about your conscience, and
whether or not you can live with what you do. On the other
hand, there are sociopaths who murder teenage girls and
have no guilt whatsoever . . . giant spiritual blind spots. My
Sunday school teachers kept repeating over and over that
the important thing for us, as good Christians, was to live
without sin. However, as I recall, there is no *Thou shalt not
lie* in the Ten Commandments. They sort of allude to it
with the bearing false witness thing, but there's no out-and-
out *no lying* commandment. And don't you think if it were
that important it would have been one of the Big Ten?

Maybe it's because there are grades of truthfulness. Fibs,
white lies, half-truths, stretching the truth (as if it were as
elastic as a rubber band), cock-and-bull stories, even a
whopper doesn't have the stench of unadulterated evil. It's

like telling someone you're sick if you just want to stay home, eat popcorn, and watch the Home Shopping Network. Or telling someone they look great when they've gained a ton of weight, or oohing and aahing over your friend's newborn even though it looks like a hairless monkey. Or telling someone they're smart when they're not. Everyone in the universe does it—except for animals. Then again, look at Sam. If you can talk, it's unavoidable.

And I'm not saying this to justify my actions. What was I supposed to do? Tell the employment agency that I didn't dare take the SAT—that I only got my high school equivalency and that, even now, if I don't focus when I read, the words are jumbled. They wouldn't care how far I've come, they'd only look at my resume. They wouldn't care that I've finally learned how to read like a normal person, just slower.

I enter University Hall and approach a young woman sitting behind the low wood reception desk. She has shiny, shoulder-length blonde hair cut to sweep her shoulders just so, a fawn-colored sweater, and she's wearing pointy red flats that stick out from under the desk. She looks like she could get away with anything. Even cruise out of Wal-Mart (as if she would ever go there) with a cart full of unpaid-for items and the security guard would just smile and say, "Have a nice day."

That would never happen to me. When we were still in high school, my best friend, Tiffany, and I decided on a dare to go to the 7-Eleven on the corner and lift something. I trotted to the register with a small diversion purchase, a pack of gum, as Tiff slipped a few candy bars down her blouse pretending to adjust her bra. I was so nervous I blew the whole deal, but the manager never called the police. He had a thing for Tiff. Everyone always had a thing for Tiff. She was just one of those girls. Like the receptionist who's waiting for me to say something. I smile real friendly like.

"Hi. I'm the one they called about from the agency. You know, for the job opening."

"Excuse me?" she intones with a withering stare.

"I'm Cassie Shaw. I have an appointment with a Mrs. . . ." Oh God, what's her name. I fumble for the piece of paper. "Pearce?"

"You mean, *Professor* Pearce?" With the emphasis on, You moron, she's a professor.

"Yeah, I guess so." She picks up the phone and gives me a quick smile, as if she's thinking of some private joke.

"Hey, this is Alison. Does the professor have an appointment with someone this morning?" Silence. "Okay, I'll tell her." She looks at me like I'm a piece of lint.

"You must have the wrong department. This is Psych. Sorry." She dismisses me and goes back to her reading.

"I'm sure this is the right place. I was sent over by the Right Hand Gal Agency."

"Oh." Her look says it all.

"Hey, it's Alison again. She's from the Right Hand Gal Agency?" Pause. She laughs. It's not a nice laugh.

"She's a little busy right now. You can wait over there," she says with an air of distaste, pointing to a small reception area in the back.

Tiff and I have a list we like to call the Guinness Book of Rude Behavior. The items include things like people hogging two parking spaces at the mall. Or leaving their shopping cart wherever so it blocks everyone's car. Or sitting in their car guzzling on water bottles, adjusting their seat belts, reapplying lip gloss, even making calls on their cell phones while you wait there for what seems like hours for their fucking space. Or the salesperson who's having a conversation with another salesperson while you're waiting for them to help you. Or the clod who rolls his suitcase over your toes and doesn't even say boo. The elevator witch is also on this list. She's the one who stands there, stone-faced, while you plead with her to keep the door open as you try to swipe your hand through the ever-narrowing space. She looks straight through you as she shuts you down. Like you're invisible.

I look out the window. There's a small courtyard in the middle of the U-shaped ivy-clad red brick building. Students are lounging on benches or lying in the grass with their heads resting on backpacks, nuzzling each other in the sunlight. It looks like they have all the time in the world to throw Frisbees, drink Coca-Cola, and read thick novels.

They remind me of the fresh-faced, optimistic volunteers who used to work at the wildlife center. Most of them were college kids on internships. A brief stop on their way to somewhere else. The center was an old cabin that used to belong to some famous writer with a floor-to-ceiling river rock fireplace. We'd all sit around the potbellied stove, drink gallons of coffee, and talk for hours. They always had so many plans. A semester in South America to study the rain forest or in Austria to study ravens. A vacation in Hawaii for spring break. Boyfriends in law school. Girlfriends in pre-med classes. Endless possibilities. They went on and on about "following their passion." I'd just try to get through the day.

I came to the conclusion they were members of some club and I would never belong. It hit home in dozens of little ways as I'd go about my duties. Class rings left by the bathroom sink. Treasure hunts for lost diamond studs. Fancy cars with environmental stickers and college parking passes lined up next to my banged-up piece of shit. And then I met Frank, and we all know how that turned out.

Now I hear something that sounds like fat, meaty bugs

smashing against a windshield. I glance out the window. And then I see him. He's tall and lean with sandy-colored hair that flies in his eyes as he chases down a tennis ball and swats it against the side of the building. The ball ricochets off the wall and sails off into the sky. Without missing a beat, he grabs another ball from his back pocket and begins again. Thwack! His arms are long and muscular and he's wearing faded red shorts with a worn navy T-shirt. He exudes pedigree, like a well-bred ridgeback. Not classically handsome, but someone who demands attention.

"Hey, Sampras!" someone yells from a second-floor window. "You ready? We gotta go." He squints up into the sunlight and smiles. I see him sweep his arm across his forehead, still gripping his tennis racquet as he walks into the building.

"Hello, Professor Conner," Alison purrs, flashing shiny perfect white teeth. Her whole demeanor has changed. As he walks by, he leaves a scent of cut grass, mixed with sweat and aftershave. I notice that, on closer inspection, he has a firm, self-possessed air that belies his messy hair and distracted look. He bounds up the stairs.

Now it's just the mean princess with nice clothes and a job, and me. She glances over with an "are you still here?" kind of look. I pick up an academic journal on the table and pretend to read. Her cell phone rings some new agey Chinese gongs. (Tiff just changed her ring tone to a '56 Chevy burning rubber.) She now gets into a discussion with her pal "Lanie" about the "extravagantly minimalist" exhibit she saw at some gallery last night.

"Looking at the images made me realize why I love Chekhov." Pause. "No. I told him I was busy tonight." Pause. Giggles. "Shut up. Good-bye." More giggles. I want to scream. I've been sitting here for almost an hour.

I march up to the desk. "Excuse me. I have another interview. Could you please see what's going on?" Alison wraps it up and rings upstairs.

"You can go up now." She starts to walk down the hall, leaving me wondering where exactly "up" is.

"What room, please . . . ?"

"Two-five-four, second door on the right," she yells over her shoulder. I hate her.

I hesitantly climb the stairs, trying to rein in my heroic doubts, and knock on the door. A clipped voice on the other side says, "It sticks, just give it a whack and it'll open."

I give it a little hit, nothing. Then I pound it with my fist. The door flies open and bashes against the wall.

"Brilliant. Come in," Professor Pearce says with a marked British accent and a welcoming smile—not at all what I expected. She's around seventy with dark, bright eyes and wild curly gray hair that has so much static it almost sticks straight up from her head. She wears thick black owl-like bifocals and a stiff, wide-lapeled Queen Elizabeth suit in a pheasant shade of teal. She could be some grand lady in a portrait holding one of those misshapen pug-faced little lapdogs, except for the hair and the glasses.

Her office has the same look—dignified yet odd. Wood-paneled bookshelves line the walls, framing a red brick fireplace with carved mantel. Classical music is playing. Papers and journals are piled high on her desk, along with a bunch of little oddities scattered here and there. Antique fireplace instruments with horse head handles. Ceramic bulldogs with blood red tongues. Pictures in fancy frames. Group shots of distinguished-looking people in tuxedos and academic robes. Smiling, confident, and successful.

"Sorry about the wait. Apparently some mix-up on the time. So here you are. What can you do for us?" she says, glancing up at me over her lenses with an air of familiarity and authority.

"Oh. I was told the job was just office work, but I'd be happy to do whatever you need. I can do all sorts of things. Even change your tires." Ha ha. I laugh nervously. She doesn't crack a smile.

"Why don't you tell me about yourself?"

I take a deep breath. "Well . . . I used to work for my husband in the automobile business—office stuff mainly, but he recently died, and I thought I'd try something totally different."

Her face softens. I'm just a broken record. When things get tough—play the widow card.

"There you go, then. We have something in common. I lost my husband five years ago. It's not easy, is it? Was he ill?"

"No. Never. He had a fireman's pulse. Drove his car right off a cliff. And that was the end of him, stone cold dead."

"How dreadful," she says, giving me an odd look. "My husband had Huntington's. Sometimes I think it's better the other way," she adds, as she opens her drawer, pulls out two little teacups and a silver flask with a *P* etched on the front.

"Sherry?" I'm thinking, is this some kind of test? Who drinks sherry at this hour? I'm just going to be polite.

"Oh, thank you," I say, carefully. Pearce is already pouring.

"Well, the job is mainly working for me and Professor Conner, filing, transcribing, phones and mail, helping coordinate department events, and some special projects. He's been wanting his library organized, for example, before it spills out into the hallway and carries us all into chaos," she says, lifting her see-through porcelain cup to her lips with a flourish, raising her deeply arched eyebrows, and downing it in one gulp. There are chains of little violets circling the cup, gathered up in pink ribbons and bows.

"He's got Descartes next to Deepak Chopra, and Muir next to Miller. Henry, that is, not Arthur." Pearce starts to laugh. I nod nervously, trying to remember which one is which. I haven't really read a serious book of literature since stumbling through it in high school.

She asks me a few perfunctory questions about my non-existent education, the wildlife center, and then she spends the rest of the interview telling me about her years at Oxford, her books, her children, her other two husbands, and a "dear friend" of hers who just moved to town. I notice that she fills her cup several more times before she excuses herself to go to the restroom. This is the best interview I've ever had. I'm buzzed, I haven't said two words, and I think I have the job.

When Professor Pearce bustles back into the room, cheeks flushed, eyes twinkling, it feels as though everything's been decided.

"I've so enjoyed our little chat. You'll start tomorrow?"

I'm about to answer when Professor Tennis Player sticks his head in the door. He's changed into a white button-down oxford shirt, jeans, and a beat-up leather jacket, and he has a thick manila folder under his arm stuffed with papers. His eyes are an undecided shade of blue, and there's a natural glamour about him. I can't exactly say why, but he makes me feel self-conscious. Looking at him makes me think of East Coast things like grandfather clocks, silver cocktail shakers, or that girl from high school who got early admittance to Smith and told everybody about a million times that her ancestors came over on the *Mayflower*.

"You coming?" he asks Pearce, as she motions him in with a brisk, imperious wave.

"We just have to wait for Samantha, if you don't mind," he adds as he walks into the office, sets down his folder, and cups his eyes for a moment from the glare of sunlight streaming through the window. Then he sees me. I wonder, just for a second, whether this man's brain matches his folder—a brain stuffed with knowledge, and literally brimming over with it.

"Oh, hello there," he says, smiling at me with interest. His voice has the rich, basso weight of an opera star—maybe a villain or a tragic king. He leans against one of the overstuffed chairs as Pearce tells him about a meeting next week and then gives him some gossip about a "seriously deluded" woman in the psych department. He listens half-attentively, half-absently, following me with his eyes. And then I notice something familiar.

He's patting his pockets in that way Tiff's brother used to when he was feeling for his pack of cigarettes. Yes, he's doing it again. He pats deeper, more deliberately, and finally plunges his hand inside his pocket and jangles some coins. He sees me watching him and casually leans into my face, narrows his eyes, and whispers, "Don't ever start." He walks over to his bulging folder and fishes inside. "Just as well," he mutters, pulling out nothing.

"Meet Cassie, our new girl," Pearce says, as she hands Conner my resume and summarily shoves the two little teacups back in the desk drawer.

"Conner is our expert on animal behavior," Pearce says, gesturing regally at him.

"Nice to meet you," he says, shooting out his hand and clasping mine with a sure, tight grasp.

"Teatime, ladies?" he adds, knowingly, as he holds my gaze for a minute and then focuses his eyes on the resume.

"U of Michigan," he reads as I tense. "Oh, it says here

you worked in the wildlife center in Topanga—heard about that place. When were you there?"

I'm about to answer when I hear "knock, knock" in a lush, smoldering voice. I look up and standing at the door is a tall, willowy blonde holding a twisted black pearl necklace in one hand and an unlit cigarette in the other. She's wearing a sleeveless black cocktail dress with a scoop neck and her collarbones are rounded and sturdy, like a pair of handlebars.

"I'm not interrupting?" She smiles as she walks right in.

"Not at all. We've been waiting for you," Conner answers politely. She walks up to him, holding out the necklace. Without comment he takes it from her, walks around behind her, lifts up her hair, and fastens it on her neck. When he's done, she slings her arm on his shoulder and gives him a brief kiss on the lips.

I think about that kiss for a long time afterward. It's the kind of gesture that seems the opposite of intimate—just a casual acknowledgment of someone's presence, like at a wedding . . . or a funeral. Sam's parrot kisses are a whole lot warmer. Conner introduces us and she gives me a society smile.

I can't take my eyes off her, but Conner's gaze is fixed on her long, slim fingers twirling the cigarette in a giant tease.

"It's my last one," she says as she slides it into his pocket. "The things I do for you." She laughs. A gay little laugh. Like those people in British movies where they take a house in Italy for the summer and all sit around drinking wine and reading Russian novels.

"How was your game?" he asks, gathering up his fat file, turning his back toward her, and barely listening.

"Not great. Stacey went on and on about how I have to stop running around my backhand and then we had lunch at the club. Now I'm beat," she says, breezily.

"Oh!" she says, as she dramatically stops and listens. "Smetana's Second."

"You are absolutely right!" Pearce says.

"Samantha can hear a piece of music just a few times and remember it," Conner informs us as Samantha feigns discomfort.

"You're embarrassing me, Conner," Samantha says coquettishly. "But it's true. I just have that type of brain. I used to amaze everyone at school. The teacher would play a few notes and I'd get the title right every time. It's a gift."

"I have a parrot like that," I say quietly.

"What?!" Samantha says, eyes narrowing to a slit.

"My parrot does the same thing," I repeat.

"No kidding," Conner says with a hint of a smile.

"Yes. If he listens to a song just a couple of times, Sam—that's his name too, isn't that a coincidence?—will remember the title and even the singer." Conner starts to laugh.

"Isn't that just something," Pearce says, trying to stifle a smile as she snaps open her purse and combs her gray frizz with a wide-bristled brush that does nothing at all. Then she unceremoniously stands up.

"Yes, well, Cassie. You'll fit in nicely around here. We're off to a reception now, but say tomorrow around nine? Is that good?"

"Thank you," I say, a slight catch in my throat.

I got the job. I feel like a schoolgirl with a hopping heart. As I turn, I see that Conner and Samantha have already started down the hall, where there is an immediate flash of fire, then exhaled smoke.

"We have smoke alarms here, but she could give a damn," Pearce murmurs under her breath, but just loud enough for me to hear.

"So much for the patch," she adds as she grabs a small round brass alarm clock, and throws it in her purse. She catches me staring at her.

"I never could wear a watch," Pearce says brightly. "Bring comfortable shoes."

CHAPTER 3

The first thing I see when I get home is a note pasted on the refrigerator door. "Big Rat in Kitchen!!! Do NOT leave fruit out. Rat likes it. Put bread and cereal in the freezer."

The note ends with a sad face. My mother hates killing rats. At the wildlife center they give them names like Monterey Jack (Monty for short) and Brie, a "darling" little white female with cream fur and little white clawed feet. Those long, eely tails and hairless ears make my skin crawl. Plus, they can squash themselves down to flat, furry pancakes and ooze like black muck under doors and windowsills. My mother has all these half-baked methods of getting rid of the suckers, but none of them work. Usually, she puts out a Havahart trap, one of those stupid catch-and-release boxes. But then you have to open the other side and let the rat out. I did that once and it flew, with a fury, in my face. I'm *never* doing that again. Now I usually wait until she leaves for work and then just put out a regular trap, load it with a chunk of cheese, and obliterate the plague-ridden vermin. Bon ap- pétit. I'm an animal lover, but these creatures are dark and evil and the opposite of natural.

The thing is, in Topanga, everyone has rats and every- body has a "rat story." It's just a fact of life, like roaches in NY or liars in LA. Speaking of liars, what if I walk in to work tomorrow and they *know*? Alison would be thrilled. Professor Pearce would give me a pitiful look and offer me a parting shot of sherry. What am I doing? The eu- phoria has definitely worn off.

"What do you think, Sam?"

"You're gorgeous." Sam's in fine spirits. He's always in fine spirits when I get home. Plus, I bought him a new toy after the interview. It's a peekaboo stuffed parrot with a hidden mirror under its wings. He'll ruin it in a couple days.

I close all the windows and doors and open Sam's cage. He hops out and follows me around like a hungry hound until I get his food together. I pull out his dinner—seeds, bits of apples, lettuce, carrots, and a little of whatever we ate last night—pudding, pasta, sweet potatoes. He partic- ularly likes cake batter. He'll sample it and say, "What's that? Want some."

After dinner, Sam marches over to the couch and finds his favorite lookout spot. Frank used to leave the window open hoping a neighborhood cat would get him, but Sam's too smart for that. I'm about to give him dessert when the phone rings.

It's Tiff. She always calls at this time. She's cur- rently working as a paralegal for two young guys named Seigelman and Stein. They have a general practice that includes trip and falls, divorces, wills, DUIs, low-level criminal stuff, and anything else that walks in the door.

"Guess what?" I say. "I got a job."

"You didn't tell me about a job."

"Well, it all happened so fast." I'm *not* going to tell her I lied.

"You mean you just walked in and boom—they said, you're hired? What kind of job is it?"

"An assistant at Stanfield University. I start tomorrow at nine."

"What are you going to wear?"

"They told me to wear comfortable shoes."

"Well, look nice. You usually dress like you're ten years older. And those long skirts. You have really good legs, you should show them off. Let me loan you something."

I tell her "No thanks" because there isn't one simple unadorned piece of clothing in her wardrobe. She can't wear anything that doesn't have a whiff of performance art about it. It's a throwback to her competition days when her childhood dream was to become a professional figure skater. Ever since I could remember, she got up at four a.m. so that she could be on the ice by five. For years, the family spent every dime they earned on coaches, skates, entry fees, and those velvet jeweled competition outfits. But, sadly, Tiff never did make the grade. Sam suddenly starts squawking in my ear. He gets jealous when I talk on the phone, just like a three-year-old.

"Can't you shut him up?" Tiff doesn't have the fondness for animals one would hope. "I hate that noise! It's so annoying."

Now Sam has moved into high gear. It's ear-splitting.

"Where are you?" I ask.

"Almost at the house. Come for dinner. Leave Sam home."

Tiff and I are as close as can be but we couldn't be more different. It goes all the way back to when we were kids and we'd read those stories in animal picture books. She always identified with City Mouse and I with Country Mouse. For her, the flow of life is not outdoors—it's in places that have roofs and walls and music and people. Whenever I've tried to pull her over to the Green Side, it's been a disaster.

For example, several years ago, when we went down to the Malibu Lagoon, I reveled in the sight of a rare white egret, while she ogled a group of ripped surfers at a nearby beach. Sometimes I can still get her to go on weekend hikes, but usually, by the end of the day, I'm thinking it's not worth it. The sunlight hurts her eyes. The forest is "teeming" with mosquitoes and ticks. The sand scratches and irritates her skin. And the boggy meadows are wet and dirty, filled with poison ivy, snakes, and Lyme disease.

Tiff looks at our dilemma in a different way. I am basically alone, she reasons, because I'm over the top about nature, and men, as a rule, do not find this at all attractive. In fact, in Tiff's mind, men view women like me as "weird and unappealing, even threatening."

"The next time I fix you up," she'll preach, "do *not* go on and on about the wildlife center. For one thing, Cassie, no one wants to hear about the roadkill you call your 'patients.' Especially when you describe how you chop up frozen rats for food. For another, your long, detailed *Wild Kingdom* stories are a total yawn. You're just kicking yourself right out of the market."

Or, "You know, Cassie, when you do that thing with the food in your mouth and your parrot sticks his beak in between your teeth and pulls it out—you know what I'm talking about?—I know you think it's sweet, but trust me, it's not. It's gross."

"You're wrong, Tiff. Everyone who has a parrot does it," I argued.

"Well, don't do that with a guy around, okay?" she added, not letting up. "Promise me, Cassie. Let them find out later, after they like you, that you're not normal."

Okay, so maybe she's right. But here's the thing: I find comfort in the color green, the glossy heart-shaped leaves of the philodendron, abundant and generous, a handful of mint, the lobed leaves of the oak shining like taffeta, and the tiers of maidenhead ferns that lift and dive, capturing the light. I rarely talk about my feelings in this area, especially to Tiff, who has no love for the great outdoors. She doesn't get that urge to break away and blend right into the landscape, like a caterpillar on a piece of bark.

"I'm sorry, Cassie," she'll say, sympathetically, "but have you ever noticed that you and your mom have absolutely no sense of humor about anything natural? There's always this undercurrent of doom and gloom—like global warming will eventually cause mass extinction. Really, I can't take it. Even if you're right. Why can't you just ignore it like everyone else?"

It's a disappointment to me, really it is. I do love her, however. The same way I love Sam—even though both of them are pretty much hopeless in the green department. It's ironic, when you think about it, that I love a bird who has absolutely zero talent for living in the wild. Sam, like most domestic parrots, has a fixed, profound sense of home, and if I were to let him fly free, even in the backyard, he'd get lost and never come back. Sad but true.

Still, green is the most important part of my nature, as much a part of me as my skin. When I feel hollow inside, I swear to God, I go outside, inhale the fresh earth smells, and feel a part of something holy. Not like I feel most of the time. A creature apart.

All that goes away when I'm in the woods enveloped in the violet afternoons or watching the day heroically bursting forth. I feel boundless and eternal, as if I could stop at any point and perform miracles.

CHAPTER 4

I head off into the darkening woods for the path that leads to Tiff's house. The grass is mashed down into the dirt, and there is the clean smell of earth and just-watered flowers. The breeze is flirting with the leaves, they flutter and skip and slide, and there's the crackle and snap of brittle branches under my feet as I pick up the pace. I used to keep a small flashlight in my parka, but for some reason it isn't there when I fish around in my pockets. Only a wad of Kleenex and a few quarters.

My mother and I still hike here from time to time, and I spent my childhood delighting in her wild imaginings and listening to her soothing, dreamlike voice. She had a way of opening her ultra-blue eyes very wide, like a sphinx. Then she'd begin her tales, introducing me to an ever-expanding cast of characters and veering off in all directions from the Green Man in the forest to subversive, drunken fairies, psycho dryads, and Herne the Hunter. She made up worlds like

Euphoria, the Dreaming Den, Elfland, and, my favorite, the Changeling Sea—the place you dived into and disappeared when you needed to start over, a concept I was always happy to believe in.

It was near here, last year, on the top of a giant rotting tree, that I first discovered the ivory-billed woodpeckers. It was quite by chance, really, the kind of discovery that people tend to make when they aren't looking for anything at all. And then bingo, their shoe happens to kick aside a rock and underneath is a map to a buried treasure, a hidden bag of cash, or a lost diamond ring—a new future that comes out of the blue and you never know why. I'd like to say right now that I do *not* believe in supernatural visitations, not one bit, but I still felt as if I was staring at a couple of ghosts. The largest, most elusive birds in North America had risen from the dead and were strutting their stuff right in front of me. I never dreamed I would see one, let alone two, in my lifetime. What strange, magnificent creatures they are, I thought, and completely out of their realm.

The bird has been called many names, the ivory-billed woodpecker, the Lord God Bird, the Grail Bird. People spend their whole lives searching for it, hoping to catch a glimpse, as if it were the Golden Fleece. It's still not officially listed in the national extinct list that's pasted to everyone's desk at the nature center, but the last time it was caught on film was in Florida in the 1940s. The birds vanished forest by forest, swamp by swamp. Ran out of habitat like most extinct species. People claim they've seen them since, but it's never been proven. A sighting here. A sighting there. None of which pans out. And the stories, always the stories. The search has reached mythic proportions—the last big deal sighting in 2004 when the bird was supposedly caught on video in an Arkansas swamp. Renewed hope of a momentous discovery. But in the end, a controversy erupted—the same old dispute over whether the sighting was, in fact, legitimate. Visions, fractions of light. Maybe wishful thinking. Maybe nothing at all.

I watched the two of them—what appeared to be a male and female. The male looked like a punked-out rocker with slick black and white feathers and a spiky red Mohawk crest. God, was he handsome. I held my breath and froze, but I felt like doing cartwheels and somersaults and screaming "Eureka." He had an oversized, gleaming white bill—a magical white—and I remember thinking he reminded me of those flamboyant guys at Mardi Gras who parade down the middle of the street, dipping and swirling and flouncing around in their garish boas and glitter hats. He was bright, way too bright, even for an angel.

I stood there, motionless, for what seemed like an eternity, as they went about their mission—boring through the decaying bark of the tree with their massive bills, sending chips flying through the air. Searching for food. You could almost hear the insects scrambling for their lives. The birds called out loudly with a strange sort of bleat, pounding like crazy on the bark and passing grubs back and forth as if they were chocolate kisses. Mr. Grubman and Mrs. Grubette—bickering away like an old married couple in their superhero capes and golden eyes. I don't know how long I stood there before the male hitched down the tree and spotted me. I could see his eyes cut like a cold rebuke. I'd invaded his realm, crashed the costume party. Too bad for me.

Unfolding his three-foot-wide wings, he let out a diatribe of double-note whack-like tones as the female instantly froze. She was so still that she literally looked stuffed, like those birds with glassed-over eyes and faded feathers downtown at the Natural History Museum. Lost, extinct and lonely, so lonely. My mother and I never went back to that exhibit—something about those phony wildlife scenes with dead birds. Like embalmed bodies in satin-lined coffins. I must have moved my feet just then, because a twig snapped and that did it. The bird streaked straight up in the air like a mythical Fury and his mate followed.

These are creatures of the deep forest, of gloomy swamps and river bottomlands. Why are they here? There's no record of them ever being seen in California. But they've also been described as nomads with powerful wings, able to fly thousands of miles. And these mountains have dozens of habitats. So it's not impossible.

I sat for so long that my legs cramped up, and I stumbled to my feet. Then I waited some more, but these birds weren't coming back anytime soon. I walked away as fast as I could without breaking into a run—like someone leaving the scene of a crime—ducking under low branches, tripping on the uprooted vines. The Park Service tries to maintain these backwoods trails for hundreds of miles, but most get overgrown and stay that way for years. Sometimes hikers perish without a trace. Trails like this one are virtually impassable, especially when it rains, and that thought gave me comfort. This mountain range is the largest wilderness park near a city in the world, a place that could hide a secret for years, keep these birds unseen and undiscovered.

That day, I took the trail all the way down, sidestepping the pools of water and swampy muck, and then slowed to a walk. All the while, I was planning what to bring the next morning—binoculars, warmer clothes, a notebook, pen. And so I went back, the next day, and the next.

It was freezing most mornings as I huddled up in my heavy parka, wrapped myself in a blanket as the fog blew off the chilly Pacific waters and hugged the soggy ground for hours. The smell of the trail permeated the air—the balm of fir and pine and decay of fallen trees, the heavy dampness bubbling under the forest canopy. There is no riot of color in a California fall, but still, the greens deepen, and mushrooms of all colors explode into the tall grass.

I watched the ivory-bills go about their daily routine, as the clouds congealed like white foam in the sky. Sometimes the rain was as soft as goose down, other times it was like a spray of buckshot. But I didn't mind. I poured out my thoughts and kept notes on everything they did, their beautiful yet unsettling forms just visible through the very tops of the trees.

When I was young I would come out here and pretend I was the first person on earth. I could learn just as much by listening to the woods and the sounds of its beauty as by reading—all that life bubbling under the surface, forming ring after ring around those massive tree trunks. Now there's even more. Secrets and more secrets.

I hear the far-off growl of thunder in the distance as I reach Tiff's front door. If I were superstitious I would say it was a sign. Maybe I went too far today to get the job. What if they find out? Keeping things hidden is like living with guilt. It overshadows everything.

CHAPTER 5

When I get to Tiff's place, I see everyone lined up on the couch watching CNN. Their satellite dish, which probably cost more than their business, got washed away in the last mudslide, so now they have this black-market cable box that Tiff's brother, Guy Jr., rigged up right before he enlisted. Tiff calls him her baby brother even though he's twenty-two, which she says "is *just* not possible." He's been trouble ever since I can remember. He used to steal the Baby Jesus and the manger from the town square and now, because of him, they don't put them out anymore. He wasn't the most studious kid, but then he shaped up, joined the Marines. Everyone was thrilled until he got shipped to Iraq.

I love their house. It's in the middle of a stand of giant eucalyptus trees with leaves that hippies keep stealing to put in their hot tubs. It's a typical Topanga house. Spanish mission with a red tile roof, big wooden doors, and beams. Tiff's family has been there since she and Guy Jr. were born. You can see their baby handprints in the concrete driveway with their names scrawled above them.

Tiff used to live with this lawyer she met at work, but they broke up last year and now she's back home with her parents. Everyone in the neighborhood calls them Aunt Ethel and Uncle Guy. Which is also the name of the bowling alley they run near Ocean Ave—Aunt Ethel and Uncle Guy's Lovers' Lanes. Uncle Guy runs the lanes and Aunt Ethel is the cook for the coffee shop in the back. Well, not a cook. She's a chef really. It's the only bowling alley in the country that serves field greens and goat cheese.

This is their sixth bowling alley since I've known them. They're always on the verge of bankruptcy, closing up one place and then opening another. During one particularly dark period, Frank gave them a car. It was the only nice thing he ever did. Although he did get it from an illegal immigrant who was too scared to come back and pick it up from the towing lot because he thought he'd be deported.

I offer to help with dinner, but Aunt Ethel scoots Tiff and me outside. We sit on the back deck and watch the sun slip behind the tree line. The color of everything burns for a moment of intensity and then it's dark. Tiff has peeled off her work clothes and is now wearing jeans and a sweatshirt, her long platinum hair pulled straight back in a simple ponytail. Not a lot of girls can get away with that, but Tiff has doll-like features, dewy porcelain skin, just a hint of a nose, and robin's-egg-blue eyes. Cosmetic counter salesgirls always offer her free makeovers. Tiff usually says yes and then winds up buying all the crap they put on her face. I end up with half of it. The truth is, Tiff doesn't need makeup to look good.

She hands me a Corona, squirts a lime in the bottle, and says, "So how much are they paying you?"

"I don't want to discuss it."

"That bad, huh?"

"I didn't exactly have a lot of choices."

"But still."

"Maybe they're paying me a million dollars."

Tiff is quiet for a minute, then starts to laugh.

"Okay," she says, "here's the scene. A man comes to your door. It's Publishers Clearing House. Are you Miss Cassie Shaw? Yes? Well, this is your lucky day! You've just won *one million dollars!* Tears! Rejoicing! Holy macaroni! What are you going to do with all that money? Give it to the poor? Save the whales? (Your mother would love that.) So many choices."

I see Tiff's hands fly up to her face in genuine excitement. I love her when she gets like this. It's so much fun.

"Well, I know what *I'd* do," she goes on. "Go straight to the mall. Get a real Prada purse, not a knockoff, and a big flawless diamond. Then I'd go buy a brand-new car. A BMW or a Mercedes with butter leather inside. And every time I went to the gas station, I'd fill it up and not ask for twenty dollars' worth. And then I'd book a week at a spa. Manicures, pedicures, facials, massages, Godiva chocolates. Maybe I'd buy my mom a flat screen. And a Viking range, she's always wanted one of those."

"What if we buy two condos in the city?" I interrupt. Now she's got me going.

"No more living with our parents!" she shouts gleefully.

"And they'll have showers that never run out of hot water!" I add.

"And an indoor spa for me and a five-acre garden for you with all those little labeled sticks that your mother loves to use, tarragon, rosemary, lavender." We're both laughing now, giddy with the possibilities.

I see the sky pop with lightning like a burnt-out bulb as Aunt Ethel calls us in to dinner. Gray clouds are sitting in furious silence. They're predicting a major storm tonight and it's not going to be good. We've already had two land-slides this season and they're still shoring up the hillside to keep the mud off the road.

The TV stays on all through dinner. They used to watch *Jeopardy!* and *Wheel of Fortune*, but now they've switched to CNN, which is all about the war these days. Bad news and more bad news. Aunt Ethel turns off the TV.

"Enough of that," she says, forcing a smile.

"So when is he coming home?" I whisper.

"Maybe Christmas," Tiff whispers back. "Don't tell Mom, it's a surprise."

Now it's raining in that windy, ugly way that only gets worse, so Tiff drives me home. I'm thinking that if it's bad weather tomorrow morning, it's going to take me twice as long. I'd better get up at six to give myself plenty of time. And I hope to God I don't have to read reams of material quickly because if I do, I'm fucked. And I hope they have a computer for me to use. I'm bringing my laptop just in case. If it's just filing, answering phones, and cataloging things, I'll be fine. I'll bet that's what it is. They're not going to give someone like me anything else. But wait. I'm not like me. I'm a college grad with a degree in psych. Oh shit.

CHAPTER 6

There's a fair amount of dread attached to stormy mornings in my neighborhood. One minute everything is normal, the next, a house collapses down the cliff into the highway or an enormous boulder dislodges from God knows where and crushes a commuter on the way to work.

I wake up at least twenty minutes before the alarm to leaden skies, the rush of water on the roof, the ever-present thunder. It's a cheerless morning, the sky is as gray as a zombie's face, and the fog presses against my bedroom window like a ghost trying to get in. And then I realize, I am not alone. Curled up in a ball on the other side of the bed is a big black sopping wet dog. He smells like a decomposing something and snores like an old man. His muzzle is gray and he has somehow managed to cover himself up with my favorite blue comforter.

"Do I know you?" I ask. He lifts his head and

yawns. A few of his teeth are whittled down and his gums are black. I think, great, another dog in my bed.

My mother leaves the back door slightly ajar most nights. It's a canyon thing, and I guess this poor old guy probably got freaked by the storm and pushed his way in. No collar, although that doesn't mean much around here. Still, I don't recognize him. When I walk to the kitchen to feed Sam, the dog leaps off the bed and rushes to the door. But when I open it and he sees the rain, he sits back on his haunches and looks up at me. He's not going anywhere.

Now I hear a deafening clap of thunder, which is Sam's cue to start stamping his feet and screeching, "Help! Help! Let me out! Let me out!"

He always gets this way during a thunderstorm. Another clap of thunder. Now he's frozen with fear, standing like a statue with one foot in the air and the other gripping his toy. I drag his cage into the other room and cover it, getting birdseed and dirty water all over my nightgown. I turn on the radio, his favorite channel, the easy-listening station. Barry Manilow always comforts him. There's another, more pressing problem. I forgot to put away the fruit and bread last night and now it's scattered like confetti all over the kitchen counter and floor. Sprinkled in for good measure are brown rat droppings and chunks of apples with tiny little bite marks. Fuck.

I can feel the sweat trickle down my chest as I run around cleaning up, and then bring Sam his breakfast of Cheerios and bananas. Normally, we sit at the table. Sam likes company when he eats. He'll just have to cope today. The highway will be jammed and I have to get out of here. I hurry to my room to get dressed as I call my mother on my cell. She's been working the night shift at the wildlife center for the past few weeks.

"Mom?"

"Haven't you left yet?"

"No. I'm about to, but a dog got into the house and he won't leave, Sam's freaking out, I forgot to put the stuff away last night, and there's rat droppings all over the place."

"Calm down, Cassie. Just get on the road. I'll come down there in a bit."

I hate it when someone tells me to calm down. It just makes me more anxious. There's nothing I can do to calm down. I can't exactly call the office and say, "Hey, guys, I'm running a few minutes late," when it's my *first* day of work. I should've gotten up at five. I knew it was going to storm. How could I have forgotten to put the damn food away? Why didn't I lock the door? My mother always says that "should'ves" do you no good. "You are where you are." And I am totally fucked.

I take a two-minute shower and throw on the clothes I laid out last night—a plaid pleated skirt, a white blouse, a cardigan, a pair of Easy Spirit black loafers, and a leather purse I borrowed from my mother. I glance in the mirror. I look like I go to school with Harry Potter. But it's too late to change.

I grab an umbrella and dash to the car. My windshield is blanketed with wet leaves, twigs, and mud. I swipe it quickly with the classifieds from yesterday and get in. The windows are fogged up and the defroster is busted, so I have to lean my head out the window as I drive down the canyon.

When I finally reach Pacific Coast Highway, the traffic is backed up for centuries and the news report says there's a power outage somewhere in the city. Now I'm positive I won't make it. As it turns out, I arrive only about fifteen minutes late, but then I drive around looking for a space on the side street with no meters because, after pawing through my purse and then dumping it on the seat, I realize I left my money in my backpack at home. I don't even have one dime.

Alison is at her desk, a cup of steaming Starbucks sitting on a coaster by the telephone, flawless and unsmiling. Her hair is swept up in a strategically tousled French twist. She's wearing a black turtleneck, gold hoops, and high-heeled black leather boots. Perfect. She's fiddling with her BlackBerry.

"Oh, Cassie, they're looking for you upstairs. Weren't you supposed to be here at nine?" she says, in that offhanded way people have of calling you a fuckup. I start to say something and she cuts me off.

"Oh, never mind, it's just that we start on time here."

As I rush past her, she sniffs, "Could you wipe your feet on the mat over there? The floor gets slippery when it's wet." I notice long black dog hairs stuck to my sweater.

I race up the stairs trying to brush them off and knock on Professor Pearce's door.

"Come in."

I jiggle the handle a minute and then remember, and give the door a big shove. It flies open and bashes into the wall with a loud thwack. The sudden peace is jarring. I have fallen into an eighteenth-century drawing room, Lord Buckingham's private library. The fire is behaving nicely, the ceramic bulldogs look sated, and Pearce is sitting in a winged, saddle-leather armchair sipping tea and reading the *London Times*.

"My dear, you're drenched!"

"I'm sorry I'm late," I say, apologetically.

"Don't worry. It was impossible to get around the city this morning. Unless you live two blocks away like Alison. Everyone was late." Lucky piece of shit, Alison.

"Come sit, dear."

I perch myself on a red velvet ottoman as she tells me that

she's teaching two senior seminars this semester, Cognition and Free Will, and Subliminal Persuasion, along with her usual freshman class, Social Psych. I'll be her personal assistant, in addition to helping Professor Conner, who would like me to start organizing his bookshelves this afternoon.

"Your lunch break is twelve, Alison's is one. Whenever she leaves, you fill in. You two work it out." That should be easy.

I spend the next few hours sorting the mail, typing a few letters, and manning the desk. Most of the professors are either teaching classes or just not around.

Around noon, I break for lunch. The rain has stopped and there are big, puffy cartoon clouds in the Windex blue sky. It's always so clear and sparkly in this town after a rain, like someone's lifted gauze off a lens. My problem is I'm starving and I have no money, so I decide to run to the bank across the street. At least I have my ATM card.

It's always a crapshoot whether my card will work. I can never keep track of my balance and half the time I get that notice on the screen that says: "Your request exceeds your balance. Please try again later."

It's deflating, but better than the waiter or salesgirl telling me politely that my card doesn't work. Do I have another?

Okay, it's been denied. Sometimes if I put it in again, it works. I shove the card in again. Now there's someone behind me. I hate that. Peering over my shoulder. It makes me want to go slower. Denied. I'm going to try one more time. Fuck it. What is this? Where's my card!

"Please see your bank" flashes indignantly on the screen. I push the button to try to get my card out. Nothing. I hit the machine hard with my fist.

"God damn it!" I whisper. "Give me back my card."

I hear a voice behind me. "Forget it. Once they confiscate

it, you have to go to your bank and get it back." Why doesn't he mind his own fucking business? I whip around.

"I never heard that," I say to some student in an alligator shirt with floppy sweatpants and a backpack slung over his shoulder. He has sapphire blue eyes with a fringe of lush black lashes that sweep across his face like a swatch of velvet. Straight nose. Pouty lower lip. He can't be more than twenty, with the open guileless face of someone who looks like he hasn't had a day of worry in his life.

"It happened to me in Prague once."

Oh, I had the same problem in Paris, myself. Ha ha ha. Fuck him. I turn back around.

"Well, it's never happened to me before," I mutter, as I close my purse and start to walk away.

"Hey!" he shouts in a loud voice. "You need some cash?"

"What?"

"I can loan you some money." What a nice kid. Shame on me.

"No. That's okay. I have money in the car," I lie. "Thanks, though."

"No worries." He smiles like an angel.

I head for my car and see if I've left any change in the side pocket or the trunk. Slapped against the wet windshield under the wiper is a soggy parking ticket. Street cleaning. What else can happen to me today? I find three quarters on the floor of the trunk. At least I don't have to put them in the meter.

I remember there was a snack center near the mail room, so when I get back to the office I head down the stairs following the eternal hum of the vending machines. There are offerings of candy bars, chips, Little Debbie donuts, Kit Kats, shrink-wrapped sandwiches. Everything's over a buck except for the gum, not that a starving person gives a shit.

When I get back to the reception area, Alison's on her cell.

"Let's meet at that new Italian place. I feel like pasta. Ça va?" Ça va, give me a break. "Oh. She's here now. See you in ten."

"Hi. Listen, I have it all in order, so please don't move anything." She gathers her Burberry coat, her matching umbrella, and her purse, which has *G*'s screaming all over it. Tiff has the exact same thing, a copy she bought downtown out of some guy's trunk, but her *G*'s are really *C*'s. You can't really notice.

Before she goes, she looks pointedly at me and says, "Oh, about the gum. They kind of frown on it here."

As she's walking away, I blow the biggest bubble I can and pop it. I know she hears me, but she keeps on going.

❦ ❦ ❦

So now it's just me, sitting here in charge of the entire psych department. Competent, professional, reliable. Students will approach me for advice. Visitors will arrive for appointments. I am the gatekeeper. But unlike Alison, I will be kind, helpful, compassionate. I catch a sudden glimpse of myself reflected off the window. My hair is frizzed and my nose is red. I look like Bozo.

In the next half hour the phone only rings once and it's someone asking for directions. Then Professor Conner calls telling me to meet him in his office at two. When Alison gets back, I spit out the gum, comb my hair, and tell her in an off-hand sort of way that I have an appointment with Professor Conner and I don't know how long I'll be. I walk past her without glancing back.

Conner's office looks like Pearce's, but after a tornado. Floor-to-ceiling bookshelves and expensive leather furniture, half-hidden by all the junk lying around. Stacked-up books, empty cans of tennis balls, and a messy pile of papers spit out from the printer and trailing like vines down to the floor. Dirty coffee mugs. Scrunched-up paper balls that have obviously missed the wastebasket. On the wall are photographs of dancing polar bears, grizzlies chewing on bloody salmon, and a big bull moose with an ivy crown. Sierra Club stuff. There's also an open canvas duffle in the corner with wrinkled, balled-up clothes and a pair of binoculars on top. I hand him his mail.

"Sorry about the mess. I call it organized chaos." I look at him skeptically as I sidestep the clutter to reach his desk.

"Honest," he says with a grin. "You should see my house. I keep it sparse. The influence of Thoreau. Simplify. Simplify."

"I got rid of everything myself last year," I say, as I think about all of Frank's crap that I threw out.

"Feels good, doesn't it?" He should only know.

He tells me he's preparing a study for some institute and he needs to categorize all the pertinent materials—everything else he wants arranged according to subject matter and author. I see a ladder on the far wall and a stack of books on the floor.

"You know how to climb a ladder, don't you?" he teases, lifting his brows.

"Sure. Just put one leg in front of another and . . . climb."

"You're too young to have seen that movie."

"It's a classic."

He stares at me a little too long and I tell myself, no way am I wearing skirts to this office.

CHAPTER 7

I t's been a few weeks since I started working in Conner's office, and I'm still on the *A*'s— Aristotle, Aristophanes, Auden, Audubon. Sometimes I go home and Google certain authors and scientists. And last week, Conner let me take home one of his dog-eared copies of Audubon's *Birds of America*. I mostly looked at the pictures.

Sometimes I get tired and just sit on the ladder and gab with Tiff. I tell her I'm surrounded by volumes and volumes of leather-bound books. Isn't that ironic? Other times, I look around at the mountains of travel logs, photographic essays of remote places around the world—the Amazon, the Galápagos Islands, the Sahara Desert—biographies, science, philosophy, and history books. And I wonder what kind of man is this? What kind of life has he led? How could he have read all these books?

Usually Conner's not here, but sometimes he leaves Post-its with odd little comments like,

"Don't put these bastards together. They hated each other."
Referring to the authors, of course. Or stuck on a book of
Auden's love poems, "Page 234 gone, ripped to shreds.
Don't ask." Or my favorite, a little happy face sticker that
said, "Good job," like you'd give a five-year-old.

Today when I walk in, he's working on the program notes
for the butterfly exhibit.

"Still on the *A*'s?" he says, looking up at me with his an-
noyingly handsome face.

"Yes. Almost finished, though," I lie.

He tosses me a book. "Here's an *A*—revisionist history of
Attila the Hun. He evidently wasn't as bad as his reputa-
tion."

"But didn't he pillage and rape?" I ask.

"Well, yes, but apparently he provided good services to
his people."

I think about that for a moment. "Would you rather I
come back later?"

"No. Actually you're just in time."

He tells me the butterfly exhibit is in the conservatory of
the science building and asks if I would come with him and
bring back some of his research. It's about a five-minute
walk and I notice he takes long, easy strides, greeting students here and there, like a celebrity. Everyone seems to
know him.

We arrive at the glass dome conservatory, which looks
like a giant greenhouse, and proceed through a hermetically
sealed passageway lined with glass panels and a few signs
cautioning visitors to "Watch Where You Walk!" The air
grows heavy and humid as we follow a serpentine path, turn
a corner, and suddenly enter a different world—a lush,
steamy, tropical rain forest landscaped with forty-foot-high
bamboos, orchids, bougainvillea, bromeliads, and a host of
other umbrella-shaped plants with dark polished leaves.

I squint in the hazy light as a tempest of motion and a whirring sound surround me. A blaze of thousands of butterflies, swarming through the air, flitting on the foliage, hovering and dancing like airborne fairies. They fly low, at eye level, shivering wings open like a fan. Gleams of flame-like reds and yellows, broad jet black rings, brilliant purples.

"If you stand still, sometimes they'll land on you," he whispers.

"I know," I say. "I did it as a child. Our house is in their migration pattern. Do you have a banana?"

"You hungry?" He laughs.

"I used to feed them," I say, as one shy little creature with trembling wings advances toward me, then changes its mind and gently lands on a nearby tree.

"Hold on," Conner says as he walks over to one of the students who is cleaning a nectar station. She looks at him quizzically, shrugs her shoulders, and then disappears.

We remain standing, silent and motionless, watching the aerial dance. The student comes back with a banged-up banana "from someone's lunch," she explains. I peel it and hand it to Conner.

"Hold it straight up in the air," I tell him. The butterflies, who have been so wary, start to gather near the fruit. One Painted Lady hops up and down on a nearby branch, flitting its wings. Conner raises his hand higher. A strange rush of iridescent color, and then slowly the Lady boldens, moving closer to Conner, circling, teasing, tantalizing.

"Heartbreakers," Conner murmurs. At that point, the butterfly surrenders, sticks her proboscis in the banana, and begins to sip.

"Hussy," I reply. Conner erupts into laughter and the Lady disappears. Like the motion of a cloud in a mist, she melts away into the swirl of glistening wings.

We walk silently through the rest of the exhibit as if we

both just had a religious experience. When we reach the exit, Conner stops to chat with a group of students. I turn back to the spellbinding display. As I'm looking up, I notice everyone else is looking down. Sticking out from under my big black shoe is a crushed orange-tipped butterfly—dead as a doornail.

CHAPTER 8

For several days, I tortured myself with this question—which rare and exotic species of Lepidoptera had I squashed? Was it, perhaps, a scrap of Painted Lady, a fragment of Monarch, or perhaps a smidgen of Black-veined White minus its antennae? I was too mortified to look closely at the crushing moment of truth, but later I was haunted by the tiny black ripples and swirls smooshed on the bottom of my shoe. I finally had to let it go—sometimes, for heaven's sake, you just step on a bug.

Fortunately, Conner doesn't mention it when he appears at my desk a few mornings later, leaning against the Xerox machine and handing me one of those pocket-sized recorders.

"Would you mind transcribing my opening lecture?" he asks, looking around at my bare desk that's wedged against the looming machines.

"It's all pretty straightforward," he goes on. "You don't have to record everything I say, just the basic material. I'm told I tend to go off on tangents, so use your judgment."

"Use my judgment," I hear myself echo as I stare down at the recorder as if it were a lie detector.

"I'm sure you'll be able to tell when I shoot the breeze. Just turn the machine off and on when I say something . . . relevant. Pretend you're back at school, taking notes from a professor—just don't fall asleep," he jokes, walking out in the hall.

"Sure, no problem," I answer, faking a little laugh.

The day of the lecture, I arrive early and take a seat up front. I feel like I'm in church. The auditorium is one of the oldest on campus, and there's a kind of hushed aura to the place as filtered light streams in from the high-paned windows. My first college lecture. They should only know.

I look around as the kids trail in. Sharp, fox-like faces, Boy Scout buzzes, layered polo shirts, hair cut at unbalanced angles, aviator glasses. A girl in a peasant top with peeling black nail polish and purple smudges under her eyes stares out the window as if she's never seen the sky. Pierced eyebrows and Goth motorcycle boots on a very young-looking girl who clump, clump, clumps as she climbs to the top row. A group of Muslim head coverings, an Indian sari.

The noise of settling in echoes and bounces around the room. Students are talking to each other, maneuvering down the aisles. Some kids open their laptops and start watching movies. I see one girl ordering airline tickets online; another punches a beach ball up into the audience and everyone swats at it, keeping it in the air like at a volleyball game. Conner walks in just as the ball hits the podium. He strides across the stage followed by a big woolly dog. No collar, no leash. It has mops of white curly long hair with the body of some kind of Lab.

"Down, Ahab," he commands, as he grabs the mike, carefully ignoring the ball.

The dog flops down, looking like a big shag rug, and juts his chin out flat on the stage. One of the cutest dogs I've ever seen. As if the girls weren't entranced with Conner enough already.

"Welcome to Animal Behavior 230," Conner says as he faces the audience, trying to get a good look at everyone. "I'm assuming you all read the book I assigned for this opening class."

Silence. Kids are looking at each other with blank expressions, thumbing through their notebooks, sinking into their seats, looking down at their desks.

"And you've also taken the required prerequisites, including organic chemistry." A few gasps. He lets the impact of his words stretch a little, controlling the silences. Then he breaks into an appealing grin, throws the ball back out into the audience, and says, "Just kidding!"

The room exhales, relieved laughter, and Conner starts right in. I turn on the tape recorder.

"So, I'm sitting on the banks of the Okavango River overlooking the Kalahari. I'd just spent the last two years in Botswana repairing broken-down farm trucks in a small village, ninety miles from the nearest gas station. There were silhouettes of impalas and giraffes on the hillside, and the cries of vervet monkeys all around me. The sun was in the perfect spot, just dancing on the horizon, and I was in a major tailspin, wondering where I belonged. I felt I had done everything, experienced everything. Used up all my resources. Life is short, right? I mean. I'd gotten three degrees, tried the Wall Street thing, done my public service, and my life was fucked."

I stare at him in disbelief. Then quickly turn off the tape. This is a tangent. You don't have to be a college grad to know that. He continues to speak with an openness that is shocking. Now he's talking faster. We're hearing about his adolescent rages, his binges, and, yes, even his women. The ones who shared his vision, the ones who didn't. The pieces of his life dissected and summarized. The words spewing out wildly like water out of a broken hydrant. You could've heard a pin drop. I clicked the tape back on.

"And then, I had this, well, hell, I'll just say it, an epiphany! I opened Melville's *Moby-Dick* and I read the first line, 'Call me Ishmael.' And it all became clear to me. Okay. So I was a little stoned." I click the tape off. "But I decided to come back, and deal with life in a different way. As Buddha said, 'Those who have failed to work toward the truth have missed the purpose of living.'"

The girl next to me smiles faintly, leans in to her friend, and mouths, "Professor McHeartthrob—is he for real?"

Her friend whispers back, "I hear he might not get tenure. He's kind of wild."

"Cool," she replies, enthralled.

Conner goes on to say that the focus of this class is "truth in nature." I click the tape on for the third time but my finger stays poised on the "off" button. He quotes Walt Whitman, Thoreau, and Emerson, "required freshman reading," shepherding us from one image to another. He asks a question. "Are animals happy? Are they happier than humans? Are they braver, more chaste, more noble, more heroic? The Greek philosopher Plutarch said that if it were not for the favor of the gods, man would be at a natural disadvantage to beasts." Conner's words are floating all around me. This guy could read the phone book and make it sound interesting.

Now he goes into "the night the pygmies slipped away

from the campsite, painted themselves with phosphorous plants, and came out celebrating the spirits of the forests. Suddenly, a bull elephant appears—angry, nearsighted, far more of a threat than a tiger. . . . I knew the single-engine Cherokee was going down—the engine chocked and faltered. . . ."

He grabs the mike, descends the stage, and starts walking up the center aisle of the auditorium like he's some kind of royalty.

"Animals and humans live in a parallel universe. Close your eyes and listen to the sweet rapture of the most complex song in the nonhuman world."

All eyes are fixed on him as he motions to a student standing near an amplifier and a few bars of a bird chorale comes over the speakers—the sounds tumbling and trilling all over each other, curlicue notes exploding into a forest of noise.

He's wearing multiple layers—jacket, plaid flannel shirt unraveling at the edges, gray sweatshirt hanging over his shoulder—all of it loose and trailing. He brushes the arm of a girl, on the end of a row, clasps her on the shoulder, and murmurs, "Sorry." It seems like a generous and gallant gesture.

At this point the students have all laid down their pens, closed their laptops, and sit mesmerized. He speaks slower now, with elegant little pauses. God, is he good!

"So what I'm really saying is—even if you suffer from major disillusionment and runs of rotten luck, you can always summon up truth through nature." Applause breaks out as the dog leaps to his feet and starts barking, soaking up the enthusiasm all over the room. Everyone is smiling and chatting as if they've seen a great show. His popularity is unquestionable.

I stand up and slide out the back door. I did okay with the tape, I think. No problem. None whatsoever.

I think about the last time I gave a shit about science. When I was in seventh grade, Tiff and I decided to get together to compete in the school's annual science fair. If we won, we'd get free tickets to Magic Mountain. So we were pretty motivated. We didn't do anything corny like those erupting plaster-of-Paris volcanoes or the effects of the rays of the sun where kids just sat out and got burnt different shades of red. Tiff and I decided to put on a show. We reenacted the movement of the solar system. We wore black leotards with tinfoil stars pinned all over them. Tiff played Saturn and twirled two hula hoops at the same time. That was a big hit. I was Mars—the cold, lonely planet. We tied for first place with Billy McCarthy, who did a really stupid San Andreas Fault diorama. And I know, for a fact, that his father, who was this successful building contractor, put the whole thing together. It still makes me mad when I think about it.

The afternoon light is blinding, like after you've gone to a daytime movie. I can hear traffic and students laughing and yelling as I walk back across campus to my office. I feel energized, happy, almost as if I was playing hooky. That's odd. I get the same feeling going to class that I used to when I cut it.

CHAPTER 9

W hat a feeling having him inside my head. His voice is rich, wine dark, primally seductive. Even when he's not on topic. He talks, I type. The rhythm. The back-and-forth. I've been transcribing Conner's lecture and it's like having an imaginary friend on a dark lonely night. Calming and consoling. His words are hypnotic as he quotes Emerson, Thoreau, Whitman, describing how nature entices the soul, its beguiling beauty and allure. He's telling me stories about the cosmic connections in the universe. Okay. So he's not talking to me, but it feels that way.

In the meantime, the same old Spelling Demon is stewing on my shoulder, screwing up the letters. When I was in school, my spelling was so far off, I couldn't even find the words in the dictionary. Thank God for spell-check. Kalomity, kalomlity, calamity—that doesn't look right, but I guess it is.

"Emerson writes that 'in the woods we return to reason and faith. There I feel that nothing can befall me in life—no disgrace, no calamity . . . which nature cannot repair.' "

"You are so right!" I say to the machine. His words run together, cajoling me, educating me. Now he's on to stories about flying flocks of Taoist priests. The shrill ring of the phone jolts me. Shit! Who's calling? I pull out the earphone and turn off the machine.

"Hey."

"Tiff. It's kind of late and I'm working."

"They paying you overtime?"

"No."

"You forgot."

"Forgot what?"

"Remember last week—I told you I was setting you up with this guy I met at work? Our double date tonight?"

"Yes. And remember I told you I didn't want to go?"

"You have to come. He seems really nice . . . but not so nice that you wouldn't want to date him. Ha ha."

"No, Tiff."

"This is exactly what we talked about—the reason your life is so boring. And don't tell me you have to stay home with Sam, either, because it's totally weird and psycho. Honestly."

"I really do have to work and, anyway, I look like shit."

"You're coming. He's a good catch. In marketing or something like that," Tiff says, ignoring me. "Wear something casual, young looking. And don't borrow anything from your mom. That's the worst."

"I'm serious, Tiff. I'm supposed to get these notes back by tomorrow."

"So get up early and finish it."

"And my hair is dirty."

"C'mon. Get dressed. And do something about your bangs. Try to make them not so flat."

"I don't know."

"Just wash them, okay? You'll look great. It'll be fun."

I'm probably making a mistake. I hate blind dates—especially those ragged little dead moments of excruciating silence when neither one of you has the foggiest notion of what to say to each other. Stuff just comes out of my mouth. It's never as smooth and funny as those guys on talk radio. I really admire them. They go on and on about nothing, but they still make it interesting. I wish I could do that. Now, Tiff, she's terrific. She can walk into a room, radiant and bubbly, and talk to anyone. She's a marvel. She really is.

Tiff swings by and picks me up at nine. She's wearing a satin camisole with a lacy bra peeking out, black jeans, and cowboy boots. Her movie-star platinum hair flows like water over bare shoulders, and even though her clothes are kind of flashy, she always has this wholesome, uncomplicated cheerleader thing going on.

"Yoo hoo, Cassie. Are you ready?"

I can tell she's not wild about my outfit. I didn't want to look like I tried too hard but, on the other hand, I didn't want to look like I've given up. I'm wearing a camel cardigan and some perfectly fine camel slacks. Tiff eyes me up and down.

"Too matchy matchy and it wouldn't kill you to put on a little makeup," Tiff says, disapprovingly.

"I did."

"Oh. Well, you need more." She pulls her makeup kit out of her purse and drags me to the bathroom. "Hi, Sam."

"Shut the fucking door!" Sam squawks.

Tiff starts to laugh. "He's so rude. Don't complain about this guy's mouth tonight. Look what you live with."

Tiff smears a pale, glowy blush called "Orgasm" on my cheekbones, and adds some liquid brown eyeliner.

"You have gorgeous eyes, but you'd never know it." She brushes coppery brown shadow on my eyes. "See how green they look now? Like giant gumdrops. And don't you have a push-up?" I look at her. Obviously, I don't.

"If you want, we can stop by my house and borrow one of mine. It'll really make a difference."

"Why bother, if no one's going to see it?"

"You never know what the night will bring. Underwear's very important. Rich girls spend a fortune on it. Anyway, I bet you ten dollars you're going to have a good time tonight."

"Okay," I say. "If you win, I pay you ten dollars. If I win, I get to go to heaven."

"At least change the shirt."

I take off the camel sweater, pull on a blue V-neck, and study us in the mirror. Tiff is pretty, pretty, blonde with a pert tiny nose, kitteny Bardot mouth, and a blinding flash of teeth. I'm tall and thin, but my features aren't as easily categorized. I like my nose, it's long and straight, but my smile is a little off center and my hair is a mousy shade of brown. We look like the "before" and "after" shots in some fashion magazine. I glance back in the mirror and stick my tongue out at myself. Sometimes I wish I were a vampire. No reflection.

"Stop it. You look great." She smiles, pumping me up.

As we head for the kitchen door, I grab her arm and whisper conspiratorially, "We need to go out the other way. I don't want Sam to see me leaving. He was looking forward to our evening home together, and if he knows I'm leaving he'll scream bloody murder."

"Give me a break."

"You have no idea how upset he gets. These guys have major separation anxiety."

"Whatever. Try to act semi-normal, Cassie."

We arrive at Shorty's about a half hour late. Rap music is screeching like a set of bad brakes in a subway station. Tiff immediately spots our dates seated at the end of the bar glued to the flat-screen football game. There are two empty glasses of beer in front of them and the gallon-sized pitcher is three-quarters empty. Tiff's date, Tom, turns, gives us a goofy grin, and waves us over. I swear to God, he looks just like a satyr, half goat, half human, with pointed ears and hook nose. His human half is just like I've always imagined—hairy body, arms, and face. All he needs are the little horns on his forehead. I make a mental note to tell Tiff later that these creatures used to lie in wait and jump on innocent nymphs.

Mine seems to be nice looking, preppy—khaki pants, polo shirt. Pleasant face. He eyes me coolly as Tiff introduces us.

"Hi there, I'm Phil," he says in a flat tone, as he stands up stiffly and shakes my hand. His expression tells it all. He's clearly disappointed.

Tiff squeezes on the bar stool with Tom. She gives him a coy little laugh. My date's eyes dart all over the room as his fingers drumroll on the bar.

"Bring over a couple more glasses," Tom says to the bartender as he grabs the pitcher and leads us to a wooden booth in the corner. Phil excuses himself to go outside and use his cell. Probably lining up something else for the night.

"Tom here's in the mattress business," Tiff says, trying to get a conversation going. My date has come back inside, and he's cornered one of the waitresses behind the bar. He should be hooded like a falcon.

"Yeah, you know what I always say . . . sleep happens." Tom laughs, elbowing Tiff, who fakes a giggle.

"So how's the mattress business?" I ask, not that I'm interested. Meanwhile, I see Phil writing down something on a piece of paper and slipping it in his back pocket. The waitress smiles as he saunters back to our booth.

"Well, here's what I always ask people," says Tom. "When's the last time you got a really great night's sleep? And if you can't remember, then you need a new mattress. People always need beds. Like coffins. You gotta sleep, right?"

Tiff downs her beer, leans in, and whispers, "By the way, did you know that Cassie's a widow?" Total silence at the table. That's always a real icebreaker. I could just kill her.

"That's too bad. So how did he die?" says Tom, unfazed.

"She doesn't like to talk about it," Tiff jumps in.

"Oh, I'm sorry," Tom says sympathetically.

"Don't worry about her. She hated the son of a bitch." Tiff flashes an innocent grin.

Now everyone's looking at me. I feel I should say I didn't murder him. My date, who hasn't said a word to me since he sat back down, asks, "How long's he been gone?"

"About three years," I answer tersely. I hate talking about this shit, although, I must say, I went through a period right after Frank died where I felt compelled to tell everyone. Even complete strangers. To the kid behind the Starbucks counter, "I never used to buy these lattes when my husband, *Frank*, was alive. Too expensive. Do you have any shaved chocolate?" Or to the woman at the perfume counter at Target, "I've been a widow now for three weeks and I need a little lift. What do you think of this fragrance?" Or at the gas station down the street, "My husband just morte. Dead. Brakes no good. Can I use your bathroom?"

But now I can't stand to talk about it. That doesn't seem to stop this dimwit.

"So what'd you do with the mattresses?" says Tom. " 'Cause some people take old, moldy mattresses, cover them, and sell them like new. Have you ever noticed a mattress that smells?"

"Not really. After my husband died, I just tipped my house over into the Pacific Ocean and threw everything out." Another silence.

"It was a car accident," Tiff adds. What that has to do with anything, I have no idea.

"I heard widows are like virgins, it's the first time all over again," Tom pipes up as he winks at his friend Phil, who could care less. Now everyone's looking at me for some kind of response. This is just so crass. I need to get out of here. I look pleadingly at Tiff.

"You know what?" Tiff announces abruptly. "We can't stay. Cassie needs to go home and finish up her work."

"Oh. We were just getting started here . . ." Tom says, deflated.

"Next time. Nice meeting you," we both say as we scramble out of the booth.

Tiff and I try to squelch our laughter until we get into her car, but don't quite make it. We're both guffawing as we roll into her red Mazda. She unhooks her push-up bra and lets out a low whistle.

"You know, Phil was a lot nicer in the office. And to think how much I helped him with that DUI. What a jerk," Tiff says apologetically. "God, Cassie. I'm sorry."

"He had a DUI?"

"I didn't mention that?"

I look at my friend. Sometimes she's so clueless it drives me batty, but the one thing I know is the first time we met, we pulled together like magnets—friends for life. Back in grade school, we'd talk for hours about everything. Later on, we'd smoke cigarettes stolen from her brother and drink, always trying to figure out new combinations of liquor and mix, staying out way too late, sneaking into the bowling league with our matching satin jackets. Being with Tiff was like driving too fast someplace, the wind rushing in your face and tearing up your eyes. I could tell her anything. She was the only one who knew I wanted to go to college. With my atrocious grades, how could I mention it to anyone else? It was just too stupid. They'd laugh.

It's strange. I'm not upset about tonight. In fact, I feel okay. I had a good day and I loved listening to Conner's lecture, especially when he talked about Emerson, who found spiritual meaning in the wilderness and called it "immortal beauty." That's just how I feel. Emerson described himself as an endless seeker with no past at his back. No past at his back. It all gives me hope in a way. Like some kind of optimism based on nothing. Even undisguised rejection can't ruin my mood.

CHAPTER 10

W hen I get home, Mom has already
covered Sam's cage and Black Dog is
on a big cushiony doggy bed, wound
up in a tight breathing ball. She's washed and
brushed him and now his coat has a lovely brindle
sheen. His eyes are nice too, soft liquid brown.
He's wearing a handsome braided leather collar
and looks like an entirely different dog. A gentleman dog. And not as old as I thought. He sees me
staring at him and wags his tail as I walk over and
pat his head. Hope Sam doesn't get too bent out
of shape.

The *New York Times* is lying on the kitchen
counter. Midway through Conner's lecture, he'd
mentioned an article in the *Times* about birdsongs. When I went to his office on my last mail
run, I noticed he'd dumped the paper in his trash,
so I grabbed it and brought it home. A public service really. Recycling. When I opened it, I noticed a bunch of other junk mail inside. A cell
phone ad. Credit card application. And an invita-

tion to a gallery opening with a nice nature photo on the front. I put that on my dresser.

Then I start reading the article on birdsongs. It's in the "Science" section of the *Times*. It says that some birds are whistlers, some are drummers, some have syncopated rhythms—this guy attributes human emotions to bird sounds. Big revelation. I'll invite him over to dinner with Sam and me. Oh, here's an article about gay sheep. Now, that's interesting. Eight percent of rams seek sex exclusively with other rams instead of ewes. That can't be right. I'd have thought it was much higher. Ewes are disgusting. I'll mention this the next time my mother wears her pashmina.

Now I switch to the "Style" section. It says the "it" bag costs twenty-five hundred dollars and there's a waiting list. Speaking of sheep. I turn the page to the parties. Mrs. So-and-So has raised three billion dollars for the Animal Rights Foundation. I scribble down the name. I'll give it to my mom for her next fund-raiser. This is so much better than the local paper. I look at the price of a year's subscription. Never mind. I'll just start taking it from Conner's trash.

My mom canceled the *LA Times* last year when she got busy at work and the papers started piling up in the kitchen still in their wrappers. She said it made her feel guilty that she couldn't keep up and she preferred the *Topanga Times*, which is free and talks about neighborhood stuff like drainage, runoff, brush removal, and hippie dippy gatherings that still draw a load of blowhard stoners with fried eggs for brains.

As I head into the bedroom, I hear my mother's voice sail over the din of her TV. "How was your evening, dear?"

"Great, Mom. Really great." I never like to tell my mother the whole depressing story. She gets too upset.

"That's nice, dear."

My mother is lying in bed, engrossed in an old movie on

TV. There's a bunch of empty coffee mugs and water bottles on her bedside table along with two "universal" remotes, neither of which has worked for ages. It doesn't seem to bother her, although personally, it would make me nuts. She just gets up and changes the channel without even thinking about it. Her face is lathered in Aloe Vera Flowing Velvet night cream. It's $9.95 from the Topanga General Store, and for as long as I can remember, she's been mixing it with mineral oil and a glob of cow udder cream. It's gross, but her skin is smooth and youthful. She gives it as presents to all her friends for Christmas. At the moment she's wearing an old sweatshirt over flannel pajamas. This one happens to read "I Brake for Animals," but she has a whole collection of them in her closet, with catchy little slogans that pretty much run the gamut from saving the planet to pictures of baby seals being bludgeoned by Eskimo hunters. She'll wear them to the center when she works, but I put my foot down if we go out to dinner.

I don't watch TV anymore, but after Frank died, that's all I did. Everybody agreed it was too much, but I didn't care. Whenever Tiff called, I'd say, "I'm right in the middle of my show. Can I call you back?" Tiff was nice about it for a while but then told me that no matter what time of the day or night she called I was always in the middle of "my show." It wasn't healthy. As if I didn't know.

I'd start out in the morning right after breakfast. My favorite was *Star Kitchen Makeovers* and then all the food shows would come on, like *Extreme Pastry*, with those guys holding squishy cones that make amazing cakes with curlicue flowers and stuff. After lunch, I'd roll into the weepy, sad, "tell us all about your miserable life" shows, like *Cancer Survivor* and all those talk shows where women pour out their hearts to a TV audience that applauds whenever they make statements like, "I'll never let him hurt me again." One guy stole this woman's money and got into all her bank accounts. She thought he loved her when really he was dating her best friend's daughter. One piece of shit after another. These women were even stupider than I was. Misery loves company, that's what I always say.

My mother doesn't have much of a social life either. Like mother, like daughter. My father died when I was six. He was shaving before work and just keeled over. My mother says she heard a thud and then there was this silence. He was tall with a big voice, but sometimes I think I just remember his face from the photos in the living room. Mom never re-married, although there once was a man who'd take her to the movies and out to dinner. She'd get all dolled up while I played in her closet, but then he stopped coming around. I never heard why.

She pats the side of her bed and tells me to sit next to her.

"I'm going to Joshua Tree next week to look for Bigfoot. Want to come?"

"I can't, Mom," I say, without commenting further.

Now she starts gently massaging my neck and shoulders. This has become our little ritual. She used to read to me at night, but now, both of us widowed, she rubs my back and asks me about my day.

When I was a child, our big day together was always Sunday. We used to go to the nine-o'clock service at Malibu Presbyterian and then afterward head to the wildlife center. The early service had acoustic guitars and a folk-songy feel about it which my mother liked, as opposed to the eleven a.m. in which there was a full-fledged rock band and "too much noise."

I felt good sitting next to her in church, holding her hand and listening to her sing and recite, but I liked walking in the woods with her better, her knack of casually identifying everything that grew there and talking about the order in an untouched environment. It seemed more religious being with her there.

My mother's always been different from other people's moms, but I don't mind. Her version of reality works for her—all her fairy tales of what really goes on in the forest, in the shadows, and under the sea.

I remember a summer day when my mother first took me to the tide pool in a small cove near Ventura, where she grew up. I was about six years old, and was much more interested in the ice cream man we had passed on our drive down. We sat on the uneven rocky bottom and our feet sank into the cool muddy sand. I still remember the salty smell of the warm sea air and how it filled my nostrils like perfume.

She pointed to the universe of undulating life beneath the shallow water. The bright blue bands circling the legs of the hermit crabs that skittered under the rocks to hide. The pink, black, and green abalone so abundant in those days, the starfish, and the smooth white sea dollars. My mother saw the world through the eyes of these creatures telling me she could read their minds and understand their thoughts. At one point, she dipped her hand into the water as a jellyfish silently floated above and her fingers illuminated, like some translucent angel's wing.

Later, she told me stories about Atlantis, Poseidon, horses, and earthquakes. Her voice was full of the sea, the sky, the forest, and the underworld as she offered up tales of the gods who dwelled in these places and helped create them. Oceanus, the ancient god of the water, with his seaweed hair, dolphins leaping from his beard, and the sea streaming, like a waterfall, out of his mouth. Her imagination danced between the sublime and the ridiculous. Even today, whenever I become frustrated with her far-out theories, I try to remember my mother sitting there, in the tide pool, lit up like a moonbeam.

Right now my mother's watching that old movie *Vertigo*

for the hundredth time. I never understood what Jimmy Stewart saw in Kim Novak. She lies to him about everything, and he's still obsessed with her. I can't watch it again.

I say good night, strip off all my clothes, and step into the shower—a prefab, wavy Plexiglas affair that's stuck, like an afterthought, to the outside wall of my bedroom. When I first moved back home, my mother had a friend get it from Home Depot and install it. It's kind of long and rectangular, like a Porta Potti, and sometimes, I feel like I'm locking myself in a closet or the trunk of a car. Plus, the noise from the water hitting the base of the shower sounds like a jackhammer. I usually get about five minutes before the hot water runs out.

I collapse into bed and see the dog turn around and around and then settle on the floor with a sigh beside me. I hear *Vertigo* coming from the next room. What's it like, I think, to have a man that in love with you? Someone who would give up *everything* for you. Tiff and I have a litmus test for how much a guy really loves you. We call it our "bullet test." Would he be willing to take a bullet for you? No one's ever passed.

I just begin to nod off when the bed lurches and all hundred pounds of Black Dog land on my stomach.

"Go back to your bed," I scold. He jumps off, leaving a hollow, wrinkled dent, and stands there giving me a mournful look. No way is he going to make me feel guilty. I turn over in my empty bed and think about the two men Tiff and I dumped tonight. At least the mattress doesn't smell.

CHAPTER 11

When I walk in the office the next day, Alison's on the phone scowling like an angry child, apparently having one of those "no, I didn't; yes, you did" kind of conversations. She lets out a big sigh and snaps shut her cell phone like a Venus flytrap. She's wearing a fake black fur vest over a white turtleneck. The skunk look. She still has that weekend sunburn glow around her nose and cheeks, but her eyes are cold and cheerless. "Hi." I smile civilly. No sense letting our mutual dislike for each other bubble over the surface.

"Oh. Hey," she says tersely, barely looking up. Nice. "Could you deliver the stuff in the mailroom? Professor Pearce wants me to stay here and get the phones." Code for, let the pretty one sit out front and the hunchback skulk around in the basement. Sometimes it's a curse to have an imagination.

I trudge from office to office dropping off

mail. When I get to Professor Conner's office I hear animated voices. I'm not sure whether to interrupt or come back later.

"I don't know why they don't like me," someone complains to Conner.

"Oh come on," Conner soothes. "The *Cue Guide* isn't that important—just some student evaluation. And all the kids lie. Didn't you see that Josephson poll? Sixty percent of the kids said they'd cheated on a test last year and the same number had lied to a teacher. Over 50 percent said they'd lied to their parents, which everyone knew was low, so the conclusion was they even lied about lying."

"This is different, it's an anonymous poll and the numbers look pretty accurate to me. Ten percent say I'm engaging."

"That's good."

"Fifteen percent say I'm interesting."

"See? It's not so bad."

"And 90 percent say I'm dull!"

"Well, that's not possible. That's more than 100 percent!" Conner says, with a chuckle.

"And 85 percent advise their peers *not* to take my course. And listen to this, they think I have a poor sense of humor. Now, you know I have a good sense of humor. Aren't I funny?"

"Not particularly, Hank. But I must say your limericks are pretty clever."

I tap lightly on the door. Conner waves me in and introduces me to a short, bow-tied, middle-aged man with a Friar Tuck bald spot in the middle of his head. He's one of those guys who has no noticeable sex appeal. His pants are hitched too high on his girly-shaped hips and he has what usually comes with this package—a round, soft butt.

He's also allergic to "something in here" he says (probably the dog), and his eyes are all red and watery. He's holding the *Cue Guide* along with a wad of Kleenex and I notice he has long black hairs on his fingers. And he's wondering why the students don't find him appealing.

"Nice to meet you, Cassie. But seriously, Conner. How do you get these astronomical scores?"

"I don't know about that, I just try to make it more relatable. You can make anything interesting to anyone. I could take someone with no background and no education and turn them on to science. It's all in the presentation."

I quickly drop the stuff on his desk and turn to leave, when he suddenly addresses me. "Isn't that right, Cassie?"

"I guess so."

"You were at my lecture. Tell Hank what you thought." They're both looking at me for an answer.

"You're putting the poor girl on the spot here, Conner."

"We're not putting her on the spot. She can say anything she wants. It's a free country." They're talking about me like I'm not here.

"Go ahead, Cassie. Be honest." Conner smiles confidently.

"Well, I loved your lecture."

"Because . . ."

"Well, um, because"—I feel my face flush—"it made me feel as if everything belonged to everything else."

"There you go, she's a goddamn John Muir!" beams Conner, proudly. He's thrilled with my response. But who's John Muir? He goes to his bookshelf and tosses me two dog-eared volumes.

"Have you read these, my favorites, meditations from the 1890s about Yosemite?" I start to leaf through one of the thin volumes. He goes on.

"My point is, you have to make your lectures relate to

everyday life. 'To see a world in a grain of sand and heaven in a wildflower.' Don't you agree, Cassie?"

"Absolutely," I say robotically. His eyes twinkle.

"I don't think it matters what I do." Hank sulks. "The students just sit there staring out the window. Half the time, I want to throw the lot of them out of it. Anyway, I can't go around quoting Blake in my geology class. I'd look like an ass." He sniffs.

"But that's precisely what you should do. Bring in all the disciplines, poetry, art, quote Whitman or Emerson. 'It's a long way from granite to the oyster, farther yet to Plato.' Play Handel, Bach. Take them on hikes. Take an overnight field trip to Joshua Tree."

"I'm not taking an overnight field trip! And I hate camping except for that one time you dragged me to Yosemite, when I had issues."

"Oh, that's right. I forgot. You're at two with nature, like Woody Allen. Joshua Tree's great."

"Well, I don't know about that," I say, hesitantly.

"Have you been there, Cassie?"

"Oh yes. Lots of times with my mother. Pretty much like Death Valley, lots of poisonous, pointy things and spooky dead trees with twisty branches. When the wind blows, nothing moves. Tarantulas and lizards skewered on sticks like shish kebob . . ."

"Great suggestion, Conner."

"Well, it's not so bad at night," I backpedal. "That's when the stars come out, thousands of them. My mother's camped out there looking for the Silhouette. In fact, one night she claims she even saw him."

"The Silhouette?" Hank asks.

"Yes. She told me that she and her friends were in the woods, and all of a sudden, there was this crunching sound and the rustle of big feet on dry leaves. Then she saw him dancing around with his tree-trunk legs in plain sight. She's going back in a few weeks with a whole group to try to find him again."

"Are you talking about Bigfoot?" Conner asks, incredulously.

"Yes!" Of course. Who did he think I was talking about?

"She said it was like being in the presence of something ancient and alive and that his breath smelled like pine needles and damp earth and . . ." I glance up. The two of them are staring at me in stunned silence.

"You don't believe this, my dear?" Hank asks, in an excruciatingly polite tone of voice.

"I'm talking about my mother . . ." I say, embarrassed.

"You know," says Conner kindly, "the god Dionysus is believed to be a forerunner of Bigfoot, the Silhouette, Yeti, or whatever the hell you want to call it. The legend is that he was Lord of the Wilderness, God of Wine and Madness. Some people still believe that he exists—a symbol of everything that's spiritual about nature."

This man should meet my mother. I gather the pile of mail and start to slip out.

"Hey, Cassie," Conner calls after me, smiling. "You gave me a great idea. I'm going to do a lecture on the Green Man."

"I'll let my mother know," I shoot back. "She's got photos."

CHAPTER 12

I finish delivering the mail and then break for lunch. It's Friday afternoon and the campus is buzzing. I still feel out of place among all these students. I can't help but envy them. They're right on the cusp of starting their lives, choosing their careers. No past. No bad decisions to live down. No damage.

After lunch, I'm lost in my thoughts when I see one of those mean meter maids pulling up to a sleek silver Jag parked next to me. This is probably the same bitch who gave me a ticket my first day of work. Oh no. She's not getting her quota here. No way. I reach into my purse, grab two quarters, and quickly shove them into the meter. Gotcha! She shoots me a dirty look, gets back into her mini cart, and drives off.

Fuck her. As I head back to my office, I hear someone calling after me.

"Excuse me. Excuse me!"

I turn and see this tall tan man about my age,

cool and crisp, wearing a beautiful, pin-striped suit and monogrammed white shirt with cuff links. His hair is immaculately gelled back from his temples, and he's holding a BlackBerry to his ear.

"Did you just put money in my meter?" he asks.

"Yes. I hate those meter maids—circling every five minutes like vultures."

"That was so nice of you." He flashes a privileged smile. "Can I buy you a cup of coffee or something?"

"Not necessary. But thanks anyway."

"No. Thank *you*," he says.

Here's the weird thing. I go to the restroom and when I get back, the same man is talking to Alison.

"Hey," he says. "Hello again."

"You two know each other?" Alison asks. Maybe it's her boyfriend or something.

"Not formally. Hi! I'm Freddy, Alison's brother."

Talk about opposites. Freddy tells Alison how we met and her gracious response is, "Cassie works in the Xerox room."

Then the two of them take off. Some family gathering. I'm always glad when she's gone. She gives me a tight stomach.

Later that evening, as I wait for the washing machine to finish its berserk cycle, I think about how ticked off Alison would've been if I'd actually gone for coffee with her precious brother. I *should* have gone. I bat away the thought and Google the University of Michigan. Since I graduated from there, I figure I better know something about it. I don't even know what city it's in. I select my college, dorm (I pick the ivy-covered red brick one near the Quad), what psych courses I took, including the labs, which professors I loved, and what the team name is—Go Wolverines! I order some rah-rah knickknacks for my desk—bright yellow coffee mug with a big *M* on it and a yellow and blue frame with "Wolverines" written on the bottom. Next time someone mentions Michigan, I'll know what I'm talking about—hopefully.

I've been teaching Sam all about my "alma mater." He now says, "Go Blue!" and fluffs up all his feathers to make himself look twice as big. He's my Big Bird on Campus. When I touch him his tail flares, and I gently ruffle the feathers on his neck. His skin feels like a newborn baby. So soft and warm.

He picks up his little ball, pushes it toward me with his beak, and says, "Play."

"Okay. But just for a few minutes. I love you. Kiss, kiss." Sam gently puts his beak on my lips.

"Kiss, kiss," he says, nuzzling my ear.

After Conner's lecture, I went to the library and checked out a few books on Whitman, Thoreau, and Emerson, since they are evidently part of "required freshman reading." I brought the books back to my desk and started reading, which for me is still a chore. For one thing, I have to use my finger, following the sentences, one by one. And for another, I do much better if I read aloud, which isn't easy at work. When someone walks by, I have to pretend I'm on the phone. I'm glad I'm hidden away in the Xerox room where I can focus on the material without a lot of outside noise. But it's still too difficult to read in bits and pieces, so I decided just to wait until I got home.

I start with the Thoreau. This one is tough sledding. But there must be something interesting to it. Conner thinks he walks on water.

All of a sudden, I hear someone calling Black Dog. In my voice. "Here boy! Here boy!" Oh shit. Sam is such a royal pain. A pint-size ventriloquist with multiple personalities like Sybil. This is his new game, pretending he's me, calling Black Dog, then rushing and pecking at his head when he comes in. I throw down the book and run to the kitchen where Sam has Black Dog cowering in the corner. Some watchdog.

"Bad bird!" I say to Sam. The pupils of his eyes pin and dilate when he doesn't like something he's hearing. He starts to squawk and flings his seeds. Whenever he gets this way, I just give him some space. Frank never learned this. He used to go after him screaming and yelling. Sam would quietly wait for him to get close and then try to lop off the tips of his fingers. In those days, I was rooting for Sam.

Black Dog follows me into the bedroom, panting heavily, and flops down with a sigh as I glance at that gallery invitation on my dresser. There's a nice black-and-white photo of a stand of white birches on one side and, on the other, details for an open house cocktail reception and photo exhibition. I asked Tiff to come with me. What the hell. It sounded interesting.

She never asked how I got invited and, anyway, if I told her we were crashing, it wouldn't bother her. Then again, if I fessed up that I took the invitation out of my boss's trash, she'd figure, if he dumped it, it had to be some loser event. The photographer happens to be a popular professor at the university. Tiff thought it sounded like a snooze until I told her the invitation mentioned a margarita bar and salsa band. Now she's calling it "cool and night-clubby." And she's dressing accordingly. It's tomorrow night, and I'm not sure what to wear. But then again, I never know what the right clothes are, and I'm always afraid of making the wrong choice. As a result, I don't wear anything too fancy or daring. Tiff tells me I do it on purpose. I dress with the expectation of not being seen, and, as a result, I'm not.

CHAPTER 13

The Case Gallery is on Robertson Blvd—an expensive shopping area straddling Beverly Hills and West Hollywood. I came here once when one of the stores had a warehouse sale. The prices were about quadruple Macy's and the stuff looked like old junk—faded T's and studded belts with half the stones missing. The gallery is lit up like a gas station, and there isn't a parking space in sight. We pull up to the valet, who tells us it's seven dollars. Tiff winces. We drive around three or four times and then give up and pull back to the valet, who throws us a knowing smirk. No way was Tiff going to walk with her four-inch heels.

She's all dolled up in a velvet body-hugging dress, and her hair in an intricate updo. A little too Ice-Capadey for me. Tiff loaned me a pair of low-rise black jeans that definitely feel too tight and a pink angora off-the-shoulder sweater, which looks good, I think, but it itches and is shorter than I usually like my tops. I pulled it down in the car but Tiff said I'd stretch it out if I kept that up, so I stopped.

All I can say is when we first walked in, it was like being on the moon. The walls are bare and bright white, like the gleaming fuselage of a rocket. The floor is a black-chalk concrete, pitted with cracks and crevices, and the air-conditioning is so fierce you could hang red meat in here. There's salsa music blaring, and the women, who seriously outnumber the men, all look cold-blooded, even savage. They have on black dresses and suits with designer bags that clamp on them like armor. Their hair is blown in loose lay-ers and their jewelry kept to a minimum. I feel like burning all my clothes. Mine and Tiff's.

The girls glance at us as we walk by. They have perfect posture, and several are so thin that their shoulder blades stick out in back. They hold their feet in glorious position, as if they'd spent years in ballet classes, and have margaritas in one hand and shiny thin cell phones in the other. Some of them have Slavic accents, and I swear to God, they look like they're six feet tall. How do they all know what to say, what to wear, how to walk?

"This is so boring. There are no men here. Let's go," Tiff says, sizing up the scene in about two minutes, and starts to walk toward the door.

"Let's at least look at the art."

"What art? Are you fucking kidding me? Who came to look at the art? I thought this was a party."

"I never told you it was a party."

"Right. You told me it was a bullshit, snobby bunch of Amazons sipping margaritas, and I said great, count me in. You know, I've always tried to see the best in rich people, but sometimes, it just doesn't work."

"Drinks, ladies?" says a cute waiter with a tray of margaritas. He's tall and buff with some kind of Southern accent. Tiff perks right up.

"Could I just have a pinch more salt on my rim, hon?" She widens her eyes in an obvious, flirtatious way.

"Sweet," he replies, with a huge grin. Their eyes lock as he licks his index finger, pokes it in the salt bowl, and circles the rim of her glass.

"So where are you from?" he asks.

"Guess," she says, wrinkling her nose in that coy little way she has when she's interested in a guy. This is my cue to wander off. Where *is* the art, anyway? Not on the walls.

Maybe in the next room. I make my way through the throng. I'm now noticing subtle tattoos in places like wrists, ankles, index fingers, and lower backs. Also, one of the girls has the largest diamond stud earrings I've ever seen. I wonder if they're CZs.

Now I enter a room filled with beautiful, almost glowing, black-and-white pictures of simple, natural images. There's a snow-covered oak, a waterfall, an owl on a bare branch of a burnt-out tree, and one lonely melon. No prices, just little red dots on the walls.

"Reminds me of Adams deconstructed, don't you think? So protean." I turn to see a delicate-looking, very thin man in a black turtleneck and black slacks. His bald head is smooth and glassy like a cue ball. He's waiting for my response. My mother says when you find yourself at a loss, it's always safe to bring up the weather, or your health. But that would be bizarre. He looks at me expectantly.

"I don't know about that," I say, "but it seems to me that the artist knows just when to let things be. Everything he sees counts."

The man stares at me for a moment, with piercing black,

crow-like eyes. "Interesting. Good way to look at it. I'm Alfred Case."

"Oh, this is your gallery." He holds out his hand, which is soft and mushy like a woman's, and his nails are shiny like his head.

"I'm Cassie. Nice to meet you. Really nice exhibit."

"Well, thank you for coming. Are you on our mailing list?"

"I don't think so. A friend brought me." Tiff did drive.

"Why don't you sign in, and we'll send you an invitation for the next one?"

So this is how it's done. Now I'm on the list. That was easy.

I thank him and wander into the next exhibit, which is called "The Wasteland." Heavy-duty clamps, slashed tires, steel supports, a rusted-out carburetor. I'm hearing comments like "a richly perceptual experience." Looks like a hodgepodge of junk to me.

"Hey, look who it is. I still owe you." I whirl around and see Freddy. His handsome face is open, friendly, filled with confidence and prosperity, and his mouth is curled in a teasing half smile. He's still holding his BlackBerry to his ear.

"Considering you saved me from the mendacious meter maid, can I buy you a drink?" He winks, as he slips the BlackBerry in his pocket and plucks two margaritas from a waiter's tray.

"Thanks," I say, as I see Alison bearing down on us.

"God, Cassie, I never expected to see you here," she says, brash as ever. Her air-blue eyes are cold and appraising. She's wearing black, of course. Hair swept up in a seamless French twist.

"So who invited you?" she says, abruptly. I knew it—busted. Freddy interrupts.

"Who needs an invitation? They're probably grabbing people off the street." He smiles apologetically, giving his sister a "cut it out" look.

"I really like the photos," I say, feeling so uncomfortable I want to crawl out of here.

"I do too. A friend of mine is the photographer. Come. I'll introduce you." He takes my arm and guides me into the next room, leaving Alison standing there.

"Don't mind my sister," he says. "Sometimes she just doesn't think before she talks." And sometimes she does.

"Don't be too long," Alison snaps.

We enter the foyer, where we see the photographer surrounded by a crowd of his friends and decide to stand by the bar and wait for a lull.

"So, Cassie. Are you here with anyone?"

I think of Tiff, who at this very moment is flirting outrageously with one of the waiters, and when she's done she'll probably shove the hors d'oeuvres into a plastic bag in her purse.

"Just a friend," I reply. "Have you known the photographer long?"

"I've collected some of his work over the years. Now I'm into prewar German Expressionists."

"Are you a dealer?"

"No. It's just a hobby. I'm an investment banker. But I can't think of anything I'd rather spend money on than good art."

I'm assuming he has a place to live, and a warm jacket.

"My friends think I'm obsessed. I'm constantly prowling the auctions, and I have two dealers who tip me off when something good is about to come up."

"So what artists do you collect?"

"Just bought a little Austrian nude. The guy's going to be the next Klimt."

"Is there anything here you'd buy?" I say, looking impressed and pretending I'm crazy about Klimt, whoever that is.

"Not really." He shrugs, looking casually around the room. "I have four levels of collecting. 'Beautiful!' 'Gotta have it!' 'Can't live without it!' And, 'Jesus, I thought this was in a museum!' " I'm not sure how to respond to this. I'm wondering if this applies to women as well when, luckily, his BlackBerry goes off.

"I'm not going to get suckered into this," he says brusquely. "Tell him it's my last offer."

"Sorry." He puts the phone away again, looking at me appraisingly. "How long have you worked with Alison?"

"A few weeks."

"You like it?"

"Yeah. It's okay. But I'm thinking of going back to school at some point," I say in a tone which I hope sounds breezy, conversational—believable.

"Really," he says, genuinely interested. "Studying what?"

"Animal behavior," I answer without hesitation. "I've worked with animals for a long time."

"Is that so?" he says. I take a few more gulps of my margarita, as he slowly brushes a strand of hair which has fallen over my eye. I feel the heat rising in my face. I get it. So he's this type of man.

"Okay, then," he says, his gaze lowered in an intimate way. "I have a question . . . Do raccoons make good pets?"

I start to laugh.

"You're joking, right?"

"No, actually, I'm not," he says, looking at me with dancing eyes. "There's a raccoon that comes into my parents' backyard every night and bangs on the garbage can lids." He takes his fist and raps on the bar—no wedding ring. "They've been leaving him food."

"Oh, they should never do that! These animals have the cutest little baby hands, but they're very aggressive and have eighty-one *huge* razor-sharp teeth."

"Eighty-one, huh?"

"They also carry rabies and this indestructible strain of roundworm that you don't even want to know about. I mean, bird flu is nothing compared to what you can get from these parasites. When I worked at the wildlife center, we were very strict. No raccoons. A complete nightmare if we ended up with one."

He breaks into a grin. I notice that when he smiles, his eyes get all crinkly.

"This is really serious. I'm not kidding," I say.

"Oh, I know you're not kidding. I was never good in the sciences. And you're going for an advanced degree. I'm impressed."

"Thank you," I say. I'm fucked.

"I've been looking all over for you. I want to go home." Alison is back and she's in a foul mood. For once, I'm happy to see her.

Freddy hands her the valet ticket.

"Why don't you get the car and I'll be right out?"

"I don't have any cash," she says impatiently. He peels off a twenty from a wad in his pocket.

"See you at the office," Alison says, with a pasted-on smile. She looks at me like I just ran over her dog. Sometimes people should just say what they think. Like, "I hate that you're talking to my brother and why don't you drop dead."

"Right." I smile back. "See you."

Freddy waits until Alison is out of earshot, and then leans in to me.

"Really nice meeting you." He looks like he's going to ask

me something, but then thinks better of it and doesn't. He brushes off some of my pink angora fuzz that's sticking like dandruff to his jacket, and with a little squeeze on my shoulder, leaves. He didn't ask for my number but then again, he knows where I work. He'll never call me.

I head out to the courtyard and hear Tiff's tinkly little laugh. She's standing next to the bartender deep in conversation. I just hope she doesn't go home with him. She motions for me to come over. Now they're having shots of tequila and I join them. I don't think I've ever had it straight up like this before. It burns your nose and your temples and tastes delicious. As soon as you swallow it, there's an immediate rush. I down a few more shots. This stuff is really strong.

I start to think about Freddy. Sometimes I wish I could just flush the old life down the toilet and become who Freddy thinks I am. A smart scientist going for a graduate degree. Someone he could brag about to his friends. " . . . Guess who I met at the gallery . . . she's up for a Nobel this year . . . and she knows so much about raccoons . . . and very attractive too."

For some reason, I'm getting all weepy. I sidle up to Tiff.

"Psst. Did you see that guy and the blonde I was talking to?" Tiff puts her arm around me and gives me an affectionate drunken hug.

"She's the mean one from work."

"Well, the guy was cute."

"He doesn't like me," I say, affecting a tragic grin. "Nobody likes me."

"Cassie, can we talk about this later?" Tiff nods toward her newest conquest.

"Yeah. Sure," I say. Shit. I stumble over something and look down. Nothing there.

Oh, here comes that nice gallery owner.

"Hey." I give him a big smile and lean against the wall.

"Did you see the Wasteland exhibit in the next room?" At least someone's being friendly.

"Yes I did. Thank you for asking."

"It reminds me of the Graham installations last year. So full of restless energy, don't you think? Cassie, isn't it?" he says, staring at my fluffy chest. God, is he full of shit.

"I'll tell you what I think." My tongue is so dry. "I think it looks like my ex's wrecking yard. Well, not exactly 'wrecking,' it was really a tow company, but he did wreck a few of them to get the insurance money." I giggle, and some of the tequila comes up my nose.

"What?" he says. Wait'll he hears this.

"Well, it wasn't only the insurance money, that only worked if they were illegals. He used to steal whatever was inside the car and then act all huffy if they asked him about it. It was a real racket, I tell you." I'm so amusing. Why isn't he smiling?

"You actually ripped off the poor people whose cars you towed?"

"I didn't do it. Trust me. Son of a bitch I used to be married to did it. But he got punished royally. Drove himself off a cliff. Too bad I didn't think of that." Ha. Ha. Ha.

"Excuse me," he says, as he edges away. Well, fuck him if he can't take a joke. I down a few more hits of this delicious tequila. I notice he's looking at me and whispering something to his assistant. She walks over to me and says, "Can I help you get your car?"

I guess he changed his mind. They're fawning all over me.

"That is so nice of you," I gush. "Would you pay the

seven bucks too? Just kidding." I suddenly realize the room
is spinning. I sit down on the ice-cold concrete floor and see
a blurry image of Tiff walking toward me. I hear her growl at
a few people standing over me, "What are you looking at?!"

And that's all I remember. That's it.

CHAPTER 14

I wake up to a dismal Sunday morning. It's still dark and the splitter splatter of rain sounds like tin cans rolling down a concrete ramp on my brain. I try to ignore the waves of nausea that wash over me as I lie on the bed thinking about the wreckage of the night before. It was like the fall of Rome, or a massive pileup on the freeway. It all comes back to me in shameful fits of remorse creeping in like thick black smoke under a door. White trash. There. I've said it. That's what I am.

Another spell of nausea hits me in the gut. I pull off the matted, stretched-out, sorry angora sweater and go to the bathroom to throw up. I've always thought that people sound like they're dying when they puke. I'm getting too old for this. When was the last time I had an epic hangover? Maybe after Frank died. But that was more celebratory. Even without trying to sort out all the details, this one was just plain failure.

I make myself a cup of tea and sip it slowly, adding some of the organic honey Mom keeps for medicinal purposes. She swears it's good for everything. Her newest kick is dandelion leaves. She's always looking for good sources of fiber. And this, she says, cures cancer or something. Maybe just a little pot. I hear that's good for nausea. No chance of that here. It's the one plant my mother won't eat. Luckily, Mom wasn't here when Tiff scraped me off the floor and dragged me home.

"Boy, were you shit-faced last night!" Tiff laughs, when I call her. "You should've seen us hustled out of there."

"Oh God, Tiff. I'm so sorry. I didn't even drink that much."

"That's what all the drunks say."

"I'm so embarrassed."

"Oh, forget it. Who cares anyways?" I'm thinking, I do.

I wander outside, sit on our old rusted metal chairs, and listen to the wind's hoarse soothing voice trail through the hills. The rain has stopped, and the sky is leaden with a hint of negativity. You can almost smell the chlorophyll as the sullen day wears on. A mess of flat leather-brown leaves are pasted on our driveway, and I hear the sound of a blackbird somewhere. There's a jittery little squirrel on a telephone wire that does a tightrope dance on his toes, then leaps to our bird feeder, grabs some seeds, and somersaults backward.

There was a moment last night when I could have done it. When I *did* do it. Sophisticated, smart people thought I was one of them. When I was younger, I used to just give up without even trying. That way when I failed, it wasn't such a big deal. I'd just laugh it off. Ha ha ha. Cassie's lazy. Cassie's an oddball. Cassie doesn't care. But when you try, and blow it, then you're just a stupid loser.

I've always had this feeling that nothing great will ever happen to me. That I'm a fuckup. A real goddamn tragedy. I tried to fool myself that when I got this job things would change. But here I am. The same worthless dullard with nothing to say and no point of view.

"Good morning, my little sweetie. How was the gallery opening?" my mother asks cheerfully as she walks outside to greet me. She's wearing her old ratty robe and carrying a steaming cup of tea. I try to wipe the vomit off my sleeve.

"Really interesting," I say, with fake enthusiasm. Everything is swirling inside me, but outside I'm a vision of tranquillity.

"Can you help me today at the center? Sylvia's off to the condor sighting. Isn't that exciting?"

"No. I hate condors," I mutter. "Bald-headed vultures, feeding on rat carcasses and roadkill."

"So, say around noon?" she says, ignoring any unpleasantness, as she always does.

"Okay. Sounds good. No problem," I reply.

I remember one evening when Frank was alive, we took my mom and her friend, Sylvia, out to dinner. In the middle of the roast beef, Frank and I got into this gigantic fight. I can't even remember what it was about, but at one point he shouted, "Why don't we just get a divorce! I'm sick of this shit." Hard to believe, but throughout the entire scene, my mother sat calmly telling Sylvia about some ballet she had just seen on TV . . . the glorious costumes . . . the pas de deux . . . the music.

"It was just heavenly," I heard her say above the shouting. All my life, she's somehow been able to blissfully ignore painful moments. What a talent. She doesn't want to hear it, so she doesn't.

It's still early. I could sit here and wallow. Or I could go to the clearing. The ivory-bills seem to have taken up residence, although it's still too early for them to build their nests. I pull myself together and decide to go. For some reason, once I'm there, my spirits lift. I pull on my jeans, worm into my rubber Wellies, and completely cover myself with green, not even an inch of skin showing. The idea is not so much to blend in but to actually become a bush.

It's quiet as I head out on the trail. Everything's heavy, damp, waterlogged. I step over a jumble of twisted branches and deep rotted trees filled with silent decay and teeming with beetles and termites. The vegetation is so dense that I have to plow straight through the elbow-high grass.

I cross over the creek, mined with poison oak and velvet toadstools, and then head through the forest. The sky is filtered through a muddy light crisscrossed with dewy cobwebs. At first, all I hear is the chattering of magpies and robins and the croaking of bullfrogs. Every kind of sound except the one I'm listening for.

I venture forward, my 24× binoculars swinging back and forth around my neck, as I use my flashlight like a machete, swatting my way to my clearing. I follow a path that only I know through the dense trackless undergrowth. There is a primeval feeling here, like I'm in Middle Earth. I stand motionless and wait. Even the most minute movement thirty miles away is like a gunshot to the birds. Their sensory abilities are profound. I try not to even breathe.

Then I hear them. Loud, nasal haughty honks. And then the distinctive double knock that echoes through the forest. *Kent kent . . . kent kent . . . kent kent.* It seems to come from an otherworldly being as it swoops like an arrow in its upside-down heaven.

I focus my binoculars upward and I see the male. His unmistakable profile, the white trailing feathers, the slick, gleaming body. He is hopping from wood to wood, calling to his mate in a tinhorn voice. She calls back, and I remember reading that these creatures live for thirty years and mate for life.

As I sit here watching them trip the light fantastic in the tree, my headache eases. Time stops. How could anything this beautiful reach the brink of extinction? But, then again, it was the bird's astonishing beauty that sealed its fate. Indians thought they were magical and wore headdresses made from the white bills. Or they would crush the bills and eat them, hoping to inherit the bird's strength and power. Their history makes you sick. Everyone wanted their heads and bills. One collector killed forty-four in a week. He sold them for specimens and for feathers in women's hats.

Everyone knew about the ivory-billed woodpecker at the wildlife center. They talked about the national obsession to find the bird. Sometimes in the fall, those extreme birders would come into the center and tell us of their quest. How they just got back from Louisiana and thought they'd discovered a roost tree, or a fragment of an eggshell, or feathers. They'd scour the old-growth forests, the swamps, interrogating each other about the one that got away, like hypercompetitive alpha males trading war stories. Hunters disguised as nature boys. That's all they were.

If I told anyone about these birds, they wouldn't believe me. It's so far away from their habitat. They'd think I was crazy. But if I finally *did* convince them, all hell would break loose. Like that time someone thought they saw one perched on a Dumpster behind a Baskin-Robbins just outside Denver. Within twenty-four hours, hundreds of amateur bird-watchers got on planes from all corners of the world and descended on the area. Forestry managers, conservationists, researchers, ornithologists from universities, US Fish and Wildlife officials, the press. For sure, they'd all race down here with their telescopes, high-powered eyepieces, night-viewing attachments, telephoto lenses, thermoses of coffee, and garbage. They'd spook the birds or capture and "relocate" them. To tell you the truth, it scares the hell out of me to think about it.

I'd like to find just one person I could trust with this— someone who would do the right thing. But every time I consider it, I change my mind. I told Mom a few months ago that I thought I sighted the ivory-bill, and she said, "You and everyone else. But, my Lord, if you did see it, don't tell anyone. That bird needs freedom. Not scrutiny."

CHAPTER 15

Last weekend was such a disaster, I almost welcome seeing Alison on Monday morning, although she seems to be snottier than usual. I struggle through my routine without much conversation, while she sits ensconced at her desk, like the Queen of Sheba.

The day drags on and by the afternoon I'm beat, but I'm scheduled to work in Conner's office and start on the *D*'s. I climb the ladder to the top shelf. Darwin, Debussy, Descartes, Durrell. I'm thinking of cutting out early when I hear Conner ambling down the hall in my direction. Shit. Now I'll have to stay until five.

"Hi, Cassie, how's the weather up there?" he says cheerfully.

"Not bad. I'm on the *D*'s."

"Only the *D*'s?"

"It's because I've been doing some things for Professor Pearce."

"That's a *P*." He laughs. "How'd you like the Muir?"

"I haven't started it yet. I'm rereading Thoreau." I *am* rereading it—over and over.

"He's inspiring, isn't he?"

"His neighbors didn't think so. They all hated him. Did you know he started a forest fire in Walden right after he moved in, and burned over a hundred acres of woods?"

"Well, that shouldn't affect how you feel about his writing," he says, smiling.

"Of course it does. And furthermore, I think he was a big hypocrite. He told everyone to simplify, but he was living for free in Emerson's cabin on Emerson's land. He didn't have to work or pay rent. Simplify. Right. Just some rich guy on vacation."

"So Cassie, did you like *anything* he wrote?" he asks, baiting me.

"Well, he said the obvious. Your problems go away when you go into the woods . . ."

"I don't know if that'd be obvious to most people," he answers, shielding his eyes and looking up at me as if I'd just scaled Mount Everest. "Hey, why don't you take a break and come down here."

I climb down the ladder, dust myself off, and settle for a minute on the couch.

"Maybe you should try Emerson, you'd probably like him better. His father died when he was eight, he had a bum right eye, tuberculosis, and asthma, and he was fired from nearly every job he ever held."

"Is that a hint?" I ask.

"So far I'd have to say that you'll get tenure before me." Tenure. What a joke. I didn't finish high school. Thoreau was a hypocrite, but I'm a fraud.

"You see," Conner adds, "I'm not that great at in-house politics. Kind of like Emerson. He used to put a 'damn' in front of everyone's name . . . that damn Thoreau, that damn Hawthorne, that damn Alcott . . ."

He's chuckling now as his cell phone rings. He pulls it out of his pocket and turns away from me.

"Hey . . . I know . . ." he says, as he starts to walk to his desk. ". . . I'm sorry. . . . I just forgot. . . . You're right. . . . Sorry. . . ."

You can always tell when a man is talking to an angry woman. Also, I can hear her distinctive voice from across the room. It's Samantha. I decide to take a little break and duck out.

As I'm leaving that afternoon, I notice Conner's John Muir book still sitting in my car. Maybe I'll read it tonight. And then move on to Emerson.

CHAPTER 16

I'm supposed to have dinner with Tiff tonight, so I stop at the Topanga Center dry cleaner and pick up whatever's left of that angora sweater. They said they'd do what they could, but I'm sure it'll have one of those little notes that say, "We're sorry *but . . .*" And then, of course, I'll buy her another one.

I pull into Al's 24 Hour Cleaners. Usually Al's daughter, Flora, is behind the desk, but today I get the big guy himself. Such a meticulous profession for a former Marine.

"Hello, beautiful," he says in a gruff voice. "How's the new job going?" He flashes a wide smile, revealing a set of uneven, skid-row teeth.

"Oh, going great!" And it kind of is.

Al's been cleaning our clothes since I was a kid. Same rheumy, bloodhound eyes, same cracked red-veined nose. I still don't know how he can stand it here, the chemical smell from the machines wafts out the door and there are piles of people's dirty laundry strewn around like dead bodies in mesh bags. But he's always so cheerful, like a lot of people in my neighborhood.

"So give me the bad news."

He hands me the sweater, which is now matted, flattened, and looks like a drowned cat—a pink drowned cat.

"Pretty trashed," he says, sympathetically. "No charge. What'd you do, drive over it with a truck?" He snorts.

"Thanks, Al."

I get back into my car and call Tiff.

"Tiff, I'm here at Al's. Your sweater's dead. I'm buying you a new one."

"You don't have to. It's fine. Really. Just because it was my favorite sweater in the whole world given to me by—"

"Shut up."

We decide to meet at six at our neighborhood diner. It's wedged between the little gourmet natural food market and a souvenir shop with a tarot card reader in the back.

I arrive a half hour early, put Conner's book under my arm, and slide into my favorite greasy red vinyl booth that hisses when I sit down, like air coming out of a balloon. I open the book and start to read when I hear a commotion in the booth behind me. It's a family of three—a father, mother, and a little girl who is screaming her lungs out as she suddenly flings a purple plastic cup into my booth.

"*Agua, agua!*" the baby shrieks in panic. Now she's mad and throws her bunny as well.

"Just a minute, my sweetness, dollyface, angelheart," the mother croons softly and robotically to the baby. "Mommy will get your sippy-cup."

I pick up the cup, turn to hand it back, and recognize the couple from high school.

"Oh, hi," Stacy says. "Jim, you remember, uhm . . ." as

she searches for my name. The light in here is merciless, but she still looks good.

"Cassie." I muster a smile.

"Oh, hey, yeah, hi." Jim doesn't have a clue who I am, but he throws me a half wave. He looks exactly the same, but with a fatter face, thicker neck.

"Hi," I say, as I hand her back the sippy-cup.

"Oh, thank you," she says as she pulls out an antibacterial wipe from her purse, and gives it a good swipe where I touched it.

"Nice seeing you. Really," she lies, as she turns back to her family. I hear a coffee mug clank down on my table.

"Hey, hon. How ya doing?" Muriel says, as she shuffles over to my booth and pours me a cup of Yuban. She's been working here as long as I can remember. She's basically a mess. Ruined face, unbrushed hair, and arthritic fingers so swollen and bent, I have a hard time looking at them. She has chronic back spasms and periodically flings herself into an empty booth and lets out a weary groan. Her husband walked out a few years ago, and she likes to joke that no one ever went looking for him. People said that he was real mean, like Frank mean.

Muriel hands me the menu that hasn't changed since I meticulously memorized it when I was eight. Each time my mom would bring me in, I'd memorize a few more entrées and specials and then I'd pretend to read it to her. And she'd pretend to be impressed. It was part of the game we played.

"How's Lucky?" I ask.

"Just sits around and watches TV all day."

"Let him. He deserves it. These are his golden years."

"Don't remind me. Lucky's the only faithful man I ever had." She shakes her head and lets out a big booming laugh.

Why do people always name rescue dogs Lucky? Why

not Velveeta, a blend of who knows what? Anyway, this one's a deaf, balding, miniature poodle mix my mom gave to Muriel a few years ago. When someone first brought him into the wildlife center, he sure was a sorry piece of matted shit with a twisted screw tail. He'd been out on the highway for God knows how long and was covered in fleas and ticks. What would prompt someone to look at this bedraggled hound and say, "I'm going to name him Lucky"?

I guess it's all about the fact that things can change on a dime from disaster to bliss. Now that old "man" is sitting pretty on a velvet cushion watching the Nature Channel all day. We hear an urgent "bing, bing" and Muriel hustles off to pick up her order.

I warm my hands on the steaming cup of coffee. It's been a long day. I stare at nothing for a while, waiting for the caffeine to kick in, and then I open Conner's book and consider the photo of John Muir. He's crouched on a rock by a stream, his six-inch, frizzy beard trailing down his chest. He looks like the homeless guy down the street from my house. My mom is always giving him used tennis shoes, old blankets, and dried apricots. I thumb through the first chapter and see that Conner has written lots of notes in the margins. He must have been in a forest somewhere, euphoric, because they say things like, "Oh, yes!" and, "How true!" And certain phrases are underlined, like "don't lose your freedom" or "save yourself from deadly apathy."

What's this? Wedged between pages five and six is a carefully folded handwritten letter addressed to a woman named Pamela. I quickly stuff it in my coat pocket, and try to keep reading. But my mind keeps going back to the letter. Is it immoral to read someone's private letter? Of course it is. On the other hand, it's burning a hole in my coat. Oh hell. No one could resist this. I pull out the letter and unfold it.

"Dear Pamela, It's difficult for me to say this . . ."

Uh-oh. This doesn't sound good.

"but when we're together, the pleasures of heaven are with me and the pains of hell . . ."

Oh no! I can't read this. It's a goddamn love letter!

"I can't forget the miracle of your back, your arms, and your long beautiful limbs . . ."

Okay. I've got to stop.

". . . unspeakable, passionate love . . ."

I stifle a laugh. Come on! I can't believe this . . .

"I can still feel the warmth of your skin against mine. It's so sweet when I slide my hands down the middle of your back until I come to that place, at the base of your spine that curves so marvelously like sculpture."

Jesus. He was probably sitting up there on a rock in Yosemite, smoking something, and horny as hell. *Meditations from John Muir* couldn't help him with this. I get a pang of guilt. This isn't right. I continue reading.

"Come with me on this Mad, Naked, Summer Night."

God, he really had it bad for her!

I hear a chirpy "Hi, Muriel!"

Shit. Tiff's here! I shove the letter in the back of the book as she plops down across from me.

"I'm starved. What're you reading?"

"Oh, nothing."

"Well, what's that book?" Thank God. She was asking about the book. My hands are clammy. I'm a bad, bad person to read his letter. He never meant for anyone to see it, not even Pamela, whoever that is. I'm tossing it when I get home.

I show Tiff the book cover and she squinches up her nose in distaste. "Looks like some cult guy. What are you reading this for? Taking a night course?" She grabs the book and starts thumbing through it.

"No, someone at work gave it to me. Let's eat." I snatch it back and shove it deep in my purse.

"God, you'd think it was porno or something." Tiff laughs. She should only know.

We order turkey burgers and sprouts (everything in Topanga comes with sprouts). I don't know why, but I seem to have lost my appetite. I can't even finish half. Tiff gobbles up my leftovers.

"What's the matter with you? Still hungover?"

"No. I'm not still hungover and can we not talk about that?"

"You seem out of it."

"I'm fine. Just tired, maybe." I can't get that letter out of my mind. I wonder what Pamela looked like. Maybe like Samantha. All shiny and smooth and perfect. Classy. Maybe it was that perfect dress she wore the first time I saw her. Yes. It *was* that dress.

I half listen to Tiff as she describes her latest case, a divorce where everything was all settled until last night at two a.m. when the husband broke into the wife's house and swiped the entry rug.

"Total moron," she says.

Now she's on to a new TV series she likes called *Rescue Me* about sexy firemen who always take their shirts off at some point in the show.

"You almost finished?" I ask. I seem to have gotten a second wind. "I want to go shopping." She brightens up.

"Fine by me. I usually have to drag you."

As we walk out, we pass Jim and Stacy arguing as they load their daughter into a silver Suburban.

"But sweetheart, if we go to the p-o-n-i-e-s first, then she won't get her n-a-p."

"But we promised her. How about the t-o-y store, it

won't take as long and then she won't have another f-u-c-k-i-n-g fit."

Tiff rolls her eyes as we get into our cars. I look at them drive off and think that we live in separate universes. Theirs is filled with toys and car seats and Purell. And mine is filled with dogs and parrots and lies.

CHAPTER 17

I drop my car at home, hop into Tiff's, and we head for the Topanga mall, which is nothing like Topanga. It's huge, with two hundred stores, dining terraces, a covered merry-go-round, and a vast underground parking lot. My mother hums that Joni Mitchell song, "They paved paradise and put in a parking lot," every time we pass it on the highway. Then she'll sigh dramatically. We park on level G4 Red and head for Macy's.

They're having a big sale and Macy's sweater department is jammed, but Tiff is unfazed. She blazes through the racks, pulling, pushing, grabbing. I stand off to the side trying to look interested. Tiff picks out a few angoras in colors ranging from hot pink to lavender.

"I thought you wanted a black one," I say. But she doesn't get the hint.

"These are so much sexier, don't you think?" she asks.

"Well, I think black would be classier. I mean you could wear it with more things."

"I'm not listening to you. You have the most boring taste in clothes. And I say this with love."

"No, really, Tiff. These just aren't that . . . nice." I don't add that I think they are a little cheesy. Too fuzzy. Too purple or pink or whatever. I don't want to hurt her feelings.

So I tell her I like the lavender one, but I'm not that convincing.

"You are so not fun. What's the matter with you? Is this too expensive? You can tell me the truth. You don't have to buy me this. Really."

"No. Don't be silly. I have a big-deal job now. I'm buying it, and then I need you to help me find the perfect black dress. A dreamy, luscious black dress. The kind of dress that would make a man think I looked like a sculpture, like a miracle. Where does one find something like that?"

Tiff is speechless in the way people get when someone they know does something completely out of character. Then she gets an impish smile. "Like a miracle, huh?" And she leads me to the dress department on three.

We go through racks and racks of black. Tiff starts out enthusiastic, but now she's fed up.

"What's wrong with this one?"

"Too shiny."

"How about this one?"

"The V's too deep."

"And this?"

"Too tight in the waist."

"And this?"

"My butt sticks out."

"Come on, Cassie. This is getting ridiculous. A black dress is a black dress. What do you need it for, anyway?

Going to another funeral? Ha ha. Oh I know! It's another fucking art opening!" she says, laughing.

"Very funny," I say. "There's nothing here. Maybe Neimans will have something."

"What? You win the lottery? Trust me. You won't find anything there under a million dollars. I'm going to Target. Get some stuff for my hair. Meet me there in twenty. And don't be late."

Every time I walk into Neimans I marvel at how tranquil and serene it is. Not that I ever buy anything. But it's fun to roam around. Just beautifully dressed saleswomen waiting at their stations smiling pleasantly as I walk by. "Would you like to try Marc Jacobs's newest fragrance?"

"Oh, thank you." She sprays me. It's $120 an ounce.

I take the escalator to the second floor and see the dress from across the room. It adorns a translucent, featureless mannequin in the middle of the designer section. I slowly approach it as if it's a spiritual experience and touch the fine wool. The texture is so supple and thin it feels silky, like a dog's ear. It's seamless with a graceful scoop neck. High enough to look elegant. Low enough to look sexy. I never used to yearn for a piece of clothing. But now, I look at this dress and I want it. I want to feel the fabric against my skin. I want to see it skim my body just so. I want to wear it and walk into the room and know that people notice me. What can I say. I just want it.

The moment I put it on I feel the dust, the grit, the disappointments and failures, the fragments of my life scatter and dissipate. Memories of who I used to be—my dubious past—eclipsed by feelings of anticipation and hope.

I sit down on the overstuffed chair near the fur salon, pull out my cell phone, and call the 1-800 number on the back of my Visa. The dress is six hundred dollars. The automated voice tells me I have three hundred dollars credit left.

I ask the salesgirl if they do layaway. She smiles sympa-thetically and says, "We don't do that here. But if you'd like, I can hold it for you for three days."

I say yes. But I know I'm never coming back. And she knows it too. I'd like to say that the thrill of trying it on was enough, but it wasn't.

I take the escalator down to the shoe department and find simple black suede heels—two hundred. I hit the handbag department next, choose a black satin clutch, the perfect size. I hold it in my palm just to make sure. It feels like noth-ing. Three hundred bucks. My final stop is the stocking department. I gaze at sheer off-black panty hose the sales-woman tells me is all the rage. She holds it over her fist and spreads her fingers like a starfish to show me there is ab-solutely no shine. Weightless. Transparent. Twenty bucks. So now I know what it costs to be Samantha. I head for Target, where I belong.

CHAPTER 18

On the way home, Tiff talks a mile a minute as she does a lot of lane changing, horn honking, and blowing through yellows. When she flips someone the bird, I tell her she drives like a guy, and she takes it as a compliment.

We stop for gas on the corner of Topanga Road, and as we're pulling out, a big boat of a car swings in front of us and cuts us off. It looks like something from the fifties with fins. All we can see are two little hands clutching the wheel and a few wisps of gray hair sticking up over the seat. Her car blocks the narrow road, and she's toodling along at not more than fifteen miles an hour. Tiff's going nuts.

"Don't honk," I tell her. "It'll give her a heart attack."

"Why do they let these people on the road? Good thing I don't have a gun. Next time some fucker cuts me off. Bam! Going too slow? Bam! Right turn from the left lane? Bam!" I see her fingers poised on the outer rim of the horn.

"I'll remind you of that when we're two little old ladies on a road trip. Don't honk."

"Okay, okay. I won't honk. Jesus. But we're not getting home till midnight."

Thirty minutes later, which should have been ten, we arrive at Tiff's house. We dump our packages on the sofa and take off our jackets.

"Mom, we're home!" Tiff yells.

"In here, Tiffy," Aunt Ethel answers in a thin, weary voice from the kitchen.

Sour, after-dinner smells of cooking pollute the air and dirty dishes are stacked by the sink. Uncle Guy is hunkered down on a stool at the counter, a toothpick hanging slack from his lower lip. He wipes a hand across his forehead as thin beads of sweat roll down his tired face. Aunt Ethel is folding laundry and smiles faintly when she sees us, then blows a strand of hair from her eyes. Tension hangs over the scene like two people who just had a fight.

"Is everything okay?" Tiff asks her mother.

Aunt Ethel quietly tells Tiff that they just got an e-mail from Guy Jr.—he's in a place near Az-Zubayr, southwest of Basra. We sit down at the computer and silently read the message.

> *To start out with, I'm okay. But this is nothing like the movies—I can tell you that. Right now I'm at an internet café and the Corps says we can say whatever we want as long as it doesn't jeopardize a mission but I don't think they really mean it. I heard they're shutting down blogs right and left but I'm going to tell you all this anyways. So far, and I'm not making this up, three guys in my unit have gotten killed. Plus my good friend's wife says she's fed up and wants a divorce. And he hasn't seen his kids in over a*

year. We bombed a house the other day and ended up killing the civilians we're supposed to be saving. It's hot as hell and all the stuff we have to wear is so heavy. I know I'm here for a reason but sometimes it's tough to remember when life is just one big fucking minefield. . . .

"God, Mom. This is so depressing," Tiff says, as she starts to read the rest of it out loud.

Aunt Ethel is struggling to keep her composure, and all the while I am picturing Guy Jr. in his teens stretched out on the living room couch in his faded rocker T-shirt and over-sized jeans. In those days, he was long limbed, and muscley with big feet and hands. Handsome. Tiff and I used to hear him laughing through the walls of her bedroom, talking to his latest girlfriend. When he was sent away last year, he jokingly told us the worst that could happen was he'd get sand-burn. The letter ends with Guy Jr. saying he may be getting a leave soon.

Tiff's dad lumbers over to me, gut thrust out, arms paddling the air with loose-slung hands.

"Meet any nice guys in your new job?" he asks, averting his eyes from the message on the computer.

"She's at a university, Daddy. Of course she hasn't met any nice guys," Tiff says, forcing a laugh and wiping her nose. I see that she's upset, still concentrating on the screen in front of us. She breaks away and locks her arm in mine. Then she drags me into the kitchen, grabs a bottle of wine, and hustles me out.

Tiff's room is a wedding cake with layers of ruffles, lace, crusted dotted Swiss, and a huge pile of self-help books. She thinks that any human being can be happy and if they're not, they should do something about it. In her pursuit of happiness, she has read over two hundred self-help books ranging from Norman Vincent Peale, which her mother gave her, to *The Art of Happiness*, *Get Out of Your Own Way*, and her bible, *Woulda, Coulda, Shoulda*. She tells me that each one, even the bad ones, gives her something important, a little hint or insight into how to crack the secret of happiness.

Her room has looked the same since she was ten. There is a high scalloped shelf over the window lined with ice-skating trophies, runner-up crap prizes like silver plates, mugs, ribbons, sashes, and pictures of Tiff looking like Baby June in her different ice-skating costumes. I think it's kind of sad. Like she's already a has-been. Even though she never was a "has." Personally, I'd stash the junk in a drawer, but Tiff says as soon as she gets her own place, she's going to build a big cabinet with glass doors to display all the stuff.

She grabs the bag from Target and with a flourish pulls out an all-in-one frosting kit.

"What do you say? I've been wanting to do this to you for years." She hands me the box. The picture on the package is a blonde-haired, blue-eyed beauty with a kilowatt smile and Lady Godiva hair "kissed by the Nordic sun." I want to be kissed by the Nordic sun. Like Samantha.

"Okay. Go ahead, Tiff."

"Really? No kidding?"

"I need a change. Just like in the magazines—from mousy to magnificent!"

She laughs as she hands me the Thrill of Brazil red nail polish and says, "Knock yourself out."

A potent burst of peroxide assaults my eyes, throat, and sinuses as Tiff mixes the chalky white formula for Royal Danish ash blonde streaks. The process takes about two hours, and I spend most of that time throwing back my share of the wine and leafing through a few of her new age books that promise to zero in on the "hidden untapped power somewhere inside me," giving me the "secret" that tells me

"I'm the most powerful transmission tower in the universe." At one point I confess how much I wanted that dress. I describe the Unattainable in detail and tell her pitifully that I'll never be able to afford it.

A few hours later, I look in the mirror as I walk in my front door. My hair's not quite dry, but it's brighter, blonder. I think it's good, but Sam obviously doesn't. He freaks out when he sees me. Shakes his cage like a convict and ruffles his feathers. He keeps backing away from me when I get close, squawking, "Help! Help!"

I wish my mother had never taught him that word, because he abuses it. Like crying wolf . . . except he's a parrot. It must be the bright red nails. And the hair. Birds hate change.

"I look good. Better than I did before," I tell him, defiantly. He eyes me suspiciously and continues to sulk. On the other hand, I could be wearing a fright wig for all Black Dog cares. He nuzzles me and plants himself at my feet.

Later that night, I take Conner's love letter out of my purse, crumple it, and throw it in the trash. There. I get undressed, crawl into bed, and start flipping through the Muir book. Usually when I'm tired, I can't bring myself to read at all but I feel strangely energized by Muir's words—his description of nature as "full of God's thoughts, a place of peace and safety, a new song, a place of beginnings." I find myself reading on and on.

Outside my window two owls, with voices like kazoos, call to each other across the darkness in rich, mournful tones. They're like troubled spirits in the black pines. One has a higher pitch than the other, but if you ask me, neither one sounds like they're saying "who." Owls are night predators, like coyotes, and occasionally they kill rats, birds, or small cats. I get up to make sure Sam is safe in his cage, and

I imagine my other birds nestled in the clearing. Hawks and owls are everywhere in the canyon. They're the enemy. Invisible, but always there.

I think about the evening. Tiff puts up a good front most of the time but I know she's worried sick about her brother and, all in all, her life isn't so hot. Her family is always living hand to mouth and her brother could come home in a box. I wonder how she stands it sometimes.

A few weeks after Frank's accident, we sat up late one night in my kitchen, drinking rum and Cokes, and I finally blurted out that I had wished Frank dead barely a week before it happened. Then I saw the photos in the morgue—the ones where he looked dead, not like he was sleeping. And then it struck me—what if this was cosmically my fault?

"God, Cassie. Don't you know everyone does that?" she answered. "We all think those things without really meaning it."

"But I meant it. That's the thing."

Tiff was quiet for a moment and then she smiled. "I guess I knew that. It's okay. I already knew that." Then she added sadly, "Anyway, wishes don't come true."

Right before I nod off, I get a thought and my toes hit the freezing floor one more time. I pull the love letter out of the trash and stash it in my drawer.

CHAPTER 19

How could this happen? My hair is sticking up in stiff-barbed, yellow-gray quills. I look like a porcupine. Heavyset, short-legged, slow-moving rodents. Were we that out of it? Maybe the stuff keeps processing while you sleep. Maybe we didn't rinse it out enough. Did we even rinse it out? Sam was right. I'm a freak and I'm late for work.

I pull my hair back in a tight, low ponytail, find an old baseball cap with a sooty lining, and squash it over my rigid frosted streaks. This is the opposite of class. This is a disaster.

I get to the office fifteen minutes late. Alison is behind the desk, as usual, but she has an uncharacteristic friendly look on her face. What's up? I mean, there's no doubt at all anymore that we can't stand each other. She smiles at me as if it's a normal greeting on her part. Maybe she's happy I look like human roadkill.

"Hey. How you doing?"

"Just fine. How about you?" I'll play along.

"You know. Okay. Listen. I need to ask a favor," she purrs.

Alison lowers her voice. Pulls a chair up and swings around to face me as if we were bosom buddies. I'm getting a bad feeling about this. Maybe they found out about me.

"There's this guy," she whispers, "and I swear to God, he's perfect. I went out with him last night and now he wants to drive me up the coast. A convertible Benz." All I can register is relief.

"I'll be back around four, can you cover for me?"

"Oh sure," I say offhandedly. What the hell.

"We don't have to tell Pearce. I mean, we're all grown-ups here."

"Right."

"Exactly."

"When's he coming?"

"Any minute." She stares at me a moment. "What's with the hat?"

I pull it off and my springy hair quills stick out every-where.

"Jesus, I hope you didn't pay for that."

I didn't feel like telling her my girlfriend did it. And that we were tanked.

"Pretty bad, huh?"

"I'll say," she says, as she hastily straps her purse around her shoulder. "See you later."

As she walks out the door, I settle myself behind the reception desk, put my purse away. Damn, I should have asked her for her hairdresser's name. There are lots of bad things I can say about Alison, but her hair isn't one of them. Oh. I see she's left her little alligator Filofax next to the phone. Hmmmm. I wonder if her hairdresser has any free time late today. I casually put the book in my lap under the desk.

Let's see. Maybe it's under *H*. I think Hawthorne, Huxley, Hubbard. Conner's shelves are polluting my brain.

Stop. Hairdresser. That's what I need. Nope. Maybe under *B*. Beauty salon. Nothing. I've heard her talking to him. The man's name is something like "Frank." What a coincidence. I look under *F* and there it is, only he spells it "Franck."

I write down the number, glance up, shit, Alison's coming back. I slide the Filofax back beside the phone.

"Oh, hi! I think I left my Filofax." I hand it to her. "God! Thanks! My life's in that book."

"No problem. Have a good time," I say as I officiously answer the ringing department phone.

"Cassie? It's Freddy."

"Oh, hey." This is awkward. "Alison just left."

"Actually, I called for you." What's this about? Maybe his pal, the photographer, saw me pass out.

"So, I got a call last night from my friend the photographer." I was right. Here goes. "And one of the critics from the *Times* gave him a great review today. Did you see it?"

"Gee, no, I haven't read the papers yet."

"Well, it was a great review. Listen to this, 'gorgeously atmospheric, romantic and haunting.' "

"I bet he's happy about that." Where are we going here? He *must* have heard about what happened. Maybe he's waiting for me to make an excuse. Oh, I took a couple Sudafeds and, after one drink, got a really bad reaction. Oh, I was coming down with the flu. Everyone at my house has it. Including the parrot.

"Anyway, I know you must be busy. I'll let you go."

"Okay. Nice talking to you." No mention of the meltdown. Maybe he didn't hear.

"By the way," he hesitates, "I know this is last minute, but I was wondering if you were free tomorrow night."

I'm stunned. "Tomorrow night?"

"I have two tickets to the symphony and it's Beethoven's Sixth."

God. The symphony. He's waiting for me to say something. I finger my gargoyle spikes. I'll stall him.

"You know what? I have tentative plans, but I'll try to work it out. Can I call you later?"

"No problem," he says politely. He gives me his number and asks for my cell.

The first thing I think of is: this is Alison's worst nightmare. Then I call her hairdresser. The receptionist, Tracy, has a pronounced British accent. It's two hundred for base and highlights. More, if there's damage. I think this would qualify as damage. I ask if they have someone who's a little less expensive. The receptionist tells me that if I'm interested, tonight is training night—the assistants do the hair supervised by the stylists. And it's free. She assures me that the work is excellent and there's only two slots left. I sign up.

I wait until an appropriate hour and call Freddy back to confirm the date. It's all breezy and casual.

Then, on my way to the hairdresser's, I swing by Neimans and take another look at that black dress. I'm doing it. I haven't had a new dress in a year. And the shoes too. It doesn't make sense to have a gorgeous dress like this and Easy Spirit shoes. I can use two different credit cards. I tell the nice saleswoman that I'm going to the symphony and I don't have much time because I'm late for my hair appointment. She's all smiles. I'm all smiles. Neither one of us can even begin to afford this dress.

When was the last time I spent so much money on myself? Money I don't have. Is that a sin too?

CHAPTER 20

Freddy asked if we could meet at his place because he has a late meeting. So I bring my new black dress to work along with a duffel stuffed with makeup, stockings, heels, and a brand-new push-up bra. After I change, Alison looks at me levelly, hardly blinking, in an effort to disguise the emotion of surprise. Otherwise, she might have to say something nice. I throw her a cheerful little wave as I leave.

Before I get into the car, I tuck a towel around the driver's seat and ease myself in like I was made of china. I don't want dog hairs sticking to my dress and I definitely don't want to get a run in my black superfine panty hose. I'm nervous. I keep checking my makeup in the mirror. The last time he saw me I looked like a ridiculous pink angora fluffball.

I find a parking spot a few blocks away from his sleek, modern high-rise, although he did specifically say to park downstairs with the valet. Frankly, with my wreck of a car, I never even considered it.

I rush toward the building, expecting the doorman to buzz Freddy, but he's already downstairs, dressed in a dark tailored suit. There's a glint of a flat gold watch on an alligator strap as he holds his car door open for me and then he gives me the second whistle of my life. (Okay, the first was from a parrot.)

"You don't know how lovely you look," Freddy says, touching my elbow and gently brushing up against me. And I should. It's not just the dress. It's my hair too—soft and loose with the bangs brushed to the side. The funny thing was, when I got home last night, Tiff stopped by and gave me a big hug.

"Cassie, we did such a good job on your color. Maybe I'm in the wrong profession. I should've gone to beauty school." I'll say. I didn't have the heart to tell her how fucked up my hair was and how it took four people an entire evening to make me look decent.

On the way to the Music Center in downtown LA, Freddy asked if I'd heard Beethoven's Sixth performed lately, and I told him I rarely (like in never) went to the symphony. He nodded as if he understood. The traffic is deadly from where you live, he said. Must take a couple hours to get there in rush hour. Oh yes, I agreed. Deadly.

"I like the *Pastoral*," he went on. "Beethoven was antisocial and nearly deaf when he wrote it, but it transports you to someplace else—like Provence or somewhere, don't you think?"

"Oh yes," I lie, thoroughly intimidated. I must look so sophisticated tonight he thinks I'm the kind of person who's acquainted with Beethoven's symphonies and who's been to Provence and back. Bravo, Cassie.

As it turns out, we're early for the concert, so Freddy invites me to have a drink in the Founders Room, which he explains is some sort of private club for donors.

All I can think about when we walk in is that scene from *Phantom of the Opera* when the giant crystal chandelier comes crashing to the floor, landing at the feet of the beautiful pale goddess, Christine. We never went to the theater, but my mother splurged and took me to that show one Sunday afternoon. It was not long after Frank died and the sudden, thunderous explosion of splintering glass and shooting light rays took me right back to the night his truck hurled like a grenade down the mountain and then exploded. Now I'm gazing up at three glimmering globs of dripping, diamond-shaped chandeliers and wondering if one of them is going to slam into the floor, sending all these fancy people straight to hell.

This place is too much. Thirty-foot ceilings, Persian carpets, heavy embroidered velvet couches, and a floor-to-ceiling portrait of a regal-looking woman in a ball gown and tiara that should be titled "Let Them Eat Cake." I gaze out the windows at the Lego-like downtown skyscrapers swooping up into the darkening sky as a tuxedoed waiter passes flutes of champagne on sterling silver trays.

Freddy hands me a glass and says conspiratorially, "By the way, would you mind if we keep this date *entre nous*?"

I look at him blankly.

"I don't really like Alison to know my business. It's easier that way, you know?"

Oh, I get it. She must have said some really nice things about me.

"Okay. No problem. I understand," I say, sweetly. *"Entre nous."*

Freddy is definitely in his element as he makes his way through the throng, reaching out to shake hands with older, distinguished-looking men—men of substance who carry their success with such casual ease. And their elegant wives, all of whom seem to display a polite lack of curiosity as far as

I'm concerned. Many of them have on black, a color which I'm beginning to realize makes all others seem unfashionable. As we walk by, they call Freddy by name as they give him an affectionate squeeze on the shoulder.

A few of them stop to chat, and he graciously introduces me. I laugh a little too hard at their jokes, and I notice that their conversation is clever and off the cuff. I find myself trying to fit in, making mental notes on how they do it—trying to pretend as if I was born in this world.

We weave our way to a sofa in the corner where a table is already set with white linen, plates of smoked salmon sandwiches, a fancy cheese tray, fruit, and a bottle of wine chilling in a silver bucket. A far cry from Frank's favorite restaurant, Mantle's, where the slogan was, "The only way you can get a better piece of chicken is to be a rooster."

Freddy sits down and pats the brocade cushion next to him in an intimate sort of way. Cozy. A few of his friends join us. The women are in dresses like mine, others in black suits with large sparkly jeweled brooches on their collar. A gift from their grandmothers, maybe.

The waiter opens the wine and hands the man sitting next to me the cork, which he inhales like an addict with a line of coke. The label on the bottle looks like an old family crest, Domaine de Something or Other from the stone cellar fortress of the Phantom's wine cellar. Probably cost a fucking fortune. He ceremoniously nods. The waiter then pours a small amount in the man's glass and stands there at attention as the guy swirls the wine around, nurses it in his hand, holds it to the light, breathes it, sips it, fills his mouth with it, leans his head back, and gargles. Freddy looks at me and winks as the man, whose name is Four (his father was Three, grandfather Two, you get the picture), leans too close to me and says, "Excellent, 1975. Lake district. I treated myself to a case of it when I was in Como." He smells like Brut 2006, Buffoon District. But I keep my mouth shut.

"So, what do you do?" he says.

"I work at the university."

"Good for you." He responds with interest, as a woman from behind calls out an exuberant greeting and wedges herself between Freddy and me, draping a gold-bangled arm around him.

"Where've you been hiding?" she croons, as she grabs his arm familiarly. "God, I've missed you."

She's wearing high heels, a white satin blouse, and a tight gray flannel skirt. Sexy without pushing it. Her flaxen blonde hair is pulled back with a velvet headband. She's around thirty, tan, thin, and her face is flawless, moist and silky with a sheer film of cardinal red lip gloss.

"Hi, I'm Nan," she says to me, as she shoots out her hand like a man. Then she goes right on talking to Freddy. Her conversation is punctuated with a lot of "musts." I "must" have you come down to the beach house." I "have" to have another glass of champagne. I've "absolutely" got to get back to New York before that play is over. She's a beauty, and she knows it, but she's absolutely strangling me with all her charm. It's almost as if she's pumping all the oxygen out of the air.

I excuse myself (because I "must" go to the bathroom) and when I come back, there's an awkward silence. I have the impression there's something I should know, but it passes when Freddy quickly jumps in, telling me that Nan is a friend of his from London. He lived there for a few years in his twenties, had an apartment in Mayfair and worked at Goldman Sachs.

"My ex-wife worked in a little gallery in the neighbor-hood. That's where I bought my first painting. I had to borrow the money, because it was in the 'can't live without it' category."

Obviously the wife wasn't. I want to find out more about her and the marriage, but instead I say, "What was the painting?"

"It was a gorgeous nude. The wife got it in the divorce."

"I'm sorry."

"Don't be. I bought it back at auction."

Nan is now seated with a group of five women, all of whom have blonde hair, lovely firm arms, and drippy expensive earrings. They're laughing and whispering conspiratorially. They look like they belong to one of those clubs that don't allow Jews or blacks.

I've just helped myself to my first sandwich when the lights flash. Freddy continues talking with his friend about some big art auction coming up, ignoring the curtain call, as a parade of serene, unhurried people stroll through doors held open by uniformed waiters. I quickly pop the sandwich in my mouth and hear a few more "Hey, Freddys," as he squeezes my knee and says, "Okay. You ready?"

I nod. I'm so excited. The last time I heard an orchestra was *The Nutcracker* when I was five.

Our seats are in the first balcony, which Freddy tells me has the best acoustics in the place. Also, it's just a few steps away from the Founders Room. No hustling downstairs for this crowd. The socializing continues where it left off, even when these people take their seats. Freddy turns around, stretches his arm back, and shakes the hand of a man two rows behind us. A woman with hurricane-proof hair kiss, kiss, kisses her way down the aisle. "How are you?" "So good to see you." "Mwaah. Mwaah."

I see the musicians onstage adjusting their instruments and their music stands. Some are intently practicing little bits of music, others are fussing with their strings and mouthpieces.

Finally the conductor appears, purposefully walking across the stage to enthusiastic applause. He takes a stately bow, as the rest of the orchestra rises with respect. He's not at all what I was expecting. In my mind, conductors are supposed to look like God, ageless with long flowing white hair. But this guy is bald, wearing a Nehru jacket and shoes so shiny the light bounces off them. He's about to begin, his baton suspended in the air, when two cell phones go off in rapid succession. He stiffens, frowns, and lowers his baton. Not quite as forgiving as God.

After a brief pause, when the place is as quiet as a tomb, he raises his baton again, waiting for a few seconds to make sure we've all learned our lesson.

The first piece is wild—completely off-key with carelessly scattered notes, ferocious drumrolls, and honking bassoons—by someone modern I never heard of. Freddy elbows me halfway through and motions for me to look around. There's a sea of gray-haired men with their heads slumped over their chests clearly sound asleep—amazing considering the deafening noise.

"They don't even last five minutes." He chuckles.

The second piece is Beethoven's Sixth, the Pastoral. The music begins with a rippling quiet melody. A smile of recognition flashes across Freddy's face as he settles down for the piece, which I read in the program will last just under an hour.

I listen closely for the first ten minutes or so and then my mind wanders—the way your mind wanders when driving along a familiar highway and all of a sudden you arrive at your destination and you can't remember driving there. I wonder if there's a name for that—like auto amnesia or something.

Oh, the music has stopped now. That was fast. I'm about

to clap when Freddy puts his hand over mine and then points to the program. Only the first movement. Four more to go. I shift in my seat and cross my legs—the cushions here are plush, but there isn't that much space in the row and my legs are too long to keep this position. I uncross them and my program falls on the floor.

Freddy smiles, picks it up, and puts it back on my lap, keeping his hand on my knee. The music is getting livelier, a country festival with flutes trilling like birds. I sink down and peek at my watch. Forty minutes to go.

Now we're in the third movement. Freddy looks like he's dozing, but he could just be listening to the music with his eyes closed. I close my eyes too and float along—the same gorgeous melodies weaving in and out, repeating themselves in different ways. I'm thinking that I'd like to come back here with my mother. She'd love it.

Suddenly the mood shifts and the music builds. Freddy rouses, takes his hand off my knee, gently slips it in mine, and says, "Thunderstorm! My favorite part! I remember . . ."

"Shhhh!" An old bat seated behind us scowls. Freddy winks at me, but the good thing about it is he keeps his hand in mine. Now his thumb is circling the inside of my palm as the music grows in intensity.

It builds to a fever pitch, calms down again, and ends on a tranquil note. Freddy flashes a majestic smile.

"That was unbelievable. Thank you so much, Freddy."

He leans in and kisses me lightly on the lips. "You are so very welcome."

The audience has leapt to its feet and is still shouting bravos and clapping furiously as we head back to the VIP room for intermission. But before we enter, Freddy stops, takes me by the arm in an oddly possessive way, and whispers, "Let's get out of here."

"Really?" I say. These tickets must have cost a fortune. How can he just leave? He notices that I'm hesitating.

"Really," he says. "You'll thank me. Unless you're up for Glenn Branca's *Hallucination City*. I saw it last year. Total bore."

I can see that for him, walking out is no big deal. I've never walked out of anything—not even a shitty movie. I guess he's at a point where his time is more valuable than his money. I don't know anyone like that.

Everything's VIP here. We take the VIP escalator down to the VIP parking lot and get in the car. The dashboard has a ghostly glow with needles floating in thin air. I sink down in the deep leather, huggy seats surrounded by burled walnut. Soft jazz plays from hidden speakers—not like Tiff's shoebox-sized subwoofers mounted under the dashboard. I try to think of something amusing to say. As it turns out, I don't need to worry as he takes over and regales me with stories from work. He throws around words like interest rates, M and A's, foreign exchange ratios, big cap, little cap, and midsize companies. In the middle of all this, his BlackBerry vibrates. He looks at the screen, sees who's calling, and ignores it.

CHAPTER 21

Twenty minutes later we pull up to Freddy's building. He tells me he bought his condo a year ago, gutted it, and then added on a few more bathrooms and a media room. I've never heard of anyone gutting an apartment, but I don't ask him if that's unusual. Lots of hip Hollywood types have moved in recently, he tells me, but when he first bought it there were "mostly widows and other old people." I'll fit right in.

"How about a quick drink, and then I'll take you back to your car." He rubs my shoulder ever so slightly and a tingling spreads under my skin. I'm almost tempted.

But if I go upstairs with him, it's all over. I know how this goes. He'll be very polite the next morning, offer me some coffee, tell me he has an early meeting, and I'll never hear from him again. No. I'm not going upstairs. That would be dumb. So I do the smart thing and say I really have to get home. When I tell him my car is several

141

blocks away, he insists on driving me. Oh well, he'd see it sooner or later.

So we drive to the block where I parked my car. Slowly pull up. No car. That's weird, I'm sure it was here. I must be confused. All these streets look alike and I *was* kind of nervous when I got here. Maybe it's on the next block. We cruise up and down two more streets. Still no car. Where the fuck is it? Could I have been that out of it? We're at least five blocks from where I originally thought I'd parked.

"Do you think you parked this far away?" he asks me. And then the zinger. "Anyway, this is permit parking only."

I look up and see a row of signs with strategically placed print, "Violators will be towed at owner's expense."

I immediately flash back on all those conversations I overheard when I worked at Frank's tow place. Everyone said the same thing, "I didn't see the sign." After we'd towed them, they'd drive round and round looking for the car, not noticing the two zillion signs that said "tow-away zone." Frank used to say, "How can anyone be that stupid?"

Now I ask Freddy to drive back to the place where I first thought I left my car. I'm hoping against hope that it'll somehow miraculously appear. We pull up to the exact spot where I am now positive I parked. There is a gaping empty space and a telltale pool of oil (a leak I've never gotten fixed), and, on the curb, looking down on us like a sentry, one of those goddamn signs.

"I've been towed," I announce. "I'm so embarrassed."

"Don't be embarrassed. It's not your fault." He smiles. "Well, actually it *is* your fault. But it happens to everyone." Now he's laughing. "Well, actually it's *never* happened to me."

"This isn't funny."

"Okay, I'm sorry. Who do we call, the DMV or something?" He gets out and starts to look at the sign to see if there's a number. I'm already on the phone.

"Could I have the listings for all the OPGs in West Hollywood?"

It turns out there's only two. I know this like the back of my hand. Official Police Garage, $96.00 for towing, $48.00 City of LA release fee, 10 percent tax, and that's just for hello. Then there's the ticket for illegally parking in a tow-away zone and, of course, any outstanding parking tickets, of which there are three I can think of right off the top of my head. Maybe I'll just let them keep the car.

We pull up to the tow yard, which looks like a correctional facility—long, low concrete bunker, chain-link fence topped with barbed wire, a security camera, and lights. Chained to the wall behind the fence is a big-ass Doberman mix.

"Are you sure this is it?" Freddy asks. Luckily, he doesn't grill me about my wealth of knowledge in this area. We go inside, me in my new black designer dress, and Freddy in his impeccable suit. There's a group of losers, druggies, and dazed teenagers slumped on concrete benches against the wall. I remember all those pleading, angry, hopeless looks. They've probably been waiting here for hours. A few of them are pooling their money, emptying their pockets trying to make bail for their cars.

I walk over to the barred cashier window manned by a greasy-looking guy in his early fifties with gray shark-like skin—Frank, if he had lived. I show my license to the guy behind the window and he tells me to wait "over there." He's talking through one of those little mikes, like at the movie theaters. I notice faded signs above the window that say in English and Spanish, "We take Visa, MasterCard, or cash. No checks."

The bill adds up to over $300. My Visa is denied, of

course. No surprise. The dress and shoes shot me way over my limit.

I whisper to the greaseball, "I'll just come back tomorrow with the cash."

"It's forty bucks a day for storage, and after thirty days, we sell the car at auction," he responds loud enough for the whole room to hear.

"Is there a problem?" Freddy walks over.

"No. Not at all," I say, hastily. "I just don't want to put this much on my card."

"Well, how much is it? I'll put it on my card."

"It's really expensive, Freddy. It's no problem. I'll just come back tomorrow." I'm completely humiliated.

Freddy turns to the guy and hands him his card. "Don't be silly. You can pay me back later."

"God. I feel terrible. How can I ever thank you?"

"Well, you can have a drink with me. After this, I could use it. And by the way, leave your car with the valet." Ha ha.

The greasy guy's evil twin pulls up in my banged-up car, which somehow looks even worse than before. Freddy casually glances at it, and says, "Why is it that all you academics have junky cars?"

How ironic. If I had known my car screamed academic, I'd have parked it with the goddamn valet in the first place. The bigger irony is that this is my first real date in years and I'm back in the sewer with Frank.

CHAPTER 22

So now it's almost midnight as he punches in his security code in three different places—the garage, the elevator, and his front door. It's not like he lives in Manhattan. My mother and I never even close our door half the time. I glance furtively around. The lights are out in his apartment except for the illuminated large flat-screen TV on the living room wall, which is turned to the Bloomberg channel. A stock ticker moves silently across the bottom of the screen flashing corporate initials with red or green arrows by each listing.

"I leave this on all the time—these days it's a twenty-four hour trading environment." He turns the TV on mute and clicks on music, telling me it's surround sound. Then he slides his BlackBerry out of his pocket, checks it out, and pulls out another gadget that looks just like it only with a bigger screen. He sees me eyeing it.

"Pretty nifty, huh? Not on the market yet. My

tech guy slipped it to me. I can access my satellite TV from anywhere."

He lays them gingerly down side by side on an end table and motions for me to sit down. Then he goes to the bar, selects a bottle of expensive-looking whiskey, and offers me a shot. It tastes smooth and strong, not bitter like the cheap stuff.

Freddy collapses opposite me on the couch and takes a big gulp, grimaces, and shakes his head like a swimmer coming up after an ice-cold twenty laps.

"God, I needed that." He exhales. I sink down into the immense, sand-colored cushions, stranded in the Sahara-like dunes of a sofa, and, for the first time this evening, I start to relax. Then I notice the art. Everywhere. Each wall is a showcase with a strategically placed light, illuminating the painting.

On the coffee table are piles of art catalogs, which he tells me he leafs through at night. Sort of like Mom with her seed catalogs.

"So tell me. Which ones are which?" I ask, glancing at the paintings.

"You mean the artists?"

"No. I mean the categories. Beautiful. Gotta have it. And the ones you couldn't live without."

He smiles, looking pleased, and points to a blurry wooded landscape over the bar. "Beautiful."

Then he stands up and walks over to a simple drawing of a repeated square. "Gotta have it."

"But this one . . ." He faces a luscious pale nude, her hair wrapped in a colorful scarf. "This one I couldn't live without."

We both gaze at her for a minute.

"Was she the one?"

He nods yes. He knows I'm talking about the painting he got back from his ex-wife.

"You see how I couldn't let her go, don't you?" he says, looking at the nude with admiration. "I learned my lesson. I had a prenup the second time around."

"Freddy! How many were there?"

"Just two. And you?"

"No divorces. Just one late husband."

"Late as in . . . ?"

"Late as in dead."

His face registers surprise. Here we go.

"Oh, I'm sorry."

I want to say, "Don't be." But instead I give him a demure, "Thank you."

Here comes the second question. It's coming now.

"How did he die?" Bingo.

"A car crash. Well, actually a truck."

"How long has it been?" he asks. They always want to know that. Just in case it was last week.

"A few years," I tell him.

Now I listen to the requisite car crash story that everyone seems to have. An uncle, an aunt, a high school sweetheart, etc., etc. He stands up and puts more ice in his drink.

I feel as if I force an outpouring of pity from everyone I meet.

"Anyway. Thanks for listening. I think I'd better be going," I say abruptly.

Freddy is quiet. He bends over and gently kisses me on the cheek. "You okay?"

"I'm fine. I'm wonderful. It's been a great evening."

As we get up to leave, we pass his gleaming stainless steel kitchen. He sees me gaze at it, and asks if I'd like a quick tour of the place.

He shows me his bedroom with its spare masculine black and beige pillows on the bed, fat and undented, his walk-in closet, all neckties and shoes, with carpet smooth as mowed lawn, his library with a burled wood desk that looks like not one soul works or reads in there, his high-tech media room. Then he leads me down the hall to the master bathroom. And standing there, like Mount Rushmore, is a massive granite shower.

"I have a bad back so my architect suggested this—Dreamline Hydrotherapy Massage Shower."

He slowly opens the vault-like glass door. Inside it's a swirl of white and black stone with a low bench hugging the perimeter.

"Nine high-impact jet turbo massagers, tropical rain forest head. You can digitally adjust the temperature, pressure, speed, and angle of attack," he boasts.

I'm hearing his words, but I'm not listening to him. All I can think about right now is ripping off my clothes, turning on that hot steaming shower, and taking a trip in Freddy's multiorgasmic Dreamline train to heaven.

I'd love to say that Freddy had to sweet-talk me into it, but the next thing I knew, he turned on one of the jets and I was there. He tore at my clothes. I tore at his.

What happened next was just a rush of hydro action culminating in a rock-steady stream of water from one of the jets throbbing at 2,800 pulses per minute.

At some point in the frenzy, Freddy looks at me indulgently, smiles, and says, "Slow down, Cassie. It's not a race." He stands behind me, his chest pressed against the curve of my back, kissing my shoulders and neck, and whispers in my ear, "Tell me what you want."

In my somewhat limited romantic history, I'd become an expert in the art of being evasive, never wanting to talk about what I needed.

"C'mon, sweetheart. How much damage can we do here? Tell me everything."

And I do. It's been three years since I've made love with anyone, and I'm having this odd, out of body thing, like I've switched lives with somebody else. The person down the street, maybe, or some random woman from the symphony.

She's the old Cassie now and I'm the new Cassie. And I say things and think things that aren't really me because the real me has disappeared.

"Now, there's only one thing left to do," he pants, as we lean exhausted against the cold stone. I'm thinking, What possibly is there left to do?

"Just like in Beethoven's Ninth, when he'd done everything he could with his instruments." He pauses. "There was only one path left for the grand finale." I raise my eyebrow. He has a jubilant smile.

" 'Ode to Joy,' my dear." And then he bursts into song. In German. A big, booming, baritone voice which is magnified in the shower tenfold.

"Freude, schoner Gotterfunken. Tochter aus Elysium . . ."

He stumbles through the first chorus and then says, "Oh, fuck it."

Now it's my turn.

"Splish, splash, we were taking a bath," I belt out. I love singing in the shower.

"Long about a Saturday night!" he answers.

We go through about four more numbers when he looks at me sweetly and says, "My God, Cassie. Your voice is horrible."

"Oh, thank you," I say with mock humbleness. I look at him for a minute.

"I'll admit, I can't sing very well." I pull him to me and fold my arms around his neck. "But I can dance."

He abruptly grabs my waist and bends me over in a tango

flourish. My wet hair sweeps the floor, as he slowly lays me down.

In the end, he makes infinitesimal adjustments to the pulsing speed and pressure of the water, until I just float away.

CHAPTER 23

F reddy's out of bed before me and has already fixed the coffee. I think it's the smell that wakes me up. I look around and immediately feel uncomfortable. He breezes in, looking entitled in his gray flannel Wall Street suit, carrying a steaming mug and placing it on the bedside table.

"Morning, princess." He grins, giving me a peck on the cheek that feels like a slap. "I hate to leave, but I'm late for this damn meeting."

I look at the clock. This is ridiculous. It's not even seven yet.

"Stay as long as you want. My girl is coming later today to clean," he says, unembarrassed, gentlemanly. I give him an ironic smile.

"It's okay. I have to get to work too," I say.

"Call you," he says, nonchalantly. Then he's gone.

I'm in a strange apartment with nothing to wear but my new black dress, which is crumpled in a heap on the bathroom floor. I hear thunder. Then rain. Perfect. I'll never make it home and back in time for work. This has turned out exactly like I thought it would. The only thing that's missing is the hundred-dollar bill on the dresser placed right next to my magazine, *Chumpette Weekly*. I'm getting the hell out of here.

Now the rain is coming down with a vengeance. I quickly get dressed, put on my coat, and take one of the wood-handled plaid umbrellas jammed in a Chinese porcelain stand by the front door. As I drive to work, I pass an elementary school, kids in yellow slickers and colorful rain boots, mothers shepherding their children to class, holding their hands, kissing them good-bye. Fat drops of rain splatter across the windshield, and my car wipers can't keep up. It's like driving through a car wash.

I turn up the heat in the car and dial Tiff's number.

"You have to go over to my house right now."

"Where are you?"

"On my way to work. Can you feed Sam and Black Dog? Mom's out of town."

"Whoa. This sounds interesting—we didn't make it home last night?" Tiff giggles.

"I'll tell you about it later. I got towed."

"Is that all?"

"Pretty much." I don't feel like going into the whole thing.

"Well, did you have a good time, at least?"

"I think I made a big mistake. Call you later." I hang up and look at the duffel in the back seat stuffed with yesterday's work clothes. I'll change when I get to the office.

Last night makes me wince. I should've left. I had the perfect out. Why didn't I just get into my car and drive home? I should've never gone upstairs with him. That's where I made my big mistake. My mother tells me the should've will kill you. Move on. No regrets.

I think about the way it felt when he touched me. A firestorm of heat building up from my gut and blazing through my body. Then this morning when he hardly looked at me. Detached with a coldness that was almost clinical. So nice to have met you. Maybe we'll do it again sometime.

I pull up to the university. Grab my duffel and my silk clutch, which is on top of all the smeared receipts from last night's towing disaster. I stuff my wallet and cell phone in my coat pocket, and head for the bathroom to change. When I get to reception, Alison is already there, drinking Starbucks, on her cell, as usual.

"Hey, Cassie. No one's in yet. The rain's fucked up everything. Would you mind getting the mail? I'm on hold with the airlines."

I go down to the mail room and start sorting the packages. I'm leaving my raincoat on all day.

My cell phone rings. It's Mom.

"Hi, honey. Just checking in. It's gorgeous out here in the desert. Is everything okay? I hear it's pouring there."

"Everything's fine. Any sightings?"

"Not yet, but there's still hope. You should've seen the sky last night—the moon is in Mercury retrograde. Incredible stars. I saw Jupiter through Sylvia's telescope. We'll talk about it tonight."

We say our good-byes; I pile up the mail, take it upstairs, and begin sorting the envelopes. Alison is still on the phone. For the first time I notice a strong family resemblance.

"Okay, Mother," I hear Alison say. "I'm all set, but they're almost sold out." She mouths "sorry" to me.

"I know. I'll tell Freddy if he and Patricia want to get on

the flight they need to call right now. I think she's away on business." Patricia?! Another pause. Alison goes on. "Me too. Bye, Mom."

Who's Patricia? No obvious pictures of her cluttering Freddy's pristine apartment. Maybe she's a cousin or something. Fat chance. He was the one with all the questions. I didn't ask him anything. I mean we talked about his art, the theater, music, and oh, by the way, Cassie, before I fuck you, you might be interested to know I have a girlfriend. He must have forgotten to mention that teeny-weeny detail. It must have slipped his mind. Liar.

Alison finally puts the phone down, and says, "Thanksgiving. It's always such a hassle. No one wants to go. We fight the whole weekend."

"Is it pretty much just the family?" I'm fishing. I don't care.

"Well, yeah. Who else could stand it?"

Maybe I'm wrong. Maybe she has another sister. Yes. That's who Patricia is.

Another sister.

"Except for Freddy's girlfriend. Without her we'd probably all kill each other." Now Alison gets up and stretches.

"God, I'm so stiff. I missed yoga this morning." She stands up, holding her arms parallel to the floor, palms down. Arms straight out. Her front knee is bent, the other leg stretched out behind her. And slowly, she turns her head to the left, looks out over her fingers.

"The warrior pose. The incarnation of Shiva. Supposed to increase your stamina. Ever do yoga?" No, I don't do yoga. I don't have time to do yoga. I'm too busy bailing out my car and fucking your cheating brother.

"No, just never seem to have the time," I say, my whole body clenched. *The pissed-off patsy pose.* I knew there was a reason those women at the concert treated me the way they did—like I was beside the point. Just another one of

Freddy's amusements—keeping him busy while the girl-friend's out of town. What kind of man takes a date to a place where everyone knows he's fooling around?

Alison leaves to take care of some things for the faculty party with Pearce, and I take over the reception desk. My heart is pounding and it feels like something is pressing against my chest, suffocating me. This is what it's like to be buried alive—dark, no air, no hope. I have to get a grip. It was just a stupid date with a stupid man who was too much of a wimp to tell me the truth. Because if he *had* told me the truth, I never would have slept with him, and that would have ruined his evening. He wouldn't have gotten laid.

The problem with people who lie is that they don't take responsibility for their actions. Or worse, if they tell the truth, they don't get what they want. And that overrides everything, their morals, their religion, their loyalties to other people, everything. And there you go. I'm the biggest liar of all. I wouldn't have this job, I wouldn't have been at the gallery, I wouldn't have met Freddy, and I certainly would never have slept with him.

I'm in a deep, deep hole and if I don't start digging my way out, I'll die. I know it. Or worse, I'll be a lump of brown, moldy dust for the rest of my life. No one wants a liar work-ing for them. Nixon, Martha Stewart, Pinocchio. It never turns out well. My mind is racing when my cell phone rings.

"Hello, gorgeous!" Freddy says loudly. I can hear voices and dishes clattering in the background. He's in a restaurant somewhere.

"Hey," I say. I feel like gagging.

"Just wanted you to know that this is your 'morning after' phone call." He laughs. "I had a terrific time with you last night, seriously, and I wanted you to know that. The whole thing was just . . . top notch."

Isn't he polite? Emily Post's etiquette for one-night stands.

"Well. Thank you for the call. I had a good time too but we really can't see each other again." You piece of shit. He's speechless. I know what he's used to. After he doesn't call for a few days, the girl calls him up with some phony excuse. Someone gave me house seats to *Swan Lake*, would you like to join me? Or, I'm having a little dinner party at the beach house, you think you can come? Or I have two tickets to *Eat Shit and Die*, how about it?

"You're dumping me so fast? This is a record." He chuckles, not taking it seriously.

"It was really fun last night and I needed the break. You were great about the car and I'm sending you a check."

"That's it? The royal kiss-off?"

"Well—to tell you the truth," I lie, "I have a boyfriend." That stops him.

"Okay. Fair enough. I'll just give you some time. What's *his* shower like?" he teases, surprisingly undeterred by all this.

"Gotta go, Freddy. Bye."

I'd love to be able to tell when someone's lying. There are signs, certain imperceptible electrical pulses. A slight jump in the needle. Like a human lie detector. Sometimes it's obvious. The tone of their voice. How they choke on their words, the smallest hesitations. Or when their smile doesn't match their face. Or too much information or too many contradictions. My mother says the best indicator is just your gut reaction. But this man has such inexhaustible charm, how can you trust your gut? Why is it that some men make lying so much easier than telling the truth?

The rest of the day is a blur, except for Professor Conner, who hands me a tape of one of his old lectures and asks me to transcribe it. I did such a great job on the last one, he tells me. He's standing at my desk, fiddling with my Michigan mug and eyeing my frame with no picture in it.

"No friends or relatives?" he says, as he holds up the empty frame.

"Pretty much," I say.

"Why don't you slip your mom's photo of Bigfoot in there?" he jokes. Ha. Ha.

Why don't you shove it up your ass, I feel like saying, as I self-consciously tug on my raincoat to hide my wrinkled clothes. I hate men.

CHAPTER 24

When I get home I slosh through two giant pools of water in the kitchen. Old leaky roof. Old leaky house. I wipe up the water with a torn, faded beach towel and grab two big soup pots to place under the leaks. Black Dog's tail is wagging so hard he looks like he's doing the hula. Obviously hungry. Sam, on the other hand, is stewing in his cage and ignores me completely. I give Black Dog some leftover chicken mixed with his dry food and meekly offer Sam a carrot and a hunk of cheese. He's too hungry to hold a grudge, so he takes the food into a corner and eats it with his back toward me, still muttering peevishly under his breath.

I pull off my clothes, step into my molded Formica shower, turn it on full blast, and watch the trickle come out. Just as I sit down in my flannels to transcribe the lecture, I hear my mother's voice sailing through the kitchen door, "Honey, I'm home!"

"I'm home! I'm home!" echoes Sam.

"Cassie, open up! I'm locked out!"

Black Dog reaches the door first, jumping up on two legs and pressing his nose to the glass door panes. Then he lets out a high-pitched wail, like a tea kettle, and bounds out the door to greet her, clawing her two large shopping bags and knocking her off balance.

"Yes, yes, I missed you too, my darling," she croons as she sets down the bags and rummages through her backpack for a baggie of treats.

"Sit," she commands, holding out a rawhide stick. Black Dog jumps up and snatches it from her hand.

"Good boy," she says matter-of-factly.

Mom hands me the bags, which are filled with organic dried fruits, preserves, almonds, honey, and giant containers of dates. Every time she goes to the desert she stops at a roadside date stand, halfway between here and hell, and loads up on this stuff. She likes to tell me that these food groups are the secret of happiness—with the added benefit of keeping one regular, sound of mind, and cancer-free. Sometimes I think if I could just combine my mother's healthy body secrets with Tiff's philosophical quest for happiness, I'd be the wisest person on earth.

When I was young, my parents and I used to stop at the place across the highway from the date shack, a giant weather-beaten concrete brontosaurus. It had a fifty-foot neck you could slide down if you didn't mind the bird shit and then climb about a zillion steps back up. I remember one time my dad got so winded he finally had to sit down, take a breather, and then double back.

My mother always loved stopping at weird roadside attractions. Like the time we went to a children's science fair on the way home from somewhere and took a tour of a walk-through human heart. It was a giant, pulsating, alarmingly red exhibit, the size of a two-story house, and when you first walked in, the rampway "arteries" were pitch-black and so narrow that we were forced to crawl. A whooshing, watery heartbeat roared like the ocean from loudspeakers and I remember feeling claustrophobic, then anxious and finally paralyzed with fear. Kids behind me kept yelling, "Move it," but I crouched there, frozen in the aorta. The museum staff had to stop the soundtrack, turn on the lights, and send a guard in to lead me out. I was shaky, exhausted, fragile. The way I imagined my father felt, a year later, when *his* giant heart shut down for good.

So, somewhere in between me putting the honey in the pantry, my mother making date shakes, and then announcing she was going to take a shower, I have a vision. Well, not a vision really, more like a cinemagraphic moment of extreme, unadulterated, remorse. A "how could I?" moment that morphs into sheer insanity. There, right in front of me, like a mirage, and blocking my view of my mother filling the Waring blender, is a video replay of Freddy and me, locked in an embrace. He is pressing me against the shower wall, his thigh rammed between my legs, his hands running up and down the sides of my breasts. And to make matters worse, I suddenly feel my body ignite, a streak of poker-hot air, burning through my groin and up toward my chest.

"Cassie, I'm talking to you . . . did you hear me? Do you want ice cream in yours?"

"Oh, sure. Sounds good, Mom. How was your trip?"

She walks over to her backpack and pulls out a package of photos as I bat away the images swarming before my eyes and try to concentrate on my mother's conversation.

"We hiked out to the ridge . . . visited the mines . . . camped near the oasis . . ."

She hands me the photos and goes back to the blender. Shit. There I am again. This time in Freddy's bed, and he is crushing my ribs and chest as he pins my arms down and holds them there while his mouth closes in on mine, cutting off all the air. I have to stop this right now. I can't breathe! This is not what I want to be thinking. He's certainly not thinking about me. He probably staged the whole thing. Takes me to a fancy place, introduces me to his fancy friends, gets me drunk, pretends to be enamored. Probably done it a thousand times. But the truth is, from the moment the water hit the marble, I wanted to fuck him. I wanted it more than I've ever wanted anything.

"Cassie?" My mother is standing in front of me holding a glass.

"Oh. Thanks, Mom." I take a sip. Thick yucky date shake that clogs my throat and gags me like my shame. What I really feel like is a clean shot of whiskey. Something that will burn my gullet and sear away the sin.

"Delicious," I tell her, and offer to put everything away so I can be alone with my wretched visions. The good Cassie gives her a hug as she goes into her bedroom to unpack. The bad Cassie keeps shoving pornographic images into my face as I put away all the hippie snacks. Freddy could tell how much I wanted him. But maybe he was wrong. What if I just wanted a man? Maybe I just wanted the high of fucking someone, anyone, until you can't fuck anymore. That out-of-breath, out-of-body feeling that's like nothing else. The thing that keeps you aching with desire for hours and days afterward even though you know the man is emotionally sleazy, a complete and utter pig.

I finish up in the kitchen, cover Sam's cage, kiss my mother good night, and try to focus on Conner's transcription. I hope I can stay awake long enough to get through at least half of it.

"We're here today to talk about *Polygonia c-album*, generally known as the common butterfly. But what an uncommon beauty it is indeed. A dream of heaven dispersed into sunlight. The novelist Vladimir Nabokov was obsessed with butterflies. He called them his passion and his demons. He was most fascinated, however, by the process of their transformation. Nabokov noted the larva's growing discomfort, the tight feeling about the neck, the pain, and the difficulty . . . so when the cocoon breaks open and the butterfly finally works herself out, he found her a symbol not only of beauty but also of strength and courage. Only then ready to float into the air."

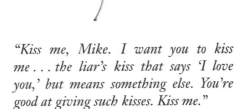

CHAPTER 25

> *"Kiss me, Mike. I want you to kiss me . . . the liar's kiss that says 'I love you,' but means something else. You're good at giving such kisses. Kiss me."*

I'm sitting in an old, shabby theater in Santa Monica that exclusively shows art films. It's in a sketchy neighborhood next to a pawnshop and a used-furniture warehouse and the street is lined with a row of decapitated parking meters. There's a homeless person wrapped in a blanket sitting cross-legged on the bus stop bench in front of the theater. I hear him mumble "motherfuckerasshole" as I walk in, so I think better about giving him my usual handout.

I must have driven past this place thousands of times without ever even considering seeing a show. Now that's all changed. We're currently at the noon showing of *Kiss Me Deadly*, which, Professor Pearce says, is a classic example of fifties film noir. The screening is part of her small senior seminar, Free Will and Philosophical Thought, and she asked me to drive her to the theater and take notes on the discussion afterward.

The movie is set in LA, but we're not talking sunny California here, that's for sure. Every scene is grim and grimmer—bourbon for breakfast, bloody bodies, garish neon lights, and a bunch of psychos, gangsters, small-time crooks, and sexy sluts all running around in the dead of night.

The story opens with a shot of some deserted highway and the sound of a woman sobbing in the background. Then the hard-boiled detective Mike Hammer hits the brakes in his cool little convertible sports car and picks up Christina, clad only in a trench. But she doesn't survive past the next charming scene in which a group of thugs hang her from the rafters of a seedy motel, torture her with a pair of pliers, and then push her off a cliff.

I have to say that I'm hooked even before Christina begs Hammer to "remember me." But the mood is momentarily broken when Pearce's alarm clock suddenly goes off in her enormous leather purse. She rustles through her bag and turns the clock off, murmuring, "So sorry."

I knew she didn't own a watch, but she also doesn't own a cell phone (brain cancer), personal computer, or a car. She tells me she'll never get used to driving on the "wrong" side even though she's lived here for decades. About once a week, I'll drive her somewhere when she can't get her friend to take her.

We've gone to several lectures at the downtown library, including one I loved on stereotyping. The visiting author was a dwarf, so you can understand his interest in the subject (okay, maybe he wasn't a *real* dwarf, but he was extremely short). And then there was the lecture on the famous psychologist Carl Jung, by someone who ranted on and on about Jung's fascination with the occult, ESP, and astrology. I was surprised how close the discussion seemed to one of my mother's coffee-klatches.

The whole atmosphere in this theater reeks of intellectual. The floor is strewn with popcorn and cigarette butts, the screen is grainy, and the sound is somewhat muffled. Watching these silvery black-and-white images is like being part of a bad dream. Nothing goes right for these people and everyone is rotten, disloyal, and murderous. In the end, they all get what's coming to them, trapped in lonely, dark alleys—dead, disfigured, despondent.

After the film, we all gather in a Venice Beach café, order triple espressos, and talk about the theme of this film and how it relates to the class. Like most people with British accents, Pearce sounds so insightful and intelligent. Tiff's friend Liza, for instance, is dumb as a post, but since she's British she gets all these great jobs. She sounds like an expert on everything and I've always believed the secret to her sex appeal is that men feel upper crust and sophisticated in her presence. If I were reading a fashion magazine on what's hot and what's not, a French or British accent would be right up there with Prada handbags and Chihuahuas.

At first I feel a little out of place. But then, I get so interested in what the group is saying, I stop typing on my laptop and just listen. They start out analyzing the morally ambiguous characters and then roll right into a discussion of, as Pearce puts it, "the lonely lawless universe" of noir.

"So is there a possibility of redemption for anyone here?" asks a solemn-faced woman dressed in black and sprawled on a velvety-maroon sofa with broken springs.

"Yes. Of course. Even though the world is tarnished, man must abide by the rules or be punished. Then again, good does not always triumph over evil," answers Pearce.

I try to digest this theory as the late-afternoon shadows flit around the faces of these bright, unassuming students who seem to have so much to say about so many things.

The topics bounce around from philosophy to science to art. Toward the end of the session, someone points out that Christina is named after a famous poet, Christina Rossetti, and that her sonnets are "brilliant." A skinny, disheveled guy, who looks like his mother just shoved him out of the nest, mentions the "existential" plays *No Exit* and *Waiting for Godot*, in which he says all the characters are just stuck in their own personal versions of hell, searching for truth. The big cosmic joke, he cracks, is that the truth doesn't exist. I nod, because the other students are nodding, but that thought confuses me and I decide to go to the library to check out books on Rossetti and on the plays. What I'd like most, however, is to just sit here for the next half-century, sip lukewarm bitter coffee, and discuss film, poetry, love, and life.

Toward the end of the conversation, Professor Pearce compares the film to German Expressionist art.

"Like Klimt?" I say, brightly.

"Exactly," Pearce says, impressed. Glad that son of a bitch Freddy was good for something.

CHAPTER 26

"So what else does Freddy have besides a big, long, hot shower?"

"This isn't funny, Tiff. He treated me like dirt."

"No, he didn't. He took you to a concert, he paid for your crappy car, and then he gave you the best shower of your life."

"He has a girlfriend. Is there anyone in America that doesn't have a girlfriend?"

"Of course there is."

"Well, I haven't met him."

It's Friday night, Tiff and I are at the diner, and then we'll probably see a movie. I tell her I just went to see a terrific film at the Royal and she casts me a curious glance.

"So we're seeing art films now?" Then she changes the subject right back to dating and Freddy. As usual, we're settling into our same old roles. Tiff thinks my standards are too high. (How she can say that after I married Frank, I don't know.) And I think Tiff has no standards.

"Are you upset because he didn't tell you the truth?"

"Yes. Of course I am."

"What's so good about the truth anyway?"

"Ask God," I say. "Unless you're thinking it's an amoral universe."

"What are you talking about? Just get rid of the girl-friend. You know how to do that, don't you?"

"Right. I'm an expert at that."

"Okay. All you do is act really sweet and understanding. Because, you know how it is, after a while, the girlfriend starts acting like a pain—bitter, complaining, where's the ring?—which is the perfect time to step in."

"I don't want to play those games."

"Let me put it in language you'll understand. You know when your dog gets old and he's limping around, never wants to play, grumpy, barks at everything. And then sadly, sadly he dies. After a while, you get a new puppy. And he's frisky, happy, playful, and affectionate. And you think what was so great about the old dog anyway?"

"I like my old dog."

"Okay. But don't you think deep down inside, Freddy really likes you?"

"I think deep down inside, there isn't any deep down inside."

I went to the bank today at lunch, transferred money out of my dwindling savings account, and sent Freddy a check for a whopping three hundred dollars. Just the thought of it bouncing makes me cringe. I try not to think about him, because mixed with all the humiliation are infuriating waves of desire. I don't think men understand that. Speaking of dogs—we're all like puppies to them. If they can't have one, they'll just take another. Oh. Stop it. I don't want to sound bitter. I hate women who sound bitter. It's such a bore. Still, I wonder what Patricia looks like.

When I get home, I put on my old PJs, look at my crumpled dress, and glance at the overflowing laundry basket in my shabby closet. Nothing decent to wear. Every day at work I look the same. I decide to check out my mother's wardrobe. Even more dismal—stuff she's worn for years. T-shirts hung up like blouses, old homemade tie-dyed skirts, wormy-looking sweats, and not one pair of pants with belt loops. All elastic pull-ons. Really bad. How come I've never noticed this before? Browns, khakis, grays, mud-colored mixtures of polyester and acrylic. I glance at myself in the mirror.

Maybe I'll wake up tomorrow and look like those girls at the symphony. A miracle will happen overnight and, voilà, Cassie's changed. She's embellished, adorned with a brilliant, iridescent sheen. Everything about her is fascinating. So articulate and well read. A singular work of art. There she goes—a creature worthy of obsession. A bit of blue heaven.

That's not going to happen. But I do need a new life. I need to travel. I need a college degree. I need more black dresses. I need money.

I've never been one of those people who worry about money, but there are so many things I want to do now, it seems all I *do* is worry about it—a little voice in my brain keeps saying, "get money, get money." It's a low, rattling, mournful wail that plagues me at inconvenient times—following me around like a shadow.

No one ever flat out tells you, "I don't have enough money," but you pretty much know it about a person—like someone laughing behind your back.

My mother's never been very good with finances. In fact, that's how she met my father. She got this threatening notice from the IRS about back taxes and, in a panic, she raced over to the Malibu H&R Block. She tearfully told her sad story of lost W-2 forms and forgotten deadlines to the CPA on duty.

He listened to her tale of woe, lent a sympathetic ear, and, after he had straightened out the whole mess, asked her out.

Not one of the more romantic stories, but he was her balding knight in shining armor, with his plastic pocket pen holder and calculator under his arm.

My mother likes to tell me that those years were the best of her life. My father doted on both of us. He was fifteen years older than my mother, a straight arrow, conservative, by-the-numbers kind of guy. She'd been a folksinger, a bicycle messenger, a coffeehouse waitress, and a lot of other related hippie clichés. After she met my dad, though, she went back to school, got her degree, and then started working in the wildlife center. She was young and beautiful. His fanciful flight.

After he died, we went back to living on the edge. Truthfully, I don't remember life any other way. He left us a little insurance money, which my mother still uses to supplement her income at the wildlife center. Taxes and budgets are always a challenge.

My mother will reminisce sometimes. "You know, your father used to tell me, 'Just save all your receipts in a shoebox.' 'God help us,' he'd say, 'if we're ever audited.' "

And every January, the shoebox comes out, but by March when it's still empty, she'll say, "The year's half gone, so what's the point."

Tiff's theory is that you need to be lucky to have money and you need to be smart to keep it. Frank was neither— look at the way he ended up—and those voices in my brain are getting louder and louder like a chorus of frogs on a summer night. I need money. I need money. So what can I sell?

There's a strong moldy smell as I flick on the lights in the garage. At first, I think there's nothing here because I sent Frank's relatives anything of value, but then I see a group of boxes in the back corner that I never bothered to unpack. All my friends who move agree, no one ever opens all their boxes. That's the thing about possessions. You decide you can't part with something, so you don't give it away, yet, after you move you never give it another thought. In fact, more often than not, it disappears altogether. Mom says that three moves equal one fire.

I rifle through some old cardboard boxes and, lo and fucking behold, here's Frank's CB and ham radio stuff he used to keep in his office—it's in pretty good condition too. Four boxes of it. Ranger CB 10 Meter Radio-150 watts, antennas, mounts, cables, connecters, power mikes, and cords. I think back to the moronic drunken messages he and his trucker friends used to send back and forth. The whole CB thing seemed so dumb. I mean they had cell phones. It was supposed to be in case of emergency, but it didn't help the *Titanic*, did it?

On the bottom of the box is his police radar detector, which some cop made him remove from his truck a few months before the accident. I know this stuff is worth something. I start to leave and then spot a box from Clay's Radio Shop half hidden by Mom's bags of organic weed retardant. How did this slip by me? Wow. Brand-new GPS navigation system. Never been used. The receipt says $799. Bingo.

So here's what I do. It's Friday night, I know exactly where Frank's friends are—the Breakers Bar in Point Dume. I heave all the boxes in my trunk, throw on some jeans, and head down the mountain for the Pacific Coast Highway. It's about a forty-five-minute drive north, and by the time I get to the bar, it's prime time, eleven p.m.

From the outside, the Breakers doesn't look like much, but all the locals know where it is. There's always a bunch of kids blowing around on skateboards outside. And inside the place is mobbed, music blasting, people crushed against the bar, and I don't recognize a soul. It's a surfer/stoner bar that draws a mixed crowd of locals, kids from Malibu High with phony IDs, and a whole group of residents that live in the trailer park in Trancas, the working-class section of Malibu. Most of the men are still in shorts and flip-flops, and some of the women wear bikini bras under their shirts. Year-round attire for this group. When the temperature plunges to sixty-five they throw on a fleece.

As I walk in, I'm hit with the familiar aroma of suntan lotion, beer, and salty ocean breezes. I remember Frank used to love this place. I did too until the kitchen was closed for rats. This year it's rated B, but I'm still not eating here. I decide to order beer and chips, and just wait. Maybe I'm a little early.

"Guess who?" someone says from behind, as he slaps his hands over my eyes.

"Who?" I say, playing along.

"It's Steve! And Carl!" I knew they'd be here—two old friends of Frank's who say they're in real estate in the West Valley but who knows. Carl's good-looking in an aging surfer sort of way. Thick, stocky body, shaggy dyed-blond hair. And Steve is one of those guys who never seem to notice that shirts have buttons. I remember they used to hang out in our house on Sundays watching every football game on the planet. Whenever their team won, they'd hoot and holler on the couch, jump up and down and do a little jig. Then they'd call their bookies. Steve had this high-pitched baby laugh, but I always used to think Carl was cute.

He was one of Frank's more interesting friends—a combination of bully and sentimental softie. We used to double-date because Frank was always attracted to his girlfriends. But I liked Carl. Maybe it's corny, but he'd always stand up when I first entered a room.

"Hardly recognize you, Cassie. You lose weight or something?" Carl says, genuinely happy to see me.

"Maybe it's my hair."

"Yeah, that's what it is. You look good. So I've been wanting to call and take you out or something since Frank and I were such good friends, but I've been traveling a lot and I couldn't get your number. You have a new number or something?"

"No," I say. "Same number."

This happened to me all the time after Frank died. I'd bump into someone we knew and they'd go into a long explanation of why they hadn't called or visited or taken me out. It got so I just wanted them to tell me the truth. "Hey, I never liked you that much in the first place," or, "Whoops. I completely forgot you exist, how embarrassing."

I take a swig of my beer, look them right in the eye, and say, "I have a proposition for you."

They look surprised and interested. I tell them about Frank's loot, how it's brand new—in mint condition—and that I'll sell it to them for half price if they pay me cash right now. And I know they have it. They always carried wads of cash. These guys make a living dealing in untraceable transactions. They look at each other knowingly. Do they feel sorry for me because they think I need the money, or are they figuring out how they can screw me?

"Four hundred bucks for the lot," says Steve, grudgingly, studying my face for a moment. He has anemic, convict blue eyes that are set close together and a cold, absent look. He's not wearing his usual surfer shorts—probably covering up his ankle tracking bracelet.

Okay. They're trying to screw me. I divide and conquer. I pull out the eBay comps I quickly looked up before I left and tell them I'll discount by 25 percent. I end up selling Carl the GPS for $500, and Steve the CB with all the other junk for $450. Almost $1,000!

Carl takes a wad of cash out of his pocket and says flirtatiously, "So, Cassie, you seeing anyone these days?"

"As a matter of fact, I am," I lie.

"Too bad," he says, as I pocket the cash. The second time this week I've lied about a boyfriend.

As I'm opening my car door to leave, I feel someone wrap their arms around my waist and pull me back from the car. All I can think about is the cash in my purse. I'm about to give him that elbow thing you learn in self-defense when he says, "C'mon, Cassie. Let's take a drive." It's Carl, and he's a little drunk. He loses his balance as I shove him away.

"You sure look great, sweetie pie, you really do."

"Oh. Thanks. That's nice of you. But my mom is waiting for me to pick her up, she's right down there by the gas station, and I really have to go."

"Okay, darlin'. What about afterwards?"

"I don't know, Carl. By the time I drive her home . . ."

"Yeah, yeah. Okay. I get it. But you know where you can find me," he says, giving up.

A year or so ago, I would've been happy, even grateful, to go out with him. But he seems less now. I finger the wad of cash that Steve and Carl gave me. I'm going to look at it as a final bequest from Frank's nonexistent estate.

PART TWO

"It is a surprising and memorable, as well as valuable experience, to be lost in the woods . . . Not till we are lost, in other words, not till we have lost the world, do we begin to find ourselves, and realize where we are. . . ."

HENRY DAVID THOREAU, "The Village," *Walden*

CHAPTER 27

The harvest moon came and went. It poured on Halloween, and the Santa Anas moved in next. Those hot, drunken winds caroused around for a few weeks, and then hunkered down into a somber mood, like a band of late-night partiers headed out into the cold.

It's almost Thanksgiving now, and the wide expanse of bramble and wood around my house is changing from green to shades of dead. In the forest, where my birds are nesting, the sap flows, and roots plunge down, wrapping themselves around each other.

These days, I think about how to do things—mostly how to keep up in class. It's been a revelation to me that college is turning out easier than high school. I can go at my own pace and take courses that have no multiple-choice tests.

I've been auditing Conner's eight a.m. class for the past month. I always slip out a few minutes early to get to my desk by nine. With the money from Frank's "estate," I was able to sign up for a nighttime extension course—only four hundred dollars. I chose Introduction to World Literature and Philosophy. It's a core course for incoming freshmen—gives you a little taste of everything. I even bought a few new outfits. I look like a mid-year student—a black backpack and matching circles under my eyes.

But my hair is looking better. I've been back to the salon several more times and I'm beginning to understand the warped concept of cutting your hair to make it grow.

I'm midway through the alphabet now in Conner's office, still cataloging away. Sometimes he and I have little discussions while I'm working. It's usually about the class I'm taking. The other day, I told him I was studying Descartes. Conner was all reason and logic, going on and on about Descartes being the father of modern philosophy, the link between mind and body and the beginning of Enlightenment.

"Sometimes," I venture, "none of it seems to make sense."

"In what way?" he replies.

"Well, for instance, 'I think, therefore I am.' I mean, I am what? Is a person who they think they are, or who other people think they are?"

He gives me a superior look, speaking slowly and deliberately. "Well . . . I think we're getting a little off-base here. To make a long story short, the point of it is the nature of certainty. Thought and being are fundamentally the same thing. So now, are we understanding it a little better?"

"To make a long story short, no." I decide that Conner has no idea about thinking and being when you're not who you think you are—I think, therefore I lie, therefore I'm not? I think, therefore I lie, therefore I am? . . . but not really. I think, therefore I am . . . oh, forget it. How can I expect him to understand—and I hate his tone.

Another time he walked into his office and caught me sitting on his couch dashing off a few notes for my extension term paper. He asked me what it was about, and I told him it was supposed to be on the subject of appearance versus reality.

"Have you seen Bertrand Russell's writings?" he asks, as he dumps his books on his desk.

"No. I'm using Plato. You know, the truth behind appearances. I'm writing about the fact that people do things to make others think they are who they aren't."

"What's your focus?" He takes off his jacket, sits down on his swivel chair, and starts checking his e-mails.

"You."

"Me?" He looks up from his laptop. Now I've got his attention. He starts swiveling his chair back and forth.

"Sort of. Let's just say . . . for argument's sake. If you didn't look the way you do, or act a certain way in class, or bring your dog, or tell wild stories about Africa—the pygmies and all—the kids wouldn't listen. Your appearance is the reason they like you. Why they pay attention."

"Just my appearance, huh?" he says, as he rolls up his shirtsleeves.

"Well, by appearance, I mean all sorts of things, your rap, your charisma. Of course, then you have to figure out what the truth is behind it."

"And have you figured that out?"

"No. I have no idea. I hardly know you."

"Fair enough. But you can make assumptions."

"Such as?" I ask.

"I'm insecure or frustrated . . ."

"Or patronizing and condescending. For example," I add.

"Exactly." He laughs. "You can do this with anyone. The truth behind appearances. Let's take you, for instance." He's flung himself down next to me on the couch. Great. Let's see how astute he really is.

"You appear to be naive and unschooled. Someone who doesn't flaunt her knowledge in the slightest—almost to a fault. But underneath, you have a skillful mind and you see things in a unique way."

"Thank you—"

He cuts me off. "In addition, you appear to be a woman who takes her beauty for granted—deliberately dressing in an indifferent sort of way. But the truth is, you still look, let's say . . . for discussion's sake . . . exceptional."

I momentarily look away. I'm not used to compliments, especially from men. And I'm embarrassed to show him how pleased I am.

"Thank you," I say. "You know, the paper's not really about you."

"That's a relief. So what's the title?"

" 'Illusions of Love.' "

❧ ❧ ❧

I can't recall exactly when it happened, maybe after I finished the hawk paper. It wasn't a sudden thing, that's for sure. But there's been a change inside me. Something's happening. Maybe I'm making too much of it, blowing it out of proportion. At any rate, I started going around to all my friends, asking if they thought I was different. In fact, I may be the only person on the planet who has actually conducted an intervention on herself. Okay, maybe not a real intervention where people stage a little "surprise" party for a loved one who is hooked on something and then sit around pleading for them to go to rehab. But you have to admit there are similarities—I was basically looking for some kind of formal acknowledgment from the people I love that I was beginning to change. So naturally, I started with Tiff.

"Tiff, do you notice anything different about me?"

"Did I say something that hurt your feelings?"

"No. I just want to know if you see any changes in me."

"In what way?" she asks cautiously.

"In any way. For instance . . . in my conversations."

"Well. Like you seem better at . . ."

"Expressing myself?" I feed her.

"Exactly. And you seem more . . ."

"At ease with other people?" I prompt.

"Yes. I've definitely noticed that. And what about your hair?" she asks confidently.

"Well, I have *you* to thank for that."

"That's true. I did do a great job."

As you can see, Tiff was no help. Neither was my mother. The general thinking on this is that parents are often the last to notice anything different about their children, even if their kids happen to be raging crackpots or pathological liars. I moved on to a few people from the wildlife center, the dry cleaner, Mom's friend Sylvia, and even the waitress at the diner.

I have to say that the universal reaction wasn't all that earthshaking. Actually, it was the total opposite of what I expected to hear. Nearly everyone said something like, "Hey, Cassie, relax. Don't you think I'd tell you if I thought you were acting strange?"

But the thing is, even if no one else notices, I have new theories and ideas about life, a new sense of how to make things work. There comes a time, a point at which you sense an imaginary boundary line—you're traveling on a road, you don't quite know where you're going but you do know it's too far to turn back.

It's disconcerting and confusing. Hard to explain. It seems as if there's never enough time. I'm restless and agitated, prone to go off on tangents, lose my train of thought, walk around with a head full of information, and rush around trying to fit it all in. Often, when I get home from work, I find myself moving from room to room, adrift and anxious, looking for someplace to alight. Sam thinks it's a game and careens along ahead of me to see what I'll do next. And I think I know what it is.

Taking these classes, working with Conner, I want to go to college for real. I want to take the SAT—the "Starting After Thirty" test. Every day, for the last week, I've Googled "SAT," logged on to the site, and answered the question of the day. I got it right four out of five times. When I was a junior in high school, nobody even mentioned taking it. Except my mother. And I blew her off. Even with all her encouragement, I just never had the confidence. Too many years of struggling with bad grades to put myself through it all over again. I wasn't college prep, so why stress? But everything is different now. I should have listened to her.

One of my professors is always talking about the things we carry with us. He should be talking about the things we don't.

CHAPTER 28

I wake up every morning by five, feed the animals, make my breakfast, and get on the road
by six. I drive in a sort of daze, following a set
of taillights down the windy canyon road, passing
the lumberyard, general store, and recycling center as the cloud cover lifts and the air gets crisp
and clear. I have a long day today, class at eight,
work until five, and then another class from seven
to nine tonight.

I race across campus, a little late for Conner's
morning lecture, where a group of us regularly sit
on the highest tier in the back. It's Friday morning, there's definitely a lighter turnout, and the
kids who are here look like they just rolled out of
bed. The girl in front of me has long wet hair,
yoga pants, fleece-lined slippers, and she's eating
a muffin from Starbucks. The kid next to me is
half asleep and has a crown of messy dark hair.
He looks like an overgrown choirboy except for
his wrinkled Led Zeppelin T-shirt and baggy
sweatpants worn low, clearly no underwear. He

183

taps me on the shoulder and introduces himself. His name is Zack.

"Hey. I know you. Remember me from the ATM?"

"Oh sure. Hi." The good-looking kid with the cash—who hangs out in Prague. He's rooting around in his backpack.

"Can I borrow a pen?"

"No problem." I pull one from my canvas bag.

"Cool," he says, as his cell phone goes off. Then he spends the first ten minutes of the lecture text messaging. He wears a thick, silver-carved ring with a skull and crossbones on his thumb.

Now my phone is vibrating. It's Freddy again. I've gotten a few messages from him in the last few weeks, and yesterday, he left me this corny message with "Splish Splash" playing in the background. I guess I'm a safe bet. Men love women who aren't available. Even though I am, and he's not.

Conner's back is toward the class and he's using a pointer with a light for emphasis. He's in jeans, a polo shirt, and a tweed jacket. Ahab is draped over a pretty girl's lap in the front row, in doggie heaven as she lovingly caresses his ears. Today's lecture is on bird migration.

"There used to be some pretty far-out beliefs about what happens to the birds when they migrated. The Romans believed swallows wintered on the moon. Other cultures thought they turned into frogs. Some even suggested calling out the troops to prevent the birds from leaving. Or shoot them all down as they left."

I feel another tap on my shoulder. Zack again.

"Can I borrow some paper?" I guess he's done text messaging. I bend down, grab a spiral notebook, and tear out a few sheets.

"Thanks. What did he just say?"

"They used to think birds migrated to the moon."

"Sweet." He gives me a hazy smile as he yanks up his sweatpants, which have sagged so low I quickly divert my eyes. Too late. I can see hair peeking out.

Conner dims the lights and rolls down a huge screen. We listen to him, as we watch a sudden surge of songbirds fly in silent formation.

"With the advent of modern travel, men finally figured out that birds didn't just disappear. They flew at incredible speeds across vast distances. At the height of migration, forty-five million songbirds arise on a single night and fly three hundred miles of Gulf Coast from Corpus Christi to Lake Charles, Louisiana. They go without resting, in the dark, through the clouds, and no one really knows why they don't get lost."

I think about my mother's hummingbird feeder and those minute creatures with misty wings who flash like emerald fireflies and then shoot off into space. My mother is always so protective of them, putting the food in spots that hawks and owls can't reach.

"All that energy and perseverance," she'd say, "and with a brain the size of a pea."

I'm trying to listen to Conner when I notice Zack staring at me.

"So. You auditing this, or something?"

"Kind of. I work in the Psych Dept."

"You a TA?"

"Not really. Just doing some research."

"Cool." He gives me a blinding, Tom Cruise smile.

"Tic Tacs?" he offers.

He taps them into my palm as we hear Conner assign a paper due in two weeks on "Predation Risk and Habitat in Southern California."

Zack flicks the pen in the air and sighs. "Shit. I'm fucked. I have two midterms next week. And I still have to make up this stuff from last semester when I had mono. What's predation risk, anyways?"

"You know, predators. Hawks. Owls. Coyotes. (Freddy.) What he was talking about last week."

"I kind of missed last week."

"Well, do the essay on red-tailed hawks. They're all over the place and eat every animal you can think of." I could knock that essay out in about an hour.

"Can I borrow your notes?" This is a first. Someone borrowing *my* notes. Even though it's a slacker. I'd better type them out and spell-check.

"Sure. Is Monday okay?"

He leans into my face, squeezes my arm, and blasts me with menthol breath. "Sure. No worries," he says.

As I walk back to the office I think about hawks—the one Frank brought into the center the first day I met him and the ones who soar through our neighborhood on updrafts of hot air searching out their prey. Sam watches out for them from his perch in front of the kitchen window—the silent sentinel. When he spots one, he mimics a hawk's warning cry, then crouches down in the corner of his cage. I make a mental note to go to the clearing tomorrow morning because I haven't checked on my ivory-bills in a couple of weeks. I'll set my alarm clock for four a.m. It's the best time to see them. Who needs sleep anyway?

CHAPTER 29

The moody, predawn light is filtering through the trees as I head to the clearing. Night crickets thunder away in my ears—a high-pitched wave of sound—the first morning of the beginning of the world. This time of year the fog is so thick it's like you're walking through Wite-Out. I trip over a chewed-out plastic irrigation pipe and get soaked. Must be the coyotes. In our neighborhood, packs of them scale people's fences and chew through the sprinklers when they want a drink. Indians used to call them "the tricksters" because they're so crafty and smart. I carry a big stick to scare them off if they try to approach me.

I make my way deeper into the forest, side-stepping pools of murky water and swampy muck filled with a million life-forms quietly ticking, ancient and fertile. At one point, I find myself surrounded by neon-colored toadstools like the *Alice in Wonderland* scene with the loopy caterpillar smoking a hookah. Acid dreams for real.

As I near the clearing, I hear a lot of fussing and preening. Happy hour in bird land. Wrens, warblers, thrashers, and goldfinches dart and swoop through the trees like neighbors visiting each other across the fence. There's a quotation on the bulletin board in the wildlife center by John Burroughs that says, "There is news in every bush." And that's what it feels like out here.

I sit down in my spot, take out my journal, and wait for the ivory-bills to appear. It's bitter cold and my ears are burning. Yesterday started out with rain but then turned into a balmy sixty-five degrees, a fine November LA day, with a definite taste of spring in the air. A nest-building day for sure. Then last night the temperature plunged to the thirties and now it's miserable once again. Every so often I look around. Strange that I never see or hear anyone in this clearing. I could freeze to death, waiting for these birds, and no one would find me for weeks. That's a comforting thought. My mother and Tiff might wander out here eventually and a few people might call—like my old buddy Carl with his oafish, froggy grin. Or Freddy.

Shit. I can't seem to shake the memory of what happened. I've morphed from a woman who didn't have sex for years and wanted it, to a woman who finally *did* have sex and wished to God she hadn't. Wait. There's the female. She's sitting in a rotting cypress about thirty feet up, her head peeking out of a freshly carved cavity big enough for a hawk to enter. She stares at me with her ancient, reptilian face as if she knows me. The male joins her out of nowhere and they both begin their jittery routine, pounding away at the bark, wallowing in their grub fest. It's only a matter of time until the male notices me and sounds the alarm. Then they'll streak off together in a holy white flash.

Meanwhile, I settle down to watch. They're an odd, reclusive couple, awkwardly hopping from limb to limb, living a life of wild uncertainty. I wonder if they're preparing to build a nest and if all the squabbling up there is just normal couple stuff. The Bickersons, taking potshots at each other. I usually stay here for hours, but it's just too damn cold. I reluctantly put away my journal and head down the mountain.

When I get home, I throw off my wet clothes, which are now icy and stuck to my skin, and take a nice hot shower. I time it. It lasts exactly three minutes before it turns cold. We really need a bigger water heater, but it's fifteen hundred dollars, so Mom said forget it.

I peek into Sam's cage. His head is sunk deep into the soft powdery feathers of his neck, his long toes tightly gripping the perch. In another hour or so he'll start his ritual morning grooming. I take out his breakfast and throw in some fresh strawberries. Sam loves those. Scraps from his dinner are splattered on the floor around his cage. Dribbles of corn, pasta, and chicken bones. Sam always flings any leftovers on the floor—he likes to keep his cage clean.

I read somewhere that Queen Victoria's parrot used to wake her with "God Save the Queen." Sam's such a grump when he gets up. Doesn't talk much before noon. I make myself a cup of coffee and sit down at the kitchen counter with my journal.

My childhood tutor was the one who first suggested I keep journals. I used to write about what I read, and how I felt about it. It was supposed to help me focus. But now I'm using them for something different. I write about my walks, my beloved ivory-bills, and what I see and what I hear.

I finish writing in my journal and then print out my lecture notes for Zack. I check the assignment. Predation Risk and Habitat in Southern California. That's so easy. Maybe I'll give him a few paragraphs—help him get started.

I spend the next few hours on the hawk paper. It just doesn't seem that hard. It's strange but in high school, whenever I had to write something, if I could go home, sit in a quiet corner, and take my time, I'd get an A. The teachers always wrote comments like "great imagination" and "well put." I remember my mother reading about some of the great writers who were dyslexic. So I guess I'm not that unusual. Trouble was, the A euphoria didn't last long. At some point I'd always have to come to class, take an exam, and get a D. But this paper took so little effort—like writing in my journals. I guess it's the subject matter. Five pages of hawks. This kid's gonna love me.

CHAPTER 30

There's a gloomy mind game everyone plays in Topanga this time of year when a spark from a car radiator or even one measly cigarette butt can ignite an entire neighborhood. If you had exactly two minutes to get out of your house, what would you grab?

It's always surprising to me what people consider worth saving. Dishes, linen, furniture, even antiques are rarely on the list. Neither is art. It's the little things people covet. An heirloom bracelet, photo albums, recipe files, lucky charms, love letters. I briefly flash on Conner's ode to Pamela. You can learn a lot about a person this way.

After I finished the hawk paper, I guess I must have crashed, because the last thing I remember was getting those waves of exhaustion around noon. I'm in that hazy, twilight state just before consciousness when your mind smears reality and dreams, and I look around my bedroom, considering my choices. The imaginary fire has leapt over the hill, incinerating everything in its wake, and the police helicopters are hovering over my roof. There's a rush of panic in the air as I hear an officer on a bullhorn ordering me to get the hell out of there (I think they use the euphemism "evacuate"). Assuming my mom and Sam are safe, I grab my favorite books about myths, my sea glass collection, and the photo of my dad holding me as a baby. I glance at my open, mini-walk-in closet. Reconsider for a moment. No, nothing else. I would happily let everything in there go up in smoke—oh, wait a minute—everything except my new black dress.

I stumble into my wreckage of a closet to grab a sweater and trip over an old bag of scuffed-up shoes I was going to get repaired last year. Jesus. I bet I haven't cleaned my closet for ten years. I lugged all my stuff over to Frank's house when I got married and then lugged it back home when he died. On display, right in front of me, is a disturbing exhibit of my pitiful past.

Here's the dress I wore when Frank proposed. Shiny and sexless. The pants and top I wore for my interview with Pearce. God, how could I? A little ensemble I used to wear to church—a long cotton flowered skirt and matching blouse—like the picture on the Old Maid card. Here's the blue brocade coat I used to live in. Looks like I'm wearing Tiff's couch. Here's the chocolate body paint Frank gave me for Valentine's Day the year before he died. Still unopened. Do these things go bad?

Leaning against the back wall, behind a bunch of empty shoeboxes, is a photo of me in a broken frame. I'm standing in front of the house in a straw-colored outfit, scowling. All I need is the pitchfork. And what's this? A nasty brown handbag with fringe, from the Village Tannery down the road. It got soaked when we had a leak in the roof and now it smells and looks like a badger. And this sweater, the result of a tragic laundry accident. Okay. I've had enough!

Conner says I deliberately dress in an indifferent way. It's not deliberate, I think, just unconscious. I read once that if you haven't worn something in two years, get rid of it. So it's got to go. I need to cleanse my soul of all this crap. I place the new outfits I bought for work and school to the side, and then start dumping everything else in giant black Hefty bags. Simplify, right?

I think about what I'm going to buy next when I have the time and the money. I want what Alison has, but without the attitude. Clean, sleek, sexy, stylish. Boots. Soft sweaters. Body-skimming skirts. Jeans that fit your butt just so. I have the urge to blow my next paycheck. Well, not my whole paycheck. I don't want to live with my mother the rest of my life. I figured out, this time next year, Tiff and I will probably be able to afford to rent our own place.

I've just finished carrying out the last bag when the phone rings.

"Hello?"

"Okay. This is the third time. How come you're not returning my calls?" It's Freddy. The voice is friendly, flirtatious.

"I was just wondering when we're going to get together. How's that boyfriend of yours?" He's got a lot of nerve.

"How's that girlfriend of yours?" Okay. I said it. Now there's silence on the other end while he obviously thinks about his well-considered reply. Then laughter.

"We've been torturing each other for some time now. And I'm almost done. D-O-N. Everything but the *E*." Now I'm laughing. You just can't embarrass this guy.

"Seriously. How about dinner sometime?" he pushes.

"Well," I hesitate.

"Tomorrow night? You pick the place." I think about it.

In the grand scheme of things, he didn't really do anything *that* bad. Maybe he was so taken with me, he decided to throw caution to the wind, and, anyhow, he's breaking up with her, isn't he?

"All right. What time?"

"I'll call you tomorrow. Make a reservation anywhere you want. Someplace nice."

Someplace nice. I make a reservation at an Italian place in Santa Monica, eight o'clock.

❦ ❦ ❦

I began the next evening with a certain optimism—an almost reckless belief that Freddy wasn't who I thought he was. I decide to wear a simple black sweater and pants—one of the few outfits I have left. Then I assemble an array of fixatives. Toners, luminizers, correctors, concealers, and primers. Things that camouflage the blemishes of your soul.

And then I wait. I turn on the TV. I turn off the TV. I put the dog out. I bring the dog back in. I lock Sam up in his cage because I don't want to get bird feathers on my sweater. At first he just moped, but now he's working himself into a fury. He hates being closed up when we're home alone together. Every five minutes he gives out an ear-piercing screech. I'm going to try to ignore him, which lately only makes things worse.

Now it's eight o'clock. Maybe I'll call the restaurant and tell them we're running late. Maybe I won't. I wait another half hour. And then another half hour. Now I'm tired. I lean back against the couch trying not to mess up my hair and makeup in case he calls. I'll act annoyed, because it's after nine, but I'll rally myself and meet him.

As the night moves forward, feelings of self-pity snowball, devouring the night's initial rush of anticipation and excitement. *Stood up.* The sad part is this rejection will have to stand in line behind a long list of disappointments. I go through a mental checklist of everything that's gone wrong the past few years. When I hit a hundred, I decide to stop. In a warped way, this busywork takes my mind off the dating debacle I'm facing. I remember the minister at our church once preached that deliverance often requires a trip into hell first.

Finally, at ten o'clock, I admit this date isn't going to happen. Now I'm mad. I hate Freddy. I hate his wrinkled khaki pants. I hate his fancy friends and their dumb names, Four, Three, Two, and Zero. I hate his sister, his mother, his father, and his fucking girlfriend, Patricia. I hate his entire apartment building and everyone in it, including the doorman. I hate his gutted condo, his ugly "gotta have it" art, his unused stainless steel kitchen, his stupid media room. And I hate his shower. Well, maybe not his shower.

The phone rings. I steel myself and answer in a terse, cold voice. "Hello?"

"You aren't going to believe what happened to me." It's Freddy. He sounds upbeat.

"You're probably right."

"I missed my flight, and I'm stuck at the airport." Sam lets out a series of seriously hostile, bloodcurdling squawks and then yells, "Help!"

"What?" I say. "I can't hear. My bird's upset."

Freddy repeats it with a little catch in his voice. "Missed my flight . . . stuck at the airport."

"Really," I say in monotone, rolling my eyes in disbelief.

"I had some business up in San Francisco." (Right. On a Sunday.) "And the meetings ran over, and then I missed my flight." (There's no phone service in San Francisco?)

"That's a shame," I snap. I feel a splitting headache coming on. I hold the phone slightly away from my ear, lie down on the couch, and begin to rub my temples. Sam, meanwhile, is doing a lot of cage rattling and wing beating. He's still screaming, "Help! Help! Let me out!"

"Forgive me?" Freddy asks. I can just see his flirtatious grin. "And I promise I'll take you somewhere wonderful to make up for it."

"Freddy. I'm not stupid." Sam is now imitating a fire siren.

"You're really upset, aren't you?"

I try to think of something truly insulting to say, but instead I say, "No. I'm just done—d-o-n-e." I laugh, but not in a nice way. In a way that says come close to me, and I'll throw you into the abyss where I myself am headed this very moment. I push the disconnect button and turn off the phone.

My taste in men has always been suspect, and it suddenly hits me that Freddy is just the flip side of Frank. Slicker maybe. A more expensive, cultured version with built-in finesse and charm, but the same lecherous, lying rat.

Tiff's boyfriend used to joke, "Tiff, hon, you're getting a big fat ass."

She'd march right over to the refrigerator, grab a half gallon of ice cream, and eat it in front of him. She had no fear. I admired that. I think about how I used to be afraid to tell Frank what I really thought. I went around every day with a tightness in my stomach, pretending I felt a certain way, pretending I was happy, believing that this was the only life available to me.

Sam starts to bellow, then lets out guttural rasps. I stomp over to his cage, open the door, and now he's livid—turning his back on me and not coming out. Okay. Be that way!

I stand up, walk to the bathroom, kick the door open, and scrub the makeup off my skin. Then I turn on the hot water full blast and dunk my whole face in the sink. Wait a minute. It occurs to me that the only emotion I'm feeling right now is anger. No self-pity, no "poor little me." I replay the conversation in my mind and I realize that I told him *exactly* how I felt. I spoke up. And I do feel d-o-n-e. And not just with Freddy.

CHAPTER 31

The academic pace is beginning to get to me. For the past two weeks I've been cramming for midterms, and the amount of material I'm studying is overwhelming. Zack actually gave me some useful tricks, 3×5 cards, nicotine gum, and Red Bull. We have a study group that meets after work at the library, or the campus bookstore. It's funny how different their priorities are from mine.

Everything these students do is for a reason—a step to lead somewhere else. They don't exactly live in the moment. Forget about that Buddhist stuff. For them, the course must qualify on three levels. It must (A) meet a requirement for their concentration, (B) help them get into a good grad school, and (C) most important, the professor must have clout. Can he or she write a letter that will help them get an impressive internship or a prestigious job?

And they all belong to clubs. Network. Network. They join the Dante Society, Italian Film

Club, Friends of Turkey, Slavic Chorus, Aerial Robotics, and the Gong Club—whatever that is. I notice there is also a Students for Organ Donation. Tiff is an official organ donor, but she only signed up at the DMV so she could put that little sticker on her driver's license to cover her age.

Some of the time, I can relate to their ambitions. But mostly, I'm removed from it all. I just want to prove to myself that I can do it, which, in light of their goals, seems so minor. They want to conquer the world, I just want to finish the assignment.

I rush to Conner's lecture and find my seat in the back of the auditorium next to Zack. The class quiets down as Conner strides in followed by his dog, who plops down in the middle of the stage and starts furiously licking his butt.

Conner glances down at him and says, "Cut it out, Ahab."

Usually, before he starts his lectures, Conner rambles on a bit about whatever's on his mind that day. Today he's telling us about his Toyota Land Cruiser, which runs on vegetable oil from the fryers of local restaurants.

"The oil from Japanese restaurants burns the cleanest," he says. "The next best thing is the Italian stuff—a little nuttier and very effective. I try to avoid the oil from fast-food places. Too dirty for my car, so I don't recommend consuming it orally."

Then he changes the subject. "I don't normally single out one piece of work, but this particular essay on predators was so well done, I'd like to share it with you."

He puts on his glasses and starts to read, "It's called 'Something Evil This Way Comes.' " Shit! This is the stuff I gave Zack.

"Hawks are murderers, deadly warriors, killing everything in their wake. Once they set their sights on something, the result is final and irrevocable—a primal nightmare. They're amoral. No conscience. Zeroing in on their prey like stealth missiles. Riding updrafts of hot air, hovering overhead, stopping on a dime, then curving into a reckless, headlong dive, talons outstretched as they kidnap baby songbirds while letting out a harrowing, hair-raising Indian warrior screech that freezes your nerves."

How rude! Zack didn't even change one word. This was supposed to be just a guide, a jumping-off point. He's copied the entire thing. Conner keeps reading. The class is at rapt attention. I look around and realize, hey, they're really liking my essay.

Conner finishes up and announces, "Zack Henderson. You there in the back. You want to stand up? Nice job." The class applauds as Zack stands up, beams, and winks at me. The little shit.

This is an example of no good deed goes unpunished. When I gave Zack my notes and essay a few weeks ago, he was so grateful. I had no idea he'd just hand it in as is. Oh, what difference does it make? I'm not taking the class for credit. Let the kid get an A. *I* know I wrote it. Still, I'm disappointed. No one will ever know about my triumph but me and him. And it's a sure bet he's not telling anyone.

As the day wears on, I actually start feeling better about the whole thing. I have a two-o'clock meeting with Conner. My fantasy is I walk in, he throws his arms around me, and says, "Cassie, I knew it was you all along! What insight! What intelligence! Let's read it again!"

Instead, I'm greeted with a half wave as Conner continues his phone conversation. He points to the couch, mouths "sorry," and keeps talking.

I sit down and his dog leaps up and flops next to me. He pushes himself on my lap and gums my forearm like a puppy. When I tussle the ringlets on his head, he rolls over on his back, and I absently scratch his stomach. I stop for a minute and he barks for more. Conner cups the phone and orders sternly, "Ahab. Down!"

Ahab completely ignores him, rolls over, and licks my face. Now the dog and I are completely entangled. I try to push him off, and he jumps back up.

"He has good taste," Conner says, wrapping up the call.

"I don't know, dogs just seem to like me." Not so great with men, however.

Conner tells me the assistant who usually helps him with his annual bird trip is unavailable. Would I mind filling in? I'll need to set up the van, confirm the motel reservations, meals, etc., etc., etc. Also accompany him and nine students next weekend, if I don't have any plans (that's a safe bet). With my experience at the wildlife center, I'm the perfect replacement.

I, of course, agree to go. Doesn't seem like work to me and I get paid overtime. When I tell Pearce about it, she says that he asks her every year and she always bows out.

"I like everything about birding except getting up before dawn, sitting in the muck, and waiting, waiting, waiting for the bloody birds who never show. Other than that, it's brilliant."

As it turns out, the day wasn't a total car wreck (although I hesitate to use that term). I go to my Honda and stuck in the door handle is a long-stemmed red rose covered in plastic with a red paper bow and one of those water capsules on the stem.

The note says: "Congratulations on your 'well done' essay. You are very cool. Zack."

CHAPTER 32

One night shortly after Frank died, my mother called a "bird whisperer" she'd discovered online. I guess she'd had enough. Sam was up at all hours, cackling, screeching, whining. He was peevish and testy and all he'd eat was pasta and parmesan. We dragged him to the vet twice at a hundred dollars a pop, and he couldn't find anything wrong with him. He wasn't molting. He didn't have a cold. It was a mystery. He wouldn't even play his favorite games. When I tried to play peekaboo with him he just said, "Dumbfuck," and knocked down his block tower.

The deal with this bird whisperer was, you'd send in a picture of your bird (dead or alive) and seventy-five dollars (by PayPal, check, or money order), and this person named Sherry Something would complete your reading within five business days. Initially, I was really mad at Mom for sending money to someone who seemed like a total psycho fruitcake. Plus, Mom told her all kinds of personal things about me. How Frank died. And how Sam hated him.

The Whisperer came right up with this brilliant analysis. Apparently, she channeled Frank, who told her he was haunting Sam's cage and we needed to do an exorcism. I'm not kidding here. My mother went for it. She always does. She said she paid the money so we might as well try it. Anyway, nothing else was working. So here's the weird thing. Every year in downtown LA, there's a big Mexican ceremony and parade called the Blessing of the Animals, which ends with a priest dipping a feather duster in some holy water and flinging it at the animals. It's a ritualistic baptism that exorcizes the demons in an animal's soul. Hundreds of people bring their pets and make a day of it, kind of like a carnival—balloons, kids, ice cream. I refused to go, but my mother took Sam anyway. And I swear to God, from that moment on, I had my old Sam back.

I'm thinking about all this as we drive down the I-15 in a crappy old van with no air-conditioning on our way to the Wilderness Tract Sanctuary. I was mortified when I went to pick it up at the rental lot. I reserved the van over the Internet. I mean, why use Hertz when Super Cheap Discount Rentals is around? Now I know why. It was too late to switch companies, and the only other van available had naked women painted on the side. When I pulled up to the school, Conner gave me a little half smile and said, "Nice van."

For the past hour or so, he's been trying to lead a discussion about communicating with animals and nature. What got me going was some joke he told about the Horse Whisperer. If he knew I was thinking about a parrot exorcism, he'd probably think I was nuts. Particularly the part about it working.

There's eleven of us in the van. Zack was sitting next to a girl named Andrea, who happens to be wearing the shortest jean skirt I've ever seen, but he moved beside me when he saw I was sitting alone. The other girls are wearing tight low-cut jeans, body-revealing T-shirts, and flip-flops. They carry fleeces with Eddie Bauer or North Face on them. I have on my old nubuck hiking boots, jeans, a fleece sweatshirt, and a solar roller sun hat I stole from my mother. I'm the only one thinking hiking here. On the other hand, they look good.

There was a festive punch in the air when we first set off, reminding me of the days we'd take field trips in school and the best part was always the bus. I mean, who in their right mind would really want to visit yet another Spanish mission in San Juan Capistrano and look at the swallow poop encrusted on the roofs? But now the multiple conversations have trailed off and nearly everyone in the van is plugged into earphones, hunkered down over something. PalmPilots, BlackBerries, iPods, video games on their phones, and a few laptops.

Zack's asleep and when I look over at Conner, he's concentrating on the endless stretch of road and seems lost in his own thoughts.

The only sound now is coming from the rear, where two girls are locked in an intense private conversation that involves one gesturing dramatically and anxiously twirling her hair while the other nods sympathetically and occasionally bursts out with "You're shitting me!" or "What a dick!"

Looking out the window is just as monotonous. Scrub oak, manzanita, yucca plants (which sound ugly because they are), tumbleweed, stiff high brown grass, and tumbles of rock.

A few hours later a weathered old man checks us into the birders' motel, where the tiny reception area reeks of Pine-Sol and stale cigarettes. Nearby is a squat building—the local diner currently belching gamey barbecue pit smells.

The rooms aren't much better—sparse, musty, no TV, a

sink in the corner, and communal bathroom down the hall. The van was my fault, but this is Conner's. He evidently *always* stays here. I look out the window and see him purposefully walking into the woods behind the building. He stops, reaches into his safari jacket, and pulls out a pack of Camels. Then he does that trick with the matches where it looks like he's snapping his fingers and a flame magically appears. There's a reason the Marlboro man is ingrained in our culture. Macho, timeless—a cowboy in tight faded Levi's, gleaming spurs, and a Stetson. Smoking's poison but sometimes it's just plain sexy. When Conner's done, he grinds the butt into the dirt, then picks it up and sticks it in his pocket. What a role model.

The plan is to take a sunset hike before dinner, so we throw our stuff in the rooms and gather in a semicircle at the trailhead near the edge of the sanctuary.

The climb is steep and rocky and the group breaks up into twos and threes, with many slinging their arms around each other or pressing their palms into the backs of the kids in front of them and pushing them forward. There's a certain camaraderie here which makes me feel wistful and even slightly jealous. I keep pace with Conner and notice he deliberately maintains a cool, social distance from the group even though he's warm and relaxed.

We finally take a break at a lookout called "Inspiration Point," and gather in a circle as Conner pulls a beat-up, leather-bound copy of *Walden* out of his backpack and starts to read aloud. His voice is deep and intimate, as if he's confiding in his listeners and the students fall silent.

" 'I wish to speak a word for Nature, for absolute freedom and wildness . . . to regard man as an inhabitant, or a part and parcel of Nature, rather than a member of society.' "

He looks at us gravely (it's part of his charm), and continues reading.

" 'If you are ready to leave father and mother, and

brother and sister, and wife and child and friends, and never see them again—if you have paid your debts, made your will, and settled all your affairs, and are a free man—then you are ready for a walk.' The purpose of this weekend, students, is to make you see what Thoreau saw at Walden—'In short, all good things are wild and free.' "

Conner then regales us with offbeat anecdotes that sound made up, like the fact that Thoreau was one of the first vegetarians, although he relished raw woodchuck. The kids don't seem to give a shit until Conner moves on to Thoreau's famous bloody description of the battle of the ants. Bingo. Dead silence.

" '. . . the struggle, the carnage . . . the ferocity . . . the severed heads of the black warrior's foes and the still living heads were hanging from either side of him like ghastly trophies . . . gnawing at the foreleg of his enemy . . . his breast all torn away . . .' "

The trail is getting steeper, narrowing down to a slim path, and we all walk single file. Conner tells the group to be on the lookout for deer, fox, bobcats, and mountain lions, although I know for a fact most of them won't come out for a few more hours.

I hear Zack's groggy voice behind me talking about some club he went to last night, and I swear to God, I smell marijuana. Whatever. Not my problem.

When we finally hit the summit, there's a rosy flush to the mountainside, and the sky is filled with voices of hundreds of birds. The noise reaches a fever pitch and then, all of a sudden, nothing. The kids are gathered in groups eating their energy bars, drinking bottles of Fiji. I pick a nice flat rock to sit on. There's a bit of shade and I take off my hat. Conner ambles toward me, throws off his backpack, and sits down. He looks at the birds zigzagging the sky.

"Don't you wish you could do that?"

"Fly?"

"Yes. I took some flying lessons once when I was in Africa. It was a biplane—fantastic. I never wanted to come down. You ever feel that way?"

Absolutely not, I think. In my opinion, birds are supposed to fly. Humans aren't. When I'm in a plane, which hasn't been that often, I imagine the birds sitting on their telephone poles watching us take off and saying, "Crash, you fuckers." He's waiting for an answer.

"Well . . . sometimes I dream about flying," I lie.

"Really . . ." He smiles seductively. "You know what Freud said—all flying dreams are actually about sex."

"Oh, c'mon," I say skeptically.

"What does this remind you of? Lifting off. Weightlessness. Ecstasy. Soaring, plunging, heaving . . ."

"Stop." I laugh. "I get it."

"You went to Michigan, right?" he asks, abruptly changing gears. "My friend Steve Anderson teaches philosophy there. You ever meet him?" Oh shit.

"To tell you the truth—it's been a while. I barely remember any of it."

"So, where'd you work after the wildlife center?" This is going from bad to worse.

"Oh, I worked for my husband."

Conner looks surprised. I see him glance at my hands. "What does he do?"

"He used to be in the automobile industry, but he died several years ago."

He moves closer. I'm waiting for the usual, you're so young, how long has it been . . . Instead he says, "A lovely widow in our midst."

I feel my cheeks starting to burn. I never know what to say when someone gives me a compliment. My instinct is to get rid of it as fast as possible.

"It must be tough," he goes on. "I've never lost anyone close to me."

I'm tempted to say, he wasn't, but at this point, two girls interrupt us. "Professor Conner, do you mind if Andrea and I start down? We're cold."

"It's okay. We'll all go. It's getting dark." He stands up, stretches his arms straight up like a swimmer about to dive, and flings his backpack over his shoulders.

I see him silhouetted against the sunset, glowing like a mythical figure. He looks at the sky. And we all look at him.

The girls are now hoofing down the hill like horses heading back to the stable. I overhear them talking and laughing about the numerous reasons they all hated their fancy summer camps—the lousy cabins with no screens, the lumpy cots, the mean counselors, the mosquitoes, and the ice-cold lake that they were forced to swim in every day. Andrea said she begged her parents to pick her up but they made her stay the full two months.

"It was a miserable way to spend the summer," she says, dramatically.

Unlike my summers. Cleaning out the cages in the wild-life center for five bucks an hour.

I get back to my single room and think about what Conner would say if he found out I lied about Michigan. The truth is, I have to keep telling myself that this was my only way in. To lie. So I did. And I'm not going to think about the consequences. I'm just not.

CHAPTER 33

A few hours later, we all march into the diner. Zack, who's now on his third helping of ribs, tells me he can't find his backpack and did I happen to see it.

"Hope I didn't leave it back on the mountain," he says. I'll bet. Especially if there's weed in it.

Conner is in an animated conversation with the one girl who seems to be interested in birds. She purposely leans over toward him, and I see teenage cleavage. And I'll bet she's not thinking blue-throated hummingbird. I'm sure this happens all the time. The girls gathering around after class, following him back to his office, looking at him with undercurrents of desire and secret crushes. But Conner never seems attracted. One-on-one with these enamored coeds, he's uncharacteristically cool and professional.

After dessert, as a harried waitress crashes our dishes together and clears our table, I work up the nerve to ask Conner if I can borrow *Walden*.

"Sounds like an interesting evening," he says in an ironic tone. Then he looks at me for a minute.

"Want to take a walk?"

We pass a few recycling bins behind the diner and sit down on a nearby bench. It feels like I'm sitting on a block of ice. He asks what I'm reading, but it's obvious he's not in the mood to banter or argue like we do in the office. Then he switches topics to the wildlife center, saying it was the most appealing thing on my resume. (Which is lucky, because the rest of it was made up.)

He tells me he used to conduct seminars at a place up north, and I find myself telling him about my duties at the center, all the while blotting out Tiff's voice in the back of my brain admonishing me to cut it out—not attractive. The hardest thing for volunteers to understand, I explain, is that in order to heal the wildlife, you have to discipline yourself to have as little contact with them as possible. Every soothing gesture puts the animals in peril. Out there in the wild, we are still the enemy, I say, and Conner nods.

The conversation drifts around to the other topics, like sick birds, poisoned sea lions—the usual—when I notice that he's gazing up at the sky.

Maybe Tiff's right. I've run on again, too long. Plus, I can see that his ears are turning purple around the edges and his snapping blue eyes are rimmed in tears from the cold.

"They have a telescope here, I think. You interested?" he asks.

"Conner, I'm freezing. Aren't you?"

"No. Well, maybe, but it's too bad. You can see most of the planets this time of year—all nine of them, or all eight, or all ten, or all twenty-three."

"Which is it?"

"No one really knows how many planets are up there

anymore. Jesus, you're right, it's cold here," he says suddenly, standing up and pulling me up with him. "Let's go."

My rear and feet are frozen and the back of my jeans are damp. We trudge a little farther and then he stops just before we reach the rooms.

"You know what," he says, brightening. "There's a little bar down the road—nice and warm and cozy—music and beer on tap. Want to ditch school for an hour?"

I hesitate, but then make a decision. "No, thanks," I quickly say. After my run of bad dates, I'm better off just being alone.

"You sure? I'm buying," he says.

"Thanks anyway. I'm beat," I lie. I want to go with him. After all, he's just asking me for a little nightcap . . . like Freddy. Forget it. I'm not going.

Later that night, after the students drift off, two by two, like in Noah's ark, I look out the window into the darkness. The moon is a pale silver disk that fades in and out through the woozy clouds, and the sky looks like a black dress with sparkles. This is the kind of night that would tempt Odysseus to follow the sweet song of the sirens, and guide his hapless ship to the crashing shore.

CHAPTER 34

The walls are so thin, I can hear every word they're saying. I can practically hear them inhaling. It's two a.m. and the Domino's guy has just dropped off some pizzas. There's a loud thump. What are they doing now? Maybe jumping on the bed? Screams of laughter. There must be ten kids in there. I hear the words "weed" and "trashed."

Spring break in Bird Land.

"Send someone down with the ID."

"I just went."

"Send Andrea. She looks way hot."

"Get Coors this time."

"I need twenty more bucks."

I peek my head out my door and look down the hall. One kid stands outside his room wearing a T-shirt with these words at waist level: "I've had it up to here with midgets."

"Hey," I say, trying to think of a nice way to tell him to shut the fuck up.

"Hey." He smiles at me, eyes glazed. "Hope we didn't wake you."

"No. Not at all." I give him a phony smile as I hear the girls screeching and giggling. I retreat back into my room. I'm such a chickenshit. Now someone's knocking on my door.

"Hey, Cassie." It's Zack. He's naked, except for his boxers, all torso with smooth-skinned washboard front and taut swimmer's legs. Johnny Stud with a bruise on one thigh, maybe a skateboard accident. "Steve says you're awake. You wanna come to Andrea's room?" There's always this air of mischief about Zack, as if he's struggling to be on his best behavior.

"Gee. Sounds great, but I'm so tired."

"C'mon. Are you sure?"

"Really sure. Thanks anyway." I shut the door and try to ignore the rap music that's now blaring from their room. "Motherfucker this, motherfucker that. I'm gonna nail that bitch." Where in the world is Conner?

Three-thirty a.m. My alarm goes off. We're supposed to meet in the lobby at four. The kids are straggling out, their eyes hooded, pretty much blotto.

"This is, like, postal," moans Zack to a girl nearby. "I have one word for the way I feel—fucked up."

The girl puts her arms around him and strokes his hair. "That's two words."

Conner breezes in, enthusiastic, all business. At least one of us got a good night's sleep. "Ambien." He winks at me. "This is my fifth year."

He has his fold-up hiker's chair laced through his backpack, his Zeiss 7×42 binoculars, his Peterson, and a miner's light on his head as he passes out brown-bag breakfasts to everyone. What these kids really need are Bloody Bulls, guaranteed to neutralize the cocktail of illegal substances they polluted their systems with last night.

Conner breathes in deeply, as we march outside—
zombies on parade. There's a bold, marshy aroma in the icy
air, and he's clearly exhilarated in the predawn excursion.
Why didn't I wear more layers? It's bitter cold and everyone
has that hunkered-down look. It can't be more than thirty
degrees out. Conner tells us we're headed for the birding
hot spot of the region—temporary home to up to forty
species of birds. He doesn't mention penguins.

Just to add to the misery, there is a steady drizzle as we
start out in the pitch dark. Some of the kids hold flashlights
and orange glow sticks. We try to keep up with Conner's
brisk pace as we trudge through slushy muck, jumping over
fallen logs, scrambling on steep, slippery ridges.

We carry on this way for a few hours, seeing nothing and,
as first light appears, there are still no birds. We talk in
hushed tones, and at certain times, with a signal from
Conner, we are ordered to stand stock-still in an open
meadow, listening. Most of the kids stop with dour expressions on their faces until Zack yells out, "Freeze tag!"

"If you spook a bird at this hour, you won't see *any* of
them," Conner says sternly.

Now it's starting to pour and we take shelter under a tree,
soaked to the skin and inhaling the smell of damp bark.

"We haven't seen one damn bird yet," grumbles a kid as
we set out again through the sludge.

After more slogging around, the sun peeks through the
clouds and the heavy fog starts to lift. Conner finds a clearing where we begin our "stakeout." It's not like my clearing,
it's a wide-open space and you can see for miles. He pulls off
his miner's light, removes his Tefal gloves, and tells us he
thinks we'll see a couple fly-ins within the next hour.

And he's right. All of a sudden it's showtime! We hear
birds calling to each other, starlings, sparrows, wrens,
finches, and crows. They appear in pairs, singly, in groups,

circling and calling, spinning off in different directions—a dazzling display of aerobatics. Rush hour in the forest. Even in their diminished state, the kids are impressed with this moment of high drama.

The sun is fully in the sky, but it's still colder than a cryonics experiment as we stop midway up the mountain on a small wooded crest. Everyone is wolfing down their breakfast, and Conner offers me his chair as he settles next to me on a slab of rock. I feel the heat of the sun on the back of my neck and down my arms. A Bengay moment. I'm so dead tired, I could doze off right now. I feel a soft tap on my shoulder. Conner has a sly little smile and holds a glinting object under his parka.

"Adults only," he says as he hands me a neat little silver flask. I take a swig. It's vodka—frigid, with a long silky aftertaste and a delicate bite. I hand the flask back to him as he turns away from the group and takes a gulp. We secretly pass it back and forth like two kids sharing a joint. I'm feeling decidedly warmer now, more relaxed and polished.

We're quiet for a minute. I'm thinking this guy may be a scientist, but he's so . . . how can I say it? Hot. I see him watching me out of the corner of his eye. He hands me the flask and I take another gulp. He puts his hands on my shoulders and starts to give me a little neck massage. What's the matter with him? His students are everywhere.

"These kids don't really care about the birds, but I try to give them just a little taste."

I think the great thing about vodka is, after a while you don't taste it at all.

"I care about birds," I say. Conner bursts into laughter.

"What's so funny? I *do* care about birds. All kinds of birds. These birds. My birds . . ."

"Nothing. You're just different." He should only know.

"Do you ever search for rare birds?" I suddenly ask.

"I used to. Then I stopped. Finally realized it didn't make me happy."

"Why do people obsess about them anyway?"

"Well, it's a bigger issue. It's rare anything. You get sucked into it. I don't know," he says, removing his parka, rolling up his shirtsleeves, digging into his backpack.

"Maybe it's something deeper that drives people to keep searching," I reply. "To discover something only they can see. Maybe it makes them feel like the Messiah—only I can talk to God or predict when the entire universe will explode into nothingness. Only I can see that telltale shadow of the Virgin Mary's profile on a taco shell. Only I can hear God's voice through the fire. Or maybe it isn't even that heavy. That fleeting glimpse is just so hypnotic, like Medusa's gaze—beautiful but could turn a person to stone."

Conner has now stopped fussing and is staring at me.

"You're right," he says. Then he's quiet. "So you see a rare bird. It doesn't unlock the secrets of life—does it? You still wake up the next day with the same shitty relationship, the same existential questions, the same damn leak in the roof. But for those few moments, you're immortal. You've beaten the odds. Reversed the natural order of things."

He pulls a bottle of martini olives out of his backpack, opens it, and holds it out to me. I pop one in my mouth. He continues in a tone that's almost religious, or maybe a little boozy. At this point, who cares?

"Frankly," he says, "the best part of bird-watching is just the quiet enjoyment of ordinary moments. The more you look, the more you see. By the way, have you done something to your hair?"

"What?"

"It looks nice."

I'm about to respond when Zack crashes down next to

me, drops his head on my shoulder, and sighs. "I am soooo wasted."

I think, so am I, as I turn my head so he can't smell my breath. Conner gives him a little shove and says, "Time to go." Zack drifts off toward the group as Conner places his hands on my shoulders, lets them slide down gently to my fingers, and pulls me up.

CHAPTER 35

"Move your fucking ass, fatso!" Zack screams out the van window as he gives the finger to the redneck driver of the black double-cab truck in front of us on the two-lane highway. The truck ominously slows down and the four guys in the cab roll down their windows and turn to us with hardened faces.

We're on our way back to LA and Conner is driving.

"Cut it out, Zack, or you'll get your ass handed to you," he yells good-naturedly. Now Zack has both hands out the window and is giving them the dancing birds.

The truck has slowed down to a crawl. A big black blob of outrage. Conner tries to pass them and just as we're eyeball to eyeball, the hulking warrior speeds up, blocking our way. Conner retreats, slows down, and gets back in the lane behind them. Then the truck slows down to

218

nothing again. It has tinted windows, so all we can see in front of us is the shadow of four massive bodies.

"I don't think we should be messing with these guys," I say helpfully. No one else is talking.

"Maybe I should just pull off the road," Conner says. I look at the stickers plastered all over the truck—the American flag, Harley-Davidson, "Support Our Troops," "Eat My Dust," and the subtle kicker, "I AM THE NRA."

"Not a good idea," I say.

"I'm going to try to pass them again," Conner says as he pulls out, and this time the truck lets us pass.

Something's up. This is just too easy. And with that, the truck roars up behind us and slams into our rear. Then, just in case we didn't notice, they do it again. A warped version of bumper cars. Classic road rage. A couple of the kids are thrown forward, their iPods and backpacks skidding across the floor. A few girls start shrieking and crying.

"Oh my God, we're going to die!"

"Call 911!" Conner says to me. I start dialing.

"Don't be a pussy, let me drive!" says Zack, as he leaps out of his seat and comes forward to the wheel. You can smell the testosterone oozing out of him.

"Shut up, Zack!" Conner whips back.

"I can run 'em off the road! I can do it!" Zack yells.

"No! Sit down," Conner says, swerving onto a dirt road as the driver of the truck lays on his air horn and guns down the highway. We pull over to the side of the road and everyone piles out. The inside of the van looks like it's been picked up by Godzilla and shaken by the neck until it's dead. There's stuff everywhere.

"So did we ever get 911?" Zack asks carefully as he eyes his backpack.

"No," I say, looking at Conner. "My cell doesn't work out here."

"Good," Zack says. And I think, Next time, leave the grass at home.

A few very quiet hours later, we drop the kids off at school. Conner has a "private little chat" with Zack, who is uncharacteristically contrite, nodding in agreement with a sheepish look on his face as Conner lets him have it. I hear the words "dumb" and "irresponsible."

Conner follows me back to return the van. By the time we get to Super Cheap Discount Rentals, the fender is loosely knocking against the chassis.

"Lucky you rented such a piece of crap. If this were Hertz, we'd be here for hours. I need a drink. Like to join me?" I don't care. I'm saying yes. I could use a drink too.

We end up at Ruth's Steak House, an old-fashioned bar that's dark no matter what time of day you get there. We slide into one of the red leather booths in the back. Conner orders a scotch, and I order a martini, then change it to a margarita, then change it to a white wine.

"Sure you don't want a Diet Coke?" Conner jokes. What does he want from me? It's the middle of the afternoon and I can't decide what mood I'm in. Do I want to get slightly buzzed, more than slightly buzzed? I have a headache.

The drinks arrive and Conner downs his in about two gulps. Then he orders another one. I sip my wine like a lady. I'm only having one and I'm *not* getting drunk.

"Jesus, that kid is so nuts," he says, exhaling loudly, and then combing his fingers through his hair in the way people do when they finally relax. We both know he's talking about Zack as he proceeds to drum his fingers on the table and then motion for a waiter. He asks if they sell cigarettes and the waiter shakes his head no.

I politely ignore this exchange.

"I think Zack's a sweet kid, just young," I say. Even though he did steal my essay.

"It's more than that. He's fearless and stupid. And entitled. Zack's the one who throws the desk through the window and never gets caught. Everyone protects him— the golden boy. Maybe it's in the genes, risky behavior, bravado." Now I know he's not talking about Zack.

"So what did *you* do?"

"What didn't I do? The school was always calling my father and having these deadly little meetings. He'd drive up from New York and we'd sit there mute as the dean ran through a laundry list of all my screwups—curfew infractions, inappropriate behavior with the opposite sex, cutting classes. My father's expression would never change. Then we'd go out for a fancy lunch and he'd never mention it again."

"He never got mad?"

"I always got the feeling that he did the same thing when he was a kid," he tells me with a fine, dry smile. "Anyway, I don't know exactly what he did. We were always so formal with each other, it was almost as if I was just some business acquaintance."

"You're lucky you didn't get kicked out."

"Oh, the grades were always fine. That's part of the reason they left me alone. That, and the fact that my father was head of the capital campaign."

"What'd your mother think?"

"She died when I was eleven. My father remarried and the new Mrs. Conner didn't give a shit. So what about your family?" he asks, obviously trying to change the subject.

I start telling him about my mother and her tree-hugging friends who believe in UFOs and run vitamin stores and make pronouncements like, "Garlic and cholesterol are natural enemies." I'm rolling into some of her adventures when I realize that Conner is looking out toward a small open balcony where several people are puffing away.

"There are still times I'd kill for a cigarette. Road rage is one of them," he says.

"Oh," I say, casually. "Pearce told me you quit."

"I did. Absolutely. Everything worked like a charm. The patch, the gum, the treadmill, the pool, meditation, yoga, acupuncture, kickboxing, compulsive buying, eating . . ."

"You know, it's so funny—a wildlife biologist and environmentalist who smokes. Plus, you have beautiful white teeth. How do you do that?"

"I stopped—remember? Anyway, thanks," he says, looking more relaxed.

"The problem is," he goes on, "there's nothing else quite as mind-expanding, quite as luxurious as a powerful inhale and exhale—with smoke. I've tried to tell several yogis this, but somehow they just don't buy it. Which is understandable."

"You're kidding, right?" I ask.

"Well, yes and no. Giving up smoking is like resigning yourself to a perpetual sense of longing with absolutely no release. Your senses ambush you all the time, egging you on when you least expect it. There will be a certain smell, a taste, even a beautiful passage in a book, or even, say, those damn butterflies we saw that day at the exhibit. God, did I want a cigarette after that. I don't know—you feel so hopeless. Never quite whole."

"Like love," I say suddenly. "Isn't that what it's like?"

Conner shakes his head with what seems like disbelief and then smiles at me.

"Yes, exactly. Like love," he says.

"So, Cassie," Conner continues, "let's cut to the chase. How long has your husband been gone?"

"About three years."

"You must have been devastated. Are you okay?" I'm so sick of that question. I feel like answering, "When the cops told me he had died, it took me a while to figure out what I was feeling. Then it hit me. It was bliss." I take another sip of my wine. Oh. It's all gone.

"We don't need to talk about it if you don't want to." He presses, as he flags the waiter and orders me another wine.

"Well, it's all right. It was a car accident. He looked down for a second. I don't know. One random move and everything changes. You press the gas instead of the brakes. Or you decide to change your flight at the last minute. It sets off an unavoidable chain reaction and turns everything into a goddamn tragedy."

"How many years were you together?"

"Around four. It seems so long ago now . . . I have a hard time talking about it." He looks at me sympathetically, and it occurs to me it's because he, like everyone else in the world, assumed I loved him.

"Well, then, we'll just change the subject." He looks away for a minute and I can tell he's gauging the situation. He makes his decision. "So are you seeing anyone?"

"Not really."

"So are you 'not' or are you 'really'?"

I start laughing. "Okay. I'm not."

"Good."

"And you?" Who's the lady in the letter? Or Samantha? And her annoying musical "gift."

"I'm not either," he says definitively, as he downs his second drink. "Can I take you to dinner sometime?"

"I'd like that."

Now he's jumping from subject to subject, from global warming to other planetary emergencies. He tells me about his friends who are protecting the panda habitat in the mountains of southwest China, preventing millions of tons of CO_2 from entering the atmosphere of the Madagascar forest, establishing hundreds of thousands of acres for the Tayna Gorilla Reserve in the Congo.

"That's what I'd like to do if I weren't teaching."

"Well, you can sign up at my wildlife center to make nests out of Dixie cups," I say.

"Every little bit counts." He laughs, squeezing my arm.

Conner finally gets the check and then tells me he has to be in St. Louis next week for a conference but he'll call when he gets back.

"It's so odd," he says, in a tone that sounds almost as if he's talking to himself. "You go to a party or whatever, and you spend the whole night zeroing in on the woman in red, the blonde in the corner, the girl with the big laugh, and then, as you're leaving, you see someone out of the corner of your eye, her hair glinting in the light, her long neck tilted slightly as she listens intently to the person next to her. And you know she's the one you *should* have talked to." He leans over and kisses me on the cheek.

And that's how I spent my first date with Conner.

CHAPTER 36

Many nights, when there's that lull after dinner, too early for TV shows, too dark for a walk, my mother will settle herself at the kitchen counter and play solitaire with Sam. Sam pecks around on the playing field, adding his two cents, and occasionally swipes a diamond or a heart (he only likes the red ones). Then he rushes into his cage, piercing the card with his beak, but he rarely gets a rise out of her. She goes right on dealing away, unfazed by Sam's bratty pranks.

"What card did you steal?" she'll ask Sam calmly.

"Black jack," Sam answers.

"Is it my deuce?"

"Black jack," he repeats. Sam prefers 21, but my mother won't switch games. It's an avian standoff.

I swipe the card back from Sam and sit down with her to play double solitaire—same rules as when I was a kid that she bends to suit her whim, same sticky, warped-edge Bicycle deck that may or may not have fifty-two cards. It's a tradition we've shared for as long as I can remember, although I tell her she can play on the Internet now without Sam's interference. She's not interested.

It's nice to spend time with her. For the past few months, she's been working several nights a week at the wildlife center, not getting home until after I leave for work. But she likes it, she says it's peaceful. And my mother does love peace.

She's home tonight because she's had a cold for the past few days and skipped work. Now she's sipping on a mug of hot water and honey mixed with bourbon and a smidgen of Vicks VapoRub. Sam keeps his distance. Parrots don't like strong smells. She lays out the cards for yet another game, her glasses hanging from a cord around her neck.

I notice she looks a little tired and wan and probably hasn't had much to eat. For all her bohemian background and naturalist leanings, she's never really been interested in doing much around the house. Like cooking and cleaning. I suggest to my mother we take a break. She goes to the bathroom to steam her head and I poke around the pantry looking for something for dinner. Whenever there's nothing else available, I can always count on spaghetti and olive oil. I'm filling a pan with water when I hear the phone ring. My mother picks it up.

She's always had one of those voices you can hear through the walls. It's not that she's loud, it's just that her tone is rich and complex, reverberating deep inside my head, like a guilty conscience. I thought it might be Sylvia at first, because I heard her mention Joshua Tree and Highway 62. There's a soft, low giggle. She's talking to a man, that's for sure. Now I hear the name Conner. Help!

I put down the pot, pick up the extension, and interrupt her mid-sentence.

"Hey," I say.

"Hey, hey, hey!!" repeats Sam, like Ed McMahon on speed. He sidles up my arm and settles on his favorite spot at the top of my shoulder.

"I was just going to call you, dear," Mom says. "Professor Conner and I are having such a nice chat."

"Hang up, Mom."

"Hang up, hang up," squawks Sam. "Close the fucking door!"

"Nice talking to you," my mother says quickly, then I hear a click.

"Is that your son?" asks Conner, as I walk into my bedroom with the phone, and shut the door.

"That's my bird. No kids."

"Oh, the African gray, right?"

"Yes. His name's Sam."

"Put him on the phone," Conner says jovially.

"You don't want to talk to him. He's so rude."

"No, really. Put him on the phone. I have a way with birds."

"Okay. You asked for it." I put Sam down on the desk, hold the phone up to his head, and he immediately starts pecking at it.

"He's on," I tell Conner.

"So, Sam, my buddy. Say 'shit,' " Conner says. Sam is silent.

"Shit! Shit! Shit!" I hear Conner repeating it like it's his ABCs. Okay. Enough of this. I grab the phone back.

"Very funny," I say. "He knows enough bad language without you adding to it."

"Well, where did he learn that from?" Conner laughs.

Okay. Why is he really calling? Why doesn't he get to the point and ask me out?

"I was talking to your mother about Bigfoot. Understand she's going back to the desert to search for him. Maybe get a few more photos?"

"Listen, Conner. I know it sounds weird, but she and her friends are dead serious about all this. It's not a joke to them. But I don't want you to think . . ."

After last night, I was searching in my mind for the right way to react when, and if, Conner ever called. But I hadn't counted on him finding out so soon that I have a strange mother and a parrot with a mouth. As opposed to beautiful Samantha with the lousy backhand and a glorious wardrobe.

"Don't worry about it, Cassie," he says, interrupting, wrapping up the chitchat. "I really just called to thank you for coming with me on the bird trip. It was nice having you there."

"Right. Thanks," I say, still waiting.

"See you when I get back from the conference." And he hangs up.

"Say shit! Say shit!" Sam screams. Exactly.

CHAPTER 37

Conner's been back from his conference for about a week, but I haven't seen him and he hasn't called. Pearce asked me to come into her office this morning to start planning this year's holiday party, and the first thing she did was buzz Conner on the speakerphone.

"Right. The damn party," he says, annoyed.

"Really, Conner. We'll take care of it. You won't have to do a thing," she soothes.

She's wearing a long burgundy velvet skirt, a white silk blouse, and a sprig of fake holly and berries pinned to her collar. She has celebratory snowflake-shaped earrings and a set of tortoise combs pulling back her wild gray hair. It doesn't seem to matter what Pearce wears, she always has an air of distinction. She's using the same tone of voice I use with Sam when I'm trying to convince him to do something he doesn't want to do.

"You always say that," he pouts. "I think it's someone else's turn."

"Come on, my love. You have such a wonderful

house," she cajoles. "We go through this every year and doesn't the party always turn out great?"

"I don't know why we even have to have a party. We should just give the money to charity like Mathematics."

"Well now, who would ever want to socialize with Mathematics? They don't even want to socialize with each other."

She gives me a wink. "I'm sending Cassie to Costco with the list. She'll call the string quartet—"

"Spare me from hearing them sawing away at Pachelbel or the *Brandenburg Concerto* for the nine hundredth time. Can't we do something a little different?"

"Whatever you want. We'll take care of it, right, Cassie?"

"Oh. Is Cassie sitting there?"

"Say hello to Conner, dear," Pearce says.

"Hello, Conner." This is awkward.

"Hello, Cassie."

Pearce winds it up and then tells me what they need for the party. Most of the guests are what she calls "social drinkers," so she tells me to buy the usual—white and red wine and rum for the eggnog. I also need to get six giant Stouffer's lasagnas, a crudité platter—which I had her translate to veggies and dip—and a bunch of other things. Use my own judgment. She wants me to go shopping next Thursday because the party is a week from tomorrow. The good part is, I get to leave early that day and shop. I'm calling Tiff.

I'm sitting at my desk, quietly reading aloud, when I look up and notice Conner standing outside the Xerox room. I quickly pick up the phone and pretend to end a conversation.

"Great. See you Friday night!" Might as well act as if I have a social life. I put down the phone as Conner knocks on the wall.

"Have you eaten yet?" he asks me. I look at the clock. Twelve noon.

"No . . ."

"Want to join me for lunch? I have an idea for another field trip, and I'd like to bounce it off you."

"It better not be Joshua Tree."

"As a matter of fact, it is. Seriously, what do you think about taking the kids there?"

"Seriously? That group? Let me just tell you they have the most outrageous raves in Southern California in that desert. And, unless you want Zack and the rest of those kids running around with neon stripes on their naked butts, and high as kites on X, I wouldn't recommend it."

He looks at me surprised. I guess he was expecting some sort of discussion about Bigfoot or the desert flora and fauna.

"Rave?"

"You know, those crazy outdoor all-night dance parties."

"Must have missed that cultural experience. Have you ever gone?"

"I've only been out there with my mother, and she's not the rave type."

"So I guess it's a no on Joshua Tree?" He laughs.

"Let's go," I say. I'm dressed in a jean skirt, sheepskin boots, and a turtleneck. Not fancy, but hip enough to go out to lunch with him. I'm wearing my hair up these days, thanks to Alison. I've learned how to do that little thing where you twirl it around your fingers and stick a clamp in it.

He takes me to a little Italian place I've heard Alison talk about. The waiters know him and give him a four-top by the window. I've been a waitress, so I know this is a primo spot. There's a fancy bottle of olive oil and vinegar and an unopened Pellegrino on the white tablecloth. No menus. The waiter comes by, takes my napkin, and lays it across my lap like a sable. Then he starts reciting the specials. I choose risotto and Conner has fish. He orders a bottle of Pinot Grigio. This is going to be some discussion.

I ask him how his trip went, and he launches into a ten-minute discussion about alternative energy sources, and the impact on heterogeneous species using words like "avian bio-geography," "systematics," and "ornithological research." Complicated. So I focus on his face, and listen to the way he pronounces his words. I like hearing him talk.

The waiter pours each of us a glass of wine all the way to the top and it leaves slick trails of tears on the rim as I take a sip. That's better.

The lecture he liked the most at the conference was one given by a psychologist who talked about the relationship between grieving for a family member and ecological griev-ing, comparing the loss of a treasured place or species to the loss of a loved one.

"Sometimes, I dream about going back in time and being able to wander through a vast, undisturbed forest where every extinct animal that ever lived is thriving."

"Like the Garden of Eden, Conner?" I say, as the waiter refills my glass. I notice that he holds his hand over his glass.

"Yes. Exactly." There's a pause. He eyes my wine and pours a little of it into his glass. Guess he changed his mind.

"What were you reading before lunch?" he asks. So now we're on to me.

"Whitman." I take a large gulp of wine.

"What do you think?"

"I just started *Song of Myself*. Doesn't rhyme. No meter. But so good."

" 'I am the poet of the body,' " Conner recites. And how, I think.

"When I was in college," he goes on, "we all identified in some way with Whitman. He overcame his problems, his class, his poverty, disabilities, and reinvented himself at age thirty-six. Gave us all hope."

"Wasn't he gay?"

"That's beside the point."

"No, it isn't. He was struggling to be himself in a world that couldn't accept him. Isn't that the point?"

Conner leans over and whispers, " 'I Sing the Body Electric.' That's the point." Shit. He's flirting with me again. "As a matter of fact," he says, "a friend of mine used to give all the girls he was sleeping with copies of *Leaves of Grass*. It's very erotic."

"Really?" I say, thinking we know who he's talking about and the name probably rhymes with Bonner. "Well, I haven't gotten there yet. It takes me a long time to read. I'm dyslexic." So throw that in the pot with your body electric.

"Some of my best friends are dyslexics." He laughs, not missing a beat. "Just kidding, Cassie. Must have been tough in school."

"It was okay." I just flunked three grades and then dropped out.

"You know John Irving is dyslexic."

"I know." There's a silence—the kind of silence that separates two people at certain moments when that so-called line is about to be crossed, the forbidden line that makes you vulnerable and dispels all the illusions and lies.

"You know what I've noticed about you, Cassie?" Uh-oh. "There's a lot you don't say when you say something. I find myself straining to hear your unspoken words."

I look down at my glass of wine so he doesn't catch my flush of embarrassment. It's true. I'm reluctant to pour it all out, but how nice that he's even interested in what I'm *not* saying.

"Most of the time you don't talk about yourself. I think this is the first time I've had a real conversation with you."

"So what do you want to know?" I ask. What the hell.

"About your life. Your marriage—the things most people go on and on about . . . I have questions."

"Okay—shoot." Now I'm looking him straight in the face, all the noise of the restaurant suddenly gone as if everyone left without us noticing.

"Well, what was it really like struggling to read? And your husband?"

"Late husband," I interrupt.

"So tell me."

"Frank and I had a bad time toward the end. He had a girlfriend. See? I'm an open book. And, as for how I coped in school, I learned to use my imagination. And I escaped—into the woods—as they say. I still do. You can be whoever you want—chatty and clever and stupid and ugly and unloved and unkissed . . . and still feel like you belong." I wait for Conner to respond, but he's mute.

Thank goodness, the food arrives.

"For the beautiful lady," says the waiter in a fake Italian accent as he sets down a steaming plate of risotto. He's probably an actor. The dishes clang. The restaurant noise comes back with a vengeance.

I give the waiter a lovely smile. Conner's still looking at me. Well, he asked for it. No more straining to hear my thoughts. Nope.

He takes a sip of wine.

"Well," Conner says. He's got that look my mother had at the racetrack when she accidentally bought a ticket for the wrong horse and it slowly dawned on her that she won.

❡ ❡ ❡

We get back to the office at around two. I'm an hour late, but Alison doesn't say anything as I walk by because I'm with

Conner. He leans in, and says to her, "I borrowed Cassie. We're working on a field trip."

"Oh, no problem." Alison smiles endearingly.

He asks me to come into his office for a minute. He has something he wants to tell me. I follow him upstairs. We walk in and there, sitting on his couch, with her reptile purse and her shiny high heels, is Samantha.

"Oh hi," he says. She gets up, and gives him a kiss on the cheek.

"I'm dropping off the parking pass for tonight. I have to get there early to set up." Conner looks at her blankly.

"And you forgot, didn't you? The theater? The party afterwards?" We both see Conner register that sheepish look that means, oh shit, I forgot.

"Oh. Right. I've been away. You remember Cassie."

"Sure. Hi, hon." Hon. That's what everyone called me when I worked as a waitress one summer. I'm leaving. Whatever he wanted to tell me he can just do it later.

CHAPTER 38

Déjà vu. I'm walking past the courtyard the next morning, delivering some papers to Admissions, when I hear a familiar thwack, thwack, bugs against the windshield. I see Conner practicing his backhand against the side of the building. And I'm pretty sure he's not running around it.

As I speed by him, I'm tempted to ask how he enjoyed the theater, but I restrain myself as he gives me a little wave. "Hey. Where's the fire?"

"Oh, hi, Conner," I say, casually, as if I didn't notice him.

"Busy?" he asks, as he keeps hitting and I keep walking.

"Just got to get these things over to Admissions."

"Shit!" he yells as the ball goes sailing over my head and just misses the window. He catches up with me.

"Nice shot," I say.

"You play?"

236

"A little." The last time was in high school on cracked concrete and saggy nets. But it was one of the few courses I passed.

"How about being my doubles partner this Saturday? My regular partner can't make it."

"That's a shame. But I stink."

"That's okay. She does too."

"No, really. I haven't played since school."

"That's fine. We just play for fun. It's not a competitive thing, really."

"Can I let you know? I usually help my mother at the center on Saturdays."

"Sure. No problem."

I guess Samantha can't make it. I go back and forth about it all day. Should I? Shouldn't I? Tiff would just tell me to go for it. But I can't help thinking this is Freddy all over again. Oh hell, I want to go.

So here I am, driving to the Los Angeles Country Club for my Saturday afternoon doubles game. La-di-da. The driveway says it all—long, windy, and bordered with a razor-cut hedge. There's a giant guard gate that screams "private" in small discreet letters, and as my car approaches, a somber, paunchy guard, carrying a clipboard, steps out of his little dwarf house.

"Good afternoon. Name?"

"Cassie Shaw. I'm a guest of William Conner." His face relaxes, he checks off my name on the list, and points me in the direction of the courts. I drive through what looks like hundreds of acres of golf course surrounding the clubhouse, which is right out of a Ralph Lauren ad except there's golf carts lined up instead of polo ponies.

I see Conner and his friends in their tennis whites (a better white, apparently, than other kinds of white), sitting around an ornate wrought-iron table overlooking the courts.

The men stand up as I approach. I notice they're all drinking iced tea in tall glasses with mint leaves. Makes me want to burst into a chorus of "Dixie."

I'm wearing pink drawstring shorts and a white T-shirt (not tennis white), and I had to scramble like hell around the house to find a suitable pair of sneakers, rather than my Vans and hiking Nikes with treads. I didn't have time to shop, and in the back of my mind, I resisted doing anything that cost one dime because, after all, he still has a girlfriend (even though he says he doesn't) and God only knows what it is exactly he thinks he's doing, leading me on all the time, talking about nature up the ass, and his spiritual connection to the world. I finally found a pair of my old tennis shoes and threw them in the car. So I won't knock 'em dead with my wardrobe. I don't know why I agreed to do this. And wait until they see how I play.

Conner introduces me to the group, and then hands me a silver graphite racquet he borrowed from the pro shop, which, he says, is state of the art.

"So don't throw it down when you miss a shot." Ha ha.

"No problem," I say, without smiling.

The other couple—the Austins, Wing and Melissa—are his regular opponents. Conner tells me Wing is his old college roommate, and he married Melissa right after graduation.

Wing is tall, blond, and lanky. Melissa is short and stumpy, wearing an enormous visor. They're both in Adidas from head to toe. Melissa gives me a big sunny hello and thanks me profusely for filling in. She may be stumpy, but she's sweet. She knows I work with Conner and even knows about the wildlife center, so he obviously gave them a rundown before I arrived. Melissa walks over to the far court, and starts slathering a thick white sunscreen all over her

body. I hear the pop and whoosh of a can of tennis balls exhaling air as Wing pulls the tab.

"So, Conner," he says, eyeing my legs, "where you been
hiding this one?"

"If I were you, I'd concentrate on the game and stop trying to butter up the opponent," Conner says.

"Well, she's sure going to be a distraction. Maybe you did
it on purpose."

"Shut up, Wing. Don't mind him, Cassie."

"I think he's perfectly charming." I smile.

Wing asks me if my grip is okay. When he comes over to
check it, Conner grabs my hand and says, "She's fine."
When we get on the court, Conner starts to stretch in that
awkward way guys do when they look like storks.

During the warm-up, everything seems so very civilized.
I volley with Melissa, as Conner and Wing good-naturedly
rally back and forth. "Good shot!" they call as they slap re-
turns to each other. The ground strokes are deep and long.
The form is perfect. The atmosphere, friendly and noncom-
petitive. "Nice hit, Slim!" Wing yells to me. "Maybe next
time," Melissa says encouragingly, as I completely miss the
shot. "Good girl!" Conner throws out, as I send back a lame,
one-handed backhand.

"Okay. Let the games begin!" Conner calls out, as he jogs
around the court collecting balls, kicking them up with his
foot and catching them in the guts of his racquet. Ping.
Ping. Ping. Melissa seems a little sluggish as she applies
more lip balm, and rubs a sunblock stick on the tops of her
hands.

Conner loses the spin, and Wing gets first serve. I see
Melissa at the net executing a subtle little hula wiggle that
signals she's good and ready. Then she lays it on thick by
rocking her racquet like a baby across her white pleated skirt

as Wing whips the serve straight down the middle. Conner pounces on it with a vengeance, rifling back a forehand to Melissa, who whacks it back to me at supersonic speed. Before I have time to think, Conner leaps in front of me and lobs it back. Wing rushes the net and smashes the ball cross-court, as Conner dives behinds me, scrapes his knee, and sends the ball spinning into the sky, landing just outside their base line.

"Fuck!" Conner screams.

"Fifteen–love!" Wing calls out.

In an instant, they've all turned into monsters, foaming at the mouth, baring their teeth and muscles, executing punishing blows to each other, one after another. This is not a game for someone with even an ounce of self-doubt or anxiety.

Wing serves to me now and I assume the ready position, without the wiggle, without the hula, without the bullshit. He floats me an easy serve, and I promptly hit it out.

"Thirty–love."

"Keep your eye on the ball," Conner snaps.

"She's choking up on her racquet," Wing yells, helpfully. "Fix her grip."

Conner adjusts my sweating fists by turning the racquet a quarter of an inch. Ah. That feels better. Now the serve is to Conner, who's bouncing around like he's tripped over a canister of nerve gas. It's a searing fireball one inch above the net. Conner grunts loudly, as he whips it back with a two-handed backhand, and then charges the net like a wild boar. Wing lobs it over his head to me. Uh-oh. Conner starts scrambling backward, screaming, "Mine. Mine, I've got it! Move!" I barely get out of the way, as he dumps a volley into the net.

Another "Fuck!"

Wing laughs. "That's what happens when you hog the ball, you bastard! Forty–love."

"Okay. Cassie and I need a time-out."

"Show her where the sweet spot is!" Wing laughs.

"Shut up, Wing!" Conner shouts as he walks purposely over to me. We turn our backs to the net in a mini huddle and he puts his arms around me. Why don't I feel comforted?

"Stay in the zone, Cassie." I'm thinking, What the fuck does that mean? But I say, "Sure thing, Prof."

"Game point, guys," Wing says, with a bemused expression as he tells Melissa, who is again applying sunscreen, to get to the net.

"Just lob it over her head, and I'll take care of the rest," Conner begs.

Wing's serve is easy and polite once again. What a nice guy. And I dutifully lob it over Melissa's giant visor. Now Wing smacks a spectacular backhand crosscourt. Shit. It's coming right at me. Conner again leaps into the trajectory screaming, "Mine! Mine!"

It's all he can do to get his racquet on it, but the ball hits his rim and ricochets into the table and chairs.

"Bull's-eye!" Wing shouts. "Game to the amazing Austins!" He high-fives his beaming wife.

Conner smirks and says, "We've only just begun. Isn't that right, Cassie?"

I'd like to say that we made a comeback, but this was clearly the high point. I don't think I hit one more shot in. After I double-faulted for the third time, Conner missed an easy lob, and threw his racquet on the ground.

"Nice," Wing says.

At six–love, Melissa announces she's had it, and heads for the locker room to "freshen up." Conner goes inside to make a phone call (no cell phones allowed on the court), and I sit with Wing, who orders us both a glass of wine. I tell him I like his name, my affinity for birds and all. He says it's a nickname, because when he was seven, he jumped out the second-floor window of a building trying to fly, broke his arms, and his family's been calling him Wing ever since.

"Really?" I say.

He winks at me. "No. Actually it's Welsh. Spelled w-i-n-q-u-e-t."

I start laughing, and we end up talking about this and that as the light fades and the air turns cold. Melissa comes back a little later, wearing slacks and a T-shirt. Her hair is pulled back in a ponytail, and she's obviously reapplied her makeup. Conner finally reappears, scowling.

"You two want to join us for dinner?" chirps Melissa, in a hostessy sort of way.

Before I can say anything, Conner quickly answers, "We really can't. Thanks anyway."

I try not to look humiliated as he walks me to the car, and goes into this long explanation of how he had previous plans he can't get out of, and how sorry he is . . . blah blah, blah. I say that's okay, because I'm busy anyway, but it doesn't sound convincing. Not even to me.

I wonder what his students would think if they saw this side of him. So much for his horseshit sensitivity nature boy image. He wanted to win. He wanted it bad. I was just the fill-in body. Well, Samantha wants him? She can have him. I see him walk away from me to his car, hands jammed in his pockets, racquet tucked under his arm. He looks down like he's concentrating on something at his feet, jerks the door open, and throws his stuff in the back. His cell phone rings, he answers it, and gets into the car.

As I drive down the manicured path of fools, all I can hear is his voice screaming in my ear, "MINE! MINE! MINE!"

CHAPTER 39

It's a busy night at Costco. There are people pushing, shoving, and lining up for freebie tastes of wieners, brownies, and sautéed chicken kebabs. It's the Christmas shopping season, which starts at this store right after Halloween. I see mothers navigating their overloaded, oversized shopping carts as their kids run wild in the aisles helping themselves to the toys on display. I've had friends come here for a head of lettuce and come home with an electric piano.

I'm not sure where the wine is, so I go to the only place that isn't crowded and ask two women sitting at a card table. One's blonde, the other's brunette, they have frozen smiles pasted on their faces, and are looking pained. Then I see the giant poster behind the table advertising their novel. Oh. Gee. A book signing.

"Would you like to buy a book?" one of them asks me hopefully.

"Maybe later," I say and make a mental note to avoid that aisle on the way back.

"Cassie!" Tiff shouts across the store.

Her cart is already loaded with poinsettias, cookies, Christmas gifts, and her newest self-help book, *Food Doesn't Make You Fat (Unless You Think It Can)*.

"Fa, la, la, la, la," she sings. "I think I've pretty much knocked off all my office Christmas presents." She looks at the wine and rum in my shopping cart and says, "That's it? That's all you're buying?"

"Well, I haven't picked up the lasagna yet . . . or the chip and dip."

"But no real booze? Looks like a fun party."

"My boss says they're social drinkers."

"What does that mean? No one's a social drinker, and if they are, they're having a shitty time. Don't you want this party to be fun?"

"Well . . . she did say I could use my own judgment."

"Perfect. Where's the tequila?"

Besides the five giant bottles of Viva tequila, 100 proof, we throw in a case of Corona, limes, plastic shot glasses, a vegetable platter, six giant Stouffer's lasagnas, guacamole dip, salsa, corn chips, and a bunch of frozen pizzas.

Tiff then adds a few boxes of Jack Daniel's chocolate-covered whiskey balls.

"People love these. You can get high on like two of them."

We roll into the checkout line. My two carts, and Tiff's one.

"So you hear from Freddy again?"

"No."

I feel like it's been so long since I confided in Tiff. If I told her it wasn't Freddy but Conner on my mind, we'd get into a whole thing and I'm not up to it.

"I'm finished with Freddy."

"Why don't you let me fix you up with this guy I met?

He's really cute. Just got divorced. You know, you've got to grab them right away. These guys don't last out there long."

"I don't think so," I say as I see Tiff's face fall. "The last one was a disaster."

The cashier now wheels over a flatbed to transfer all our junk. My sales receipt alone is over a yard long, and curls like paper Christmas ribbon. Ho ho ho!

It would've been the perfect shopping trip except for one thing. In the parking lot, Tiff whips out a tin of caviar from her bra.

"Knock yourself out. Share it with your fancy friends," she says, proudly.

"Tiff, for Christ's sake. You want to get arrested?"

"You don't want it?"

"No, I don't want it," I snap. "Take it back right now. Say you forgot."

"Oh. Okay." She dramatically crosses her arms like the Virgin Mary, lifts her eyes toward heaven, and says, "Please forgive me, I forgot." She laughs uncomfortably. "Calm down, I'll take it back."

"Good," I say, unsmiling. "I'll wait here."

"You know, Cassie, sometimes I feel like you just don't want to be with me anymore. You don't call me. You don't come over. I mean, let's forget the stealing, that was stupid. I was just messing around. But you never used to get mad. What's going on?"

"Nothing. I'm just tired. I'm working like a maniac, taking these classes. And you know what a bitch it is for me to sit down and read anything. It takes me three times as long as anyone else to get stuff done."

"I know. I'm sorry. But I feel like you don't want to be with me."

"Don't be ridiculous. I love you," I say, as Tiff starts crying. Oh God.

"I just think that you've moved on with your new job and your new life, and I'm not in your world anymore."

"Tiff. Don't cry. I'm just so distracted." I take a crumpled Kleenex from my purse and hand it to her.

"Okay. Never mind. Forget it." She blows her nose.

"No. You're right. You really want to know what's going on? There's a professor at work who I'm starting to like, he asked me to be his doubles partner last Saturday afternoon at a big-deal country club, and it turned out to be a complete nothing. He had plans with someone else that night, and he was a competitive asshole on the court. I, of course, couldn't hit a thing."

"Which country club? Really?" Tiff brightens.

"That isn't the point. The point is, I can't figure out what he wants. Sometimes, I think he really likes me, and other times, I think he's just amusing himself with some weird nature junkie from the office."

"You *are* a little weird in that department," she says. "You *know* you are. Anyway, tell me. What did you wear?"

"I looked terrible."

"I bet you didn't. You never look terrible . . . anymore. You're so smart and beautiful and you don't even know it."

We talk a little bit more about Conner and the more we talk, the more I realize that Tiff has always been on my list of hallowed souls, right up there with my mother and Sam. She bets Conner will call me because, even if I didn't wear a sexy tennis outfit, "He's an educated man who knows a classic when he sees one."

I give her a big hug. "Do you want me to go with you to return the fucking caviar?"

"Okay," she says. "Don't let me buy anything else."

CHAPTER 40

"So, do you realize if Napoleon had ever bothered to observe the flight of storks and cranes passing over his army on the road to Moscow, the whole course of European history might have been different?"

"Is that so?" I say, trying to act cool. Conner is standing behind my desk, leaning into the Xerox machine, back to his old, charming self. That angry little furrow between his brows—the one that kept appearing when I flubbed a shot—is gone, and he's obviously not in a hurry to go anywhere.

"The birds knew a terrible winter was coming, and they flew their little fannies off to the south, but Napoleon and his army marched north. It's amazing when you think about it."

It's been nearly a week since our little tennis game. I've avoided going upstairs, and, luckily, he's been in a retreat with some of his grad students most of the time, which is just as well because I've been studying like crazy. What a jerk to not even call me.

"So, Cassie, what did you think of Wing?"

"He was a good sport."

"As opposed to me."

"Well. You know what Plato says, 'You can discover more about a person in an hour of play than a year of conversation.' "

"Very nice, Cassie. What's the name of your professor again?"

"Brooks."

"Well, he's creating a monster."

"I don't think so. 'Philosophy is the highest music.' That's Plato too."

"I think he's overrated. Anyway, I'm sorry about the game. Sometimes I get carried away. But I have a compliment for you. Wing wants me to bring you around again, and I don't think it's for your strokes. I think the word he used was 'fascinating,' with the emphasis on 'great bone structure.' "

"Tell him I'd be delighted."

"I will not. He's a flirt," Conner snaps.

"I thought he seemed interesting," I say, egging him on.

"I wouldn't think he was your type."

"What's my type?" I say.

"Intellectual, articulate, unpretentious, into nature, worldly, and charming."

"You forgot to add competitive, controlling, critical, and a court hog."

"You had that much fun, huh?"

"Oh. Right up there."

"Listen. About me running off like that . . ."

"You don't have to apologize."

"Well, I had a situation going on."

"Your wife doesn't understand you?"

"Very cute. More like an ex-girlfriend."

"Does she know she's an ex?"

"She does now."

We hear footsteps and Pearce appears at the doorway, carrying a stack of papers.

"I'm not interrupting?" she asks.

"No," I say. "We were just discussing Napoleon's retreat."

"I've never been that interested in the French. Don't tell anyone. Party under control, Cassie?"

I told her I had to pick up a few more things, and as she leaves, she gives Conner and me the once-over. Nothing gets by Pearce.

"So what festivities do you have planned for tomorrow night?" Conner asks.

"It's a surprise."

"I love surprises."

"This one involves giant marimbas, tequila, and chocolate-covered Jack Daniel's balls."

"You make me smile."

"You make me mad."

"We'll have to do something about that."

CHAPTER 41

It's five o'clock, still warm and balmy. Unseasonable, even by LA standards. I roll down the window of my car as I pull up to Conner's house and a rush of fragrant orange-tree-scented air hits me in the face. I sit in the parked car, radio still running, luxuriating in that feeling one gets just before something gets going, and reluctant to turn off the engine and go inside. Through the window, I can see people moving furniture, a flurry of activity—waiters holding trays, men with buckets of ice. I think about what I used to love when I went to a party—booze, food, and cute guys, not in that order. But now I'm looking forward to trenchant conversations with academics filled with intellectual, witty remarks. Okay, and Conner too.

Alison was supposed to come help, but she told me, "I don't do cleanup." And then she gave Pearce some cock-and-bull story that she had to go out of town.

Conner's home was built in the thirties by a

silent-film star who evidently loved drama. The house looks like a mountain stone cabin. There are massive oak pillars supporting a beamed ceiling, dark barn wood floors, and a big stone fireplace which is now decorated with spruce and mistletoe.

I think back to Conner's description of his house when I first met him. Simplify, my ass. This is just as cluttered as everyone else's. The room is filled with oversized, heavy furniture which someone tells me is Indonesian teak. Brightly colored throw pillows, piles of books, folders, dog toys, and half-burned candles with globs of splattered wax hardened on the tables and the floor.

I glance at myself in the entry mirror. My goal was to look like I'd spent no time getting ready. Obviously that took hours. Washing my hair, blow-drying it, leg wax, arm wax, other wax, makeup, discreet mascara, blush, eyeliner, see-through foundation, dressing, undressing, nice underwear, push-up bra. And it all worked. I still love my black dress. Even after all it's been through.

When I told my mother we wanted something different for the faculty party, she suggested this marimba band instead of the string quartet. The wildlife center used them last year for their annual fund-raiser and it was a big hit. The musicians are now unloading their van, and it looks like clowns coming out of a Volkswagen bug. A tall one, a short one, a family of four, three teenagers, two older guys lugging a portable piano like an old tug, a bass, and then the marimbas.

The whole group looks like a tribe of aging hippies and—oh, did I mention, their screaming, barefooted children are running around like banshees? One of the kids, who's about seven, his hair in a tiny Mohawk, whizzes by me wearing huge neon green plastic sunglasses. He's hyped up Ahab into a frenzy, teasing him with stolen wieners from the kitchen.

"Raven, cut it the fuck out and come over here," one of the men yells. Raven pretends not to hear.

"Hello? Cassie? Where are you? Interesting choice of music, dear," Pearce says with a twinkle. "I just love pageantry."

She's wearing a festive red suit with a big starburst brooch. She introduces me to her childhood friend Marion, who's around six feet two with dyed foxtail red hair that looks dead. You can see where the dye stops and a layer of silver and brown is growing in. The fluorescent lights in the kitchen accentuate the orange makeup already caking on her face.

"So nice to meet you," Marion says, with a gravelly voice as she gives my hand a heavy-duty shake. She's wearing an oversized turquoise tunic which sort of camouflages her protruding belly.

"So you're the nature girl," she says, with a lopsided smile that looks like she's about to crack a joke.

"Hey, Nature Girl," Conner says, as he breezes into the kitchen with a frazzled smile, straightening his necktie. He stands back and gives me an exaggerated once-over, kisses my cheek, and whispers in my ear, "Looking pretty downtown tonight."

Pearce and Marion give each other a look.

"Hi, ladies, lovely as always."

"Aren't you the charmer, as always," Marion says to him, amiably.

"What's going on out back?" he asks as we hear one of the musicians yelling, "Move the goddamn table—you're fucking up my wires!"

"That's your musical entertainment." Pearce grins, as she adjusts his collar. "You look so handsome, and you did say that you were tired of all the string quartets." She winks at me as she shamelessly butters him up.

There's a buzz of spirited conversation coming from the

living room. The guests are arriving in a steady stream, most of them carrying potluck hors d'oeuvres. Conner moves to the door, smiling genuinely, and greeting each one with, "Can I get you a drink?" "Take your coat? Your tray?" "Glad you could come." "Great to see you."

The perfect host.

He grabs a few men with gusto—gripping their shoulders in a fraternal sort of way, very clubby—maybe old school-mates.

"Hey, Brad—you look like hell. Do I look that old?" Conner jokes with his old friend.

"No. You have hair, you son of a bitch," Brad shoots back jovially.

The band is still setting up. When I ask how much longer, the guy in charge tells me, "Chill, we're almost there." I go back to the bar and help myself to a second glass of wine. Conversations swirl around me.

"Teaching freshmen is a waste of time," says a man wearing a jolly red sweater with grinning overzealous elves slinging gifts on a sleigh.

"Sophomores aren't much better," replies his rail-thin confidant.

"Parker just got published again."

"The bastard."

"Well, his teaching schedule's so light."

"How's your novel coming?"

"Been translated into nineteen languages, including Celtic."

"That's great."

"Just kidding. I'm looking for a publisher." False laughter.

"So what's it about?"

"You know. Life. I can't really talk about it."

"Isn't it warm in here?"

There are two women huddled in the corner looking at the middle-aged man who just walked in.

". . . just separated from his wife of thirty years."

". . . living at the University Club downtown . . ."

". . . some grad student."

A couple walks in the front door, a professor and his wife with a fur-collared sweater. I hear her whisper to her husband, "Do you think it's safe to put my sweater upstairs?"

"I don't know, dear, he has a dog."

"I didn't mean that," she snaps. "I mean there are students here." Her husband shoots her a look and quietly lays the sweater over his arm.

A group of eager young grad students looking slightly uncomfortable in their suits are throwing down glasses of wine by the bar. Two of them are leaning against the doorjamb.

"I understood Rilke because he understood human suffering. He respected human suffering. But that lit professor fucked me over so bad."

"The guy was like sub-zero on the student picks. You should've never taken that class."

"Tell me about it. It was the only paper I wrote this term I was even proud of, and he basically told me it was crap. Why fucking bother?"

"Really."

They drift off toward the hors d'oeuvres table, where one of them plucks a shrimp off the plate, pops the body in his mouth, and flings the tail on the floor.

Across the room, Conner, with his back to me, is talking to a group of students. He's describing one of his adventures with his hands—earnest, animated.

Pearce and Marion wander over. They see me staring at him.

"So, dear, are you and Conner spending time together?" Pearce asks, maternally.

"Not really." I'm thinking of what Conner said about "not really." Is it "not" or is it "really"? I don't know.

"Because you know what Conner stands for, don't you?" Pearce looks at me pointedly.

"Trouble," Marion answers with a grin.

"He's a love. He really is. I'm mad about him. But you know he's a bit of a player," says Pearce.

"Never been married," Marion adds with emphasis, just in case I didn't get it. Oh, I get it all right.

"And, he has this magical effect on women. It's genius really. His courtliness, his self-deprecating humor, his splendid ability to disarm and then disappear—fatal gifts as far as you're concerned," Pearce says protectively.

"You're not upset we're telling you this, are you?" they both press.

"Oh no. Not at all. Thanks for letting me know." I force a smile. Okay. He's a ladies' man. Like I didn't know.

"Just don't volunteer to take care of his dog. It'll get you nowhere," says Marion, slipping off her flats. "God. My feet are killing me and the party's just getting started."

Now Conner hustles everyone outside to the patio, steps up to the makeshift stage, and takes the mike.

"Before we start the music, I have an important announcement to make. Hank, my colleague and good friend, has *again* won the Edward Lear Society Limerick Award—third year in a row! So, I've asked him to recite one of his winners. C'mon up, Hank!"

Everyone claps except Marion, who sticks her two index fingers in her mouth, shows a set of fiercesome horse teeth, and lets out a piercing ballpark whistle.

Hank tentatively walks up to the stage. It's the geology professor with the low rating. He's wearing an oxford striped tie and a long forest green cardigan sweater—like

Mr. Rogers. He trips as he reaches for the mike and motions for everyone to stop clapping. His nose is as red as Rudolph's and his eyes are glazed. He's three sheets to the wind already. This ought to be good.

"Which one?" he asks Conner with a shy, elfin smile.

"You choose," Conner says.

"You know, I've never enjoyed speaking in front of people, but now I'm feeling great. I guess that's the miracle of alcohol. Here goes!" Hank says.

> *"While I wooed, playing Bach was a tactic*
> *Causing orgasms intergalactic.*
> *But when Beethoven played,*
> *I never got laid:*
> *Ludwig's music was anticlimactic."*

Someone shouts "Whoa!!" from the back. Enthusiastic applause. Everyone's yelling, "More!" "More!" "C'mon, Hank!" Hank shuffles around, flush with success. He takes a big gulp of his tequila and keeps going.

> *"Excitable mathematicians*
> *Fuck in only prime numbered positions,*
> *For to factor while screwing*
> *Would so heighten their wooing*
> *As to cause premature sperm emissions."*

Conner is beaming. Pearce chuckles while Marion is neighing and snorting. I think it's laughter. The rest of the crowd is into it. "Another one!!"

"Dirtier!" they yell. You couldn't pry Hank off the stage now with a crowbar. He's just warming up.

"You asked for it!" he shouts.

> *"Demosthenes mastered oration*
> *Through the ancient Greek art of fellation;*
> *As he tried to emote*
> *With that cock down his throat*
> *He improved his syllabification."*

Everyone's screaming. Now I know what smart people do at Christmas parties. They tell dirty jokes disguised as poetry. I see Conner give Hank the "slit your throat" sign, but Hank's not finished. No way!

> *"Said Pinocchio's lover, midst sighs,*
> *My puppet's technique takes the prize.*
> *He gives me full measure*
> *Through dishonest pleasure:*
> *I sit on his face and he lies."*

Conner's finally had enough. He motions for the band to start playing. Hank finally gives up the stage in triumph, calling out, "Salut, everyone! Take one day at a time!" If he'd only do this in class, it'd be a guaranteed A rating.

Conner and I are now leaning against the wall, and as the crowd disperses, I notice Hank inching next to an attractive woman.

"Is that his wife?" I ask Conner.

"Oh no. Hank's not married. He was madly in love once, but she never cared that much about him."

"That's sad."

"It was. I took him to Yosemite to cheer him up. We drank a lot, read Muir, and I played Cyrano, writing letters to his beloved." He's smiling.

"You must have been good at that."

"Oh yes. If I do say so myself, the letter was great. Let's

see . . . I ripped off some of Whitman's lines . . . 'when I'm with you, the pleasures of heaven are with me, and the pains of hell . . . O unspeakable passionate love . . .' I think I even ended it with . . . come to me on this 'Mad Naked Summer Night.' Hank thought it was over the top, so he never sent it. The woman broke his heart."

I think about confessing to him, that at this very moment, the letter is in the drawer of my bedside table. Then I change my mind. So it was Whitman!

Conner leans in to me and whispers, "What would you think if you got that letter?" His tone is rich and decadent, and I sink back against the wall and hold on for dear life.

"I think if Hank had sent that letter, things might have turned out differently for him."

CHAPTER 42

The party had entered into the Kingdom of Feeling No Pain. The singing started out with a spirited but off-key version of "La Bamba," and rolled into an earsplitting "Ole Holy Night." Between Mom's band and Tiff's tequila we really turned this party around.

At one point Pearce and Marion climbed onto the stage, grabbed the mallets, and started pounding wildly with the band. That is, until Marion keeled over with chest pains and someone called 911. However, by the time they arrived, the chest pains had ceased and she walked demurely out the door accompanied by Pearce.

But now everyone's gone except two professors, one of whom is so drunk, he has glassy, shocked doll's eyes. You'd think they'd take the hint. Tiff always says that this kind of thing goes down in her Guinness Book of Rude Behavior— party hanger-oners. They wait until all the guests are gone, march into the kitchen as if they owned the place, rummage in the fridge for the food that's already been put away. Then they go into the bar and pull out booze that's not even been opened yet. They yak, yak, yak, until you want to scream, "Get the fuck out of here!" These two are still sitting on their asses, spouting pretentious pronouncements about music.

"Mendelssohn, Shmendelssohn, I'm talking about *real* music."

"You mean like Sibelius's Fourth? It's his best, you know."

"No. It's his *only*."

I look pleadingly at Conner as I clean up remnants of cigarette butts in the couch, tequila shot glasses in the potted plants, and smashed shrimp tails on the floor. Pearce promised him we would leave the place in the same condition as we found it. Not a chance. Conner takes the hint and hustles the guys out of there.

"Thank God," I say. "How'd you get them to leave?"

"I told them I wanted them to go home."

"Really?"

"The truth always works. They didn't mind." He takes my arm. "Come here. I want to show you something."

I follow him outside. It's still warm and the crickets are chiming so loudly they sound like sleigh bells. We sit down on the back steps and he turns to me, his collar askew, his hair going off in all different directions.

"So, I'm paying the band, telling them how great they are, giving them a big tip, and guess what they gave me?"

"A five-hundred-pound baby-grand marimba?"

"You're close." He reaches into his pocket and pulls out a jay. A big fat jay. "They tell me this is 'really good shit.' So what do you think?"

"Got a light?" I respond.

He lights up, sucking in so hard that the paper shrivels and almost collapses in on itself. He holds his breath for about a hundred seconds, his face contorting like a weight lifter's, and then exhales with a fit of gagging and spewing, gasping for air.

"It's great," he says in a strangled tone as he hands it to me.

"I can see that," I say. The last time I had grass was in high school, but I'm not copping to that just now. I stick the butt in my mouth and he holds up the match as I inhale. A great burst of light hits his face, illuminating it like a saint. I feel his hand on my thigh, and there's a whiff of imminent disaster.

We pass the joint back and forth until it gets so small it burns my fingers.

"Good stuff," I say, in what I notice is a slightly giddy tone.

"It's like a goddamn Christmas miracle." He laughs.

"You know," I say, "Mildred told me to be careful of you."

"Mildred?"

"Yeah, Pearce's friend," I say, giggling and then bursting into a fit of uncontrollable laughter.

"You mean Marion," he responds, and then laughs.

"What's her story anyway?"

"She's a flame swallower in the circus."

"No she's not. She's an Olympic shot-putter."

"She has a cat named Mr. Tickles."

"Who hunts small mice and snaps their little necks."

"She's addicted to chocolate."

"Do you have any? I'm starving," I say.

"I think we can take care of that." He disappears, and then comes back with a handful of Tiff's Jack Daniel's balls, which I gobble up. They taste like heaven.

I hold up the chocolate balls. "These things are unbelievable," I say.

"You're unbelievable," he says, as he leans over and kisses

me. I've forgotten how great kisses feel when you're stoned. There's a surprising blast of heat searing through my dress, engulfing my breasts and upper thighs with boiling lava and causing me to cross my arms tightly around my chest and blush with full-on desire. Can he tell? I open my eyes. He's staring at me. I think if he doesn't touch me, I'll jump him. He smiles and kisses me again, tugging lightly on my lower lip and then pulling away yet again, taking me to that place just shy of the begging point. How could he? Doesn't he realize that I am struggling to gain my composure here, pretending what is happening to my body isn't happening, that I can turn off the frenzied, raging urges now scorching my skin every time he touches me? Come on, I think in exasperation, praying that I do NOT have that predatory, half-crazed look a person gets in their eyes when they want it bad. Calm down. You're stoned.

"So do women just throw themselves at you?" I ask, casually, as I finally get a hold of myself. He moves his face so close to mine that I can see a thin, blue vein in his temple, throbbing slightly.

"Well, sometimes I have to throw myself at them and they don't even notice." He looks at me pointedly and abruptly stands up. Then he pops a Jack Daniel's ball and looks up at the sky.

"I've spent so many years searching after elusive creatures. Birds, animals, women. This is all I want now. Just the simple pleasures. Sitting in my backyard. Watching the sky at night." He looks at me like I'm a rare luxury item. Then he touches my cheek and almost falls into me.

"You know . . . you have a quality that's . . . I don't know . . ."

I shift back and try to figure out what the hell he's trying to say.

"It's something . . . indescribable . . . you're just pulling me in . . ." He stops himself and gives me a loopy grin.

"I don't usually talk to people like this." He pauses for a moment. "Unless I'm trying to get laid." He laughs. "Which I'm not," he lies.

"That's good," I say. "Because I'm not who you think I am."

"So who are you?"

"Well . . ." I think about it. "During the day, I'm just Cassie, but . . . at night, I turn into the exquisite, magnificent ivory-billed woodpecker. The most sought-after bird on earth."

He's quiet for a moment. I smile, and say, "Do you have any more grass?"

He robotically stands up, goes inside, and comes back with a baggie and a tall glass bong.

"So what do you know about the ivory-bill?"

"What do *you* know?" I ask.

"What does anyone know? It doesn't exist. Or it does but no one can find it."

We both take a hit from the bong, and the water on the bottom bubbles up and turns amber. It's so smooth.

"I can find it. I know where it is."

"Of course you do."

"No. Really." I want to tell him everything. "I know where to find the ivory-bill."

He leans over, sleepy, his low voice in my ear.

"The ivory-bill. What a glorious bird," he whispers.

CHAPTER 43

It's a warm winter morning. I can hear the winds blowing—as if it's freezing out—but these are Santa Anas and the air is hot and dusty. I look across the bed. Not a creature is stirring. Conner's deeply asleep like a dead body on the beach. I can't even tell if he's breathing. Ahab is stretched out on the carpet next to the bed. He lifts his head and looks at me when he hears the sheets rustle and then I hear his tail, flap, flap, flap.

I slip out of bed, and quietly tiptoe into the bathroom. The wood floor is cold on my bare feet, and I put on the white terry-cloth robe hanging on the hook by the shower. I slap some cold water on my face, and then I see there are two toothbrushes in the glass by the sink. Tiff tells me you can learn everything you need to know about someone by looking in his medicine cabinet. I open it up and survey the contents. A whole row of vitamins. Anti–snake venom, Sting-Kill, razors, shaving cream, toothpaste, an assortment of painkillers—Advil, Tylenol, Motrin. Two tubes of Neosporin, one labeled "Ahab." No sign of a woman. I look under the sink. Maybe there's a cosmetic bag. I see nothing but a plastic basket with cleaning stuff and some rolls of toilet paper.

I pad back into the bedroom and see Ahab waiting by the door. I quietly open it and he races past me, through the kitchen and out the doggie door. There's a coffeemaker on the counter. I start to fill the pot and then stop. What am I doing? I should leave. The dogs in the neighborhood are barking at early-morning joggers as I go back to find my clothes. Conner is sitting up. Shit. I'm so uncomfortable. He smiles, and pats the sheets.

"It's early, why don't you come back to bed?"

"Well, Ahab wanted to go out."

"He's out."

"I really have to get home." I stall.

"I was hoping we could go get some breakfast."

"Oh. Breakfast."

"You know, toast, eggs—last night was wonderful—juice. Maybe afterwards, we could drive to the beach or something." He gets up and puts his arms around me.

"Unless you don't want to."

"I want to."

He lends me a big woolly sweater and sweatpants, which I put on with my high black heels. I think it must be the hottest December morning on record. When he opens the door to his Land Cruiser, the steamy air fogs up my sunglasses. We get in, and he lowers the windows all the way down.

"Jesus, it's like a sauna in here," he says, as he rolls up his sleeves and then flaps his shirt up and down to create a breeze. He turns on the air, and a burst of hot comes out. We wait a minute for it to cool down, but it doesn't.

"Maybe I need antifreeze. I haven't used the air since last summer," he says.

"I should have borrowed a T-shirt. I'm dying," I answer. Also, I didn't even bother to put on my bra, and this sweater is itching like crazy.

"Truth or dare," he suddenly says, with a Cheshire grin. "Tell the truth or peel it off, baby. You didn't really find Wing attractive, did you?"

It takes me a few seconds to register what's going on. I give him a slow smile of recognition. I played this as a child. Of course, the dare in those days was eating dirt or ringing doorbells and running away. Okay. If he wants to play, I'll play.

"Truth. You're right," I throw back. "I didn't. My turn. Truth or dare. Pearce says you're a player. Are you a player?"

He pauses a minute. Leans over into the backseat, grabs a towel, and mops his forehead. "No. I'm not a player. Truth. My turn. Truth or dare. Did you date Alison's brother?"

Whoa. Not answering that one. And how did he find out anyway? I fling off my sunglasses. He laughs, as I take his towel and wipe the back of my neck. I'm dripping wet.

"My turn," I say. "Truth or dare. So you're not a player, right? How many Samanthas have there been?"

He leans his head into my lap, shoots his legs out his window, and dramatically pushes off his sneakers.

"Truth or dare," he whips back. "Did you sleep with Freddy?" Now I lean in to *his* lap, stick my legs out my window, and kick off my heels. They clatter on the pavement like leaden pearls of wisdom.

"Truth or dare," I throw out. "What's the real reason you don't have tenure?"

He winces. "Now it's getting ugly."

He takes off his shirt, rolls it in a ball, and lobs it out the window with my heels.

"Truth or dare," he pitches. "How many men have you been with?"

And I thought he was different. Every man asks that at some point—even if you're just casually dating him. But the truth is, they don't want to know the truth and I'm certainly not telling him. I look Conner in the eye and slowly lift off my sweater. He takes the towel and tenderly pats the sweat off my chest.

"Truth or dare." I dig in. "Did you sleep with Samantha before or after you broke up with her Saturday night?" We both eye his pants. He gives me a sly little grin, and says, "Truth. Neither."

It's getting positively hellish in the car. We're both naked from the waist up, and I'm waiting for one of his neighbors to come strolling by walking their dog. He could care less. His turn.

"Okay. Truth or dare." He laughs, egging me on. "Are you really as innocent as you seem?"

I slowly ease off the sweatpants, inch by inch, a flash of thigh, knee, calf, and ankle. Then I roll into an abbreviated Gypsy Rose Lee number, twirling the pants with a flourish and chucking them out the window. Good thing I wore my thong.

His face is flushed, he moves toward me, but I push him off.

"Truth or dare." I think for a minute. Why not? "What do you *really* want from me?"

He leans over, murmurs, "Truth," and starts kissing my naked chest, my neck, stroking the inside of my bare thigh. Then he slips his hands under the waistband of my thong and pulls it off as he whispers in my ear, "I can't decide, you're different every time I see you. You're strange and secretive and elusive . . ." He kisses my mouth and presses me toward him. "And filled with stories about birds and magical beings . . ." I look around and small particles are dancing in the air like diamond dust. Right before we tumble into each other, he murmurs, "And you take me halfway to heaven."

❧ ❧ ❧

It's noon. We're back in his bedroom. I see the quiet light on the dark walls, the greenness outside. Ahab is stretched out at the end of the bed, panting away.

Now we do the "morning after" recap, our heads close together like two kids whispering under the sheets. We talk about the party. Who left with who. The band. Pearce. And then he says to me out of the blue, "So what was all that last night about the ivory-bill?"

I slowly sit up and pull the hair behind my ears in a nervous protective gesture. "I was stoned."

"Funny, the things that come out."

"Isn't it." I pause a minute. "What if I told you I saw the ivory-bill?"

"You already did."

"This is a test, pretend it's true."

"I always ace tests."

"Well, I don't. Just answer."

"You're serious, right? First, I'd ask you where you saw it—I'm assuming Florida or Louisiana or something. And then I'd say, no way. That bird's history."

"Meet me at the bottom of Topanga Canyon tomorrow morning," I say. "I want to show you something."

CHAPTER 44

We met at four a.m. the next morning. He showed up with his miner's light, binoculars, and all the rest of his stuff, but it was clear he was skeptical. He kept giving me these dubious looks as we trudged deeper and deeper into the forest, but I told myself I didn't care because I knew how he'd feel when he saw the ivory-bills—jubilant, incredulous. But, instead, we're standing here, drenched in sweat, looking up through the arbor of trees at a cold blue sky. Nothing. Just a wall of hollow air, suddenly empty. We wait for two hours. Still nothing. The birds aren't here.

The silence is unnerving. He's looking at me with disbelief. A jolt of lightning crosses my eyes and cuts through my brain like shards of broken glass. There's a metallic taste on my tongue and I'm queasy. I think I'm having a breakdown.

"Why don't we get some breakfast?" Conner says, humoring me.

"Where could they have gone?" I say in a panic. I can't decide whether I'm more upset they're not here or that Conner didn't see them. I give him an accusatory look. "You don't believe me."

"I don't know, Cassie. I think you saw something."

"But you don't think it was the ivory-bill."

"It's just that they've never been this far west."

"But they *were* here. Look, you can see their holes," I say, pleading.

"There are lots of birds that do this kind of damage. Other woodpeckers, woodchucks, raccoons." He can tell I'm ready to cry.

"C'mon, Cassie. No one's seen this bird in over seventy years. They're extinct. People claim they've seen it, but no one can prove it."

"I can prove it. Just wait a little longer."

We settle back down behind the bushes, looking up at the leafy cloud land and airy canopy of the trees. I sit as rigid as a statue. Maybe we made too much noise. That's it. It's our voices.

"Cassie, what's this all about?"

"Shhhh!" I tell him. "They have extremely sharp sensory perception."

"I know that, for Christ's sake."

We sit there in silence for another half hour. Nothing. I listen in desperation for any drop of sound. He's getting impatient. "How on earth did you ever come up with this?"

"What do you mean, 'come up with this'?"

"I mean you have a vivid imagination, and you see things in nature other people don't, okay, but this is bordering on Bigfoot."

He thinks I'm a nutcase. I'm sobbing now. He puts his arm around me.

"I'll tell you what," he backtracks. "Let me give this some thought. Maybe I'll come back with my digital camera, hook it up to a tree, and see if we can find something."

"Okay," I say. I try to sound hopeful. We hike back to our cars in silence. I hear squirrels, frogs, crows, even the wail of a hawk somewhere. But all the other sounds in the forest are an affront to me now. I'm listening for that one particular, life-affirming voice. And it's not there.

When we reach the bottom, he gives me what feels like a consolation kiss, squeezes my arm, and says, "Don't take it so hard, Cassie. Maybe they'll come back."

I nod as I get in my car and watch him drive away. I sit there for a minute, turn off the ignition, and decide to go back.

When I was ten, I got lost one summer in the woods. I was on vacation with my mother and her family in upstate Michigan, where my aunt rented a lakeside cabin and then invited every relative in the country. I had to share a bedroom in the attic with a pack of bratty cousins, and I remember telling my mother in the car on the way to town one day that the room stank of dirty socks and mold and the kids never shut up.

I was cranky and tired and whined about the food, the heat, the bugs, and anything else I could think of at the time. Mom told me she had a headache and asked me to please stop, but I kept it up anyway. Finally, she snapped, turned around, and let me have it. In a fury, I demanded she stop the car so I could jump out. To my utter surprise, she did, and I fled, furious, into the woods. I could hear her voice calling me, trailing off behind me, and then there was perfect silence.

I don't know when I realized I was lost. It just hit me that I was tired, but when I turned back to the road, the road wasn't there. Just a vast expanse of wood and green, wherever I looked. I trudged glumly on, kicking over rocks, feeling like I was stuck in the place where lost things go, never to return.

I kept expecting to spot something familiar, so I walked on and on, never seeming to get anywhere. And that's when I saw him. It was pitch-black, but I felt a presence. It was a tall brown man with long dark hair and moccasins. He had this damp, bark smell and there was a comforting stillness about him.

He asked me where I came from, and then offered to lead me back to town. It turned out, I was about five miles from the spot where my mother stopped the car. My whole family was waiting at the police station. I walked in there on my own. My guide had vanished.

My mother asked me later about the man, but I couldn't tell her much. Only that he said he knew the forest, and that the trees talked to him, and that he knew what went on deep inside them.

Everyone said I was lying—about the Indian, about how far I walked, the whole enchilada. Except my mother. She told me she believed my story. Every word of it.

That made me feel better until years later when she told me the Indian was really the spirit of the forest, taking me by the hand and leading me out of darkness. Maybe, just maybe, she said, it was Bigfoot.

CHAPTER 45

I went back to the clearing hoping that somehow Conner had spooked the birds but,
miraculously, they would come out for me.
I waited and waited. No birds. I kept thinking
about an article I read about the last ivory-bill
ever sighted in America. It was a female, all alone,
in a dwindling forest. The bills mate for life and,
apparently, she called for her male for the longest
time, and then she disappeared. It made me so
sad.

I hiked back to the car thinking just a few
hours ago my life had turned around. I was
with someone I cared about, whom I could trust
with my secret. It never occurred to me the
birds wouldn't be here. And that he wouldn't believe me.

As I drove home, I thought of my past, a parade of failures, one after another. I saw Frank's
face looming over me.

"You'll never get anywhere, Cassie. Maybe if
you joined Weight Watchers. Learned how to

cook Italian. Took the real estate exam. Sold Mary Kay door-to-door."

Maybe he was right. There's a doctor on talk radio who says that women are biological marvels compared to men, and that their bodies handle stress in a much more efficient manner. Men, she says, are designed for short, nasty, brutal lives while women are designed for long, miserable ones.* I don't know. It just stuck with me.

That night I reached my lowest point. I was sitting around, pouring my heart out to Sam, when the thought suddenly occurred to me. The Bird Whisperer. Maybe she could figure out where the ivory-bills went. It turned out she remembered Sam and offered me the "return customer" discount. Fifty bucks.

"So do you think you can get in contact with them?" I asked feebly. (I didn't, however, tell her the exact kind of woodpecker or the location—I'm not that trusting.)

She told me that she could connect energetically to the birds but she needed a photo. I told her I didn't have one.

"Well," she hesitated, "it's not as easy, but I can still— through energy alone—telepathically connect with the birds and find out their thoughts, feelings, and wishes. I can also address any behavioral or health concerns."

I heard myself telling her to ask them their location . . . and then I thought . . . what in the world am I doing? I told her I'd changed my mind and hung up.

I was not looking forward to Monday. The thought of trying to have a normal conversation with Conner was just too much. It turned out I didn't have to worry. I barely saw him. He told me he unexpectedly had to go back east on some "family matter" but his TA would set up the camera and observe the area as soon as the rain stopped. Of course,

*Dr. Estelle Ramey

it was pouring. We'd talk when he got back. All very professional. All very civil. All very fucked.

The day he returned, I went to see him. When he asked if
there was any other proof, I mentioned my journals. He
looked interested, so I gathered them up from the shelf in
my bedroom, all six months' worth, and brought them to his
office the next day. When I first walked in, he was sitting at
his desk with Ahab plopped down on his feet. The dog leapt
up and bounded toward me, as I carefully put the notebooks
on his credenza. The last time Ahab saw me, I was in bed
with Conner.

"Cassie, we need to talk. Sit down." He's dead serious.
"Look, this isn't personal." (Uh-oh. I've learned that whenever someone tells you "this isn't personal," you're about
to get screwed.) "My TA is really questioning the whole
thing."

"He is?" I back up, and ease into the couch as Ahab nuzzles in beside me.

"First of all, as I told you before, this isn't the ivory-bills'
natural habitat. Cornell's sent teams of experts out for the
last seventy years trying to find them. People have devoted
their entire lives—it just doesn't seem possible they'd show
up in Topanga."

"Well, how about those birds getting thousands of miles
off course? Birds from Siberia found in Texas. I heard it in
your lecture."

"Cassie, it's just so unrealistic," he says, painfully.

"They were there. The birds were there. It's all in my
journals."

"Maybe it was the pileated woodpecker. That even fools
the experts. A lot of these birds look alike."

"The ivory-bill doesn't look like any other bird."

"Well, maybe when you did the research on it . . ." He
thumbs through one of my journals.

"I didn't do any research. These are my observations." I push the dog off and stand up. I want to scream.

"You could have copied these from anywhere!" He hesitates. "I mean, experts might think you copied these from past observations."

"I didn't. I thought you'd believe me."

"I don't know what to believe."

"You're the only one I trusted with this. I thought—"

"Cassie. It's just not possible," he interrupts in a hushed, embarrassed tone. He's lost patience with me, as if I'm a sweet but deluded child. "It's a fantasy."

"Are you saying I'm lying?"

"It's not a lie if you believe it. Let's just leave it alone and move on."

I try to think of something to say, but everything sounds so pathetic. I slam out of the office leaving the journals behind. I think about my namesake, Cassandra, and the curse Apollo placed upon her, that no one would ever believe her. An everlasting source of pain.

CHAPTER 46

The rest of the week was grim. I finally call Tiff and she offers to meet me for lunch. She has the day off and can tell that I'm down.

"What's wrong, Cassie? You sound horrible."

"We'll talk about it when I see you."

Tiff's never been to my office, so the plan was that she'd swing by, pick me up, and we'd go to that little Italian place we like. But as I'm about to leave, Pearce buzzes me and asks me to deliver something to biology, which is all the way across campus. I race out of there, imagining Tiff circling the block waiting for me, but when I finally get back to the office, I see Tiff talking to Alison, of all people. I walk toward them and Alison floats me a strange, bright smile.

"Have a nice lunch, girls. Great talking to you, Tiffany," she says this with the emphasis on "great," looking straight at me.

The second we get outside I ask Tiff, "What were you and Alison talking about?"

"She's really not that bad, Cassie. She's kind of nice, although she didn't know where your desk was."

"What do you mean?"

"She showed me one in the Xerox room with this University of Michigan frame on it, and I said this can't be her desk, Cassie wouldn't have stuff from Michigan, and Alison said, why not, she went there, and I said, she did not and I ought to know, she's my best friend."

"And then what did she say?"

"Well, she asked where you *did* go to college, and I said you didn't. Neither one of us did. Anyway, we talked a little bit about how I ended up going to paralegal school and then you showed up . . . Cassie?"

❧ ❧ ❧

So now we're in Tiff's car. Her face is ashen. Last time I saw her look like this was when her father came to school drunk to pick her up.

"Cassie, why didn't you tell me? I swear to God I never would've said what I said."

"I don't know. Maybe I wanted everyone to think I got the job on my own. Maybe I just started to believe I was who I said I was. Isn't that sick?"

"But you *are* that person, Cassie. Well, not really that person. But they love you, right?"

"Well, they love who they think I am. Oh, forget it. It doesn't matter. Alison's going to march right into my boss's office, and that'll be that. Axed. Fired. History."

Tiff bursts into tears.

"Oh, for crying out loud. How could you have known? Anyway, it was bound to happen. I should have told the truth."

"What's so great about the truth?" Tiff questions.

"I don't know. It just works better in the end."

"But not in the beginning. You'd have never gotten that job."

"Just drop me at my car, Tiff."

"Okay. I love you. Did you at least make yourself cum laude?"

I drive home thinking this is what it must feel like to get caught robbing a liquor store or stealing someone's wallet. I turn on the radio, but the music assaults me like an angry swarm of bees and I turn it off. I feel better in silence, the shame rolling all over me. There's an ache in my chest as I get on the highway. The same thought keeps tumbling over and over in my mind. What am I going to do? What am I going to do?

I get home and my mother is in the kitchen feeding Black Dog.

"You're home early, Cassie," she says, as Sam jumps around like a cricket, chirping out my name. My head hurts, and I'm about to say something, when I suddenly start heaving and sobbing, and tell her the whole story, exhaling every bit of air I've ever taken.

She listens patiently as Sam flies off his perch and onto my shoulder. He can tell I'm upset and he starts softly beaking my ears and neck. Mom doesn't say much as I finish the rant, just sits silently.

"You know, I went to your father's grave last weekend. I was there clearing the weeds, putting out some fresh flowers. Just visiting. Sometimes, I read the other stones and I notice they all have the same message. Beloved father, loving sister, trusted friend. You think any of these stones have CEO of Exxon, president of UCLA, graduate of Michigan?"

"Mine would read, 'Here Lies a Liar.' "

She shakes her head like I'm talking nonsense.

"So what do I do now, Mom?"

"Make it all true. Take the courses and get your degree. You know you can do it."

"But I loved *that* job. I loved those people. They'll never hire me again."

"Yes, they will. People tend to be very forgiving," she says, as she brushes back my hair with her hand.

"You're living in a dream world. Why do I even listen to you? You believe in Bigfoot."

"But Cassie, honey, *he's* real."

CHAPTER 47

I suppose I could've gone back the next week, argued my case, explained why I wanted the job and why I lied. But the week rolled by and I never could get up the nerve. By then, it was Christmas break and I'd made my decision. I was never going back.

I changed my cell number, and with our post office box, I don't have to worry about someone showing up at my door—not that they would. Well, Conner might. But why would he? He thinks I'm a liar like everyone else.

Most mornings, I trudge out to the clearing at dawn, hoping for some sign—like waiting for a lover who never calls. Self-pity is an emotion that should be banned from the universe. Imploded. I wear the same sweatpants and shirt that I slept in, and, if I'm still cold, I'll rummage through the hamper for another layer. My bras are all strangled up in a drawer with mismatched, stretched-out socks and panties. And it's way too much trouble to unhook everything, pull it all off, and then put it back on again. I can't remember when I last washed my hair—maybe last Thursday. I pull it back with an elastic band so it doesn't look that dirty, although my scalp's itchy and it hurts when I run my fingers through it. The blonde streaks have grown out, and there's a dark rim of ratty roots. I haven't bothered with the shower either. It looks cold and forbidding, smells of mold, and the tile floor is caked with crusted clumps of soap scum. Anyway, it's too early when I leave to start messing with the portable heater and searching for a towel that hasn't already been used. Or a razor. I give off a slight odor of rot, the scent of the lost and lonely.

By the time I get back from the clearing, my clothes are sticking to my skin and beads of sweat trickle down my chest and under my arms. At least Sam's happy I'm home. He preens his feathers on my arm, swipes his beak on my pants legs, leaving gelatinous trails of seed and bird spit. When I finally get around to thinking about cleaning up, I'm too tired and then it's almost dinnertime, and why bother because, hey, it's not like I'm going anywhere. The next day, it's the same, and the next and the next. It's been about a week now, and I've stopped going to the clearing. There's no more mystery. The birds are gone.

I guess I'm just like the rest of the forsaken ivory-bill crowd—bewitched and abandoned. Searching for a clue or some reason to keep the faith. I feel as if I've been cheated out of something or even dumped. Forgive me, Father, for I'm not worthy.

❦ ❦ ❦

I can tell my mother's worried, because she's signed me up to start working in the wildlife center after the first of the year, although she's adjusted the schedule so that if I want to continue with my courses, I can. To tell the truth, I'd rather drown than show up at that campus again. Just before I changed my cell phone, Freddy called. Alison naturally told him about my "misleading" resume. He left a message that it's "no big deal—everyone fudges everything, and how about Saturday night?"

"You see?" he said. "I told you I was going to break up with the GF." What a prince. I didn't call him back.

Then there's Tiff. She keeps trying to get me to go with her to the mall, or to the diner, or to a movie. Her treat. We talk on the phone, but she inevitably brings up what happened in the office, going over and over it as if she could've said something else that would've changed my fate. It drives me nuts.

"This thing's eating me alive, I should've realized what was up," she says. "I don't know why I kept insisting you didn't go to college when Alison said you did."

I have to hold myself back from yelling at her, because I know it wasn't her fault, but eventually I just tell her to stop. There's an awkward silence, then she says, "Please don't hate me." Then *I* feel guilty that she feels guilty and we hang up.

Somewhere in the middle of all this, Tiff and her family got good news. Guy Jr. scored a leave for the holidays, so the two of us just dropped the drama and did some last-minute rushing around to make her house look festive. Every year they dig out the ornaments as if they were buried treasures. It's comforting. Almost as if life in their household will never change. Just lots of merry music, good tidings, and cheer to wash away the fuckups of the past year.

Tonight is Christmas Eve, and it's taken the whole day to pull myself together. Tiff volunteered to redo my hair, and I finally had to come clean and tell her about the salon makeover. Franck's assistant had an opening this morning and I grabbed it. I had to wash my hair *before* I went in, that's how bad it was.

When I was a child, Mom hated the idea of a chopped-down fir dying in the living room, and she wouldn't have an artificial one, plus the bulbs used up too much power. But every Christmas Eve we'd drive around looking at all the lit-up houses. We'd turn the radio on and listen to "White Christmas" and "Winter Wonderland" as we'd drive past palm trees and billboards with orangey-bronze girls in bikinis advertising tanning salons, which always seemed crazy in a town where it's sunny three hundred days a year.

At four o'clock Mom and I, loaded down with gifts, homemade cranberry sauce, and a sweet potato casserole, walk over to Tiff's. The night is clean and clear, a lot better than the past few days, where the air particles were the size of shredded wheat. We pass our neighbor's house, which has so many cement sculptures littering the lawn you can hardly see the front door. Standing among the droopy badminton net and old plastic pool covered with leaves are gnomes, dwarfs, birdbaths, and a life-size Abe Lincoln complete with top hat. Tonight the owners have strung little colored fairy lights all over the figurines, and it looks like a miniature golf course.

You can see Tiff's Christmas tree through the window, all dolled up with strands of multicolor bubble lights and drippy silver icicles. The personalized needlepoint stockings are strung across the fireplace, as usual, as if the kids were five and six. Uncle Guy used to make ornaments out of Marlboro's red and white flip-top boxes, but now it's politically incorrect, even for them.

Guy Jr. is in the basement rec room with a buddy playing video games on a new Xbox 360 that Uncle Guy had all set up for him before he arrived. You can hear excited, booming voices echoing down the halls and then gales of laughter mixed with really raunchy swear words.

"Guy, Cassie's here!" Aunt Ethel calls down to him, as she ushers my mom into the kitchen.

I walk down the stairs and see Guy and his friend sitting all tensed up on the chewed-up brown plaid couch, legs wide apart, controllers in their laps, frantically jerking the joysticks up, down, and sideways as if they're two epileptics driving a race car at a hundred miles an hour.

"Fuck! Are you using a sniper rifle, you desperate homo?" screams his friend.

"Head shot! Ha! I don't need a cheap ass sniper to get your nasty, Nazi ass! Instant death—keep talking, keep talking."

"You totally suck—I'm going to blow you the fuck away."

"Shit. I saw that. You're looking at my screen, you cheating pussy!"

"Oh hey, Cassie," Guy Jr. says with a wave, still ramming the joystick up and down with manic finger work. I notice a new tattoo on his biceps that says, "Sacrifice."

"Hey, Guy," I say and give him a peck on the cheek. The screen is bloody as hell with bullet-ridden World War II American soldiers and Nazis. When someone dies, the screen ignites in gushing sprays of crimson. I hear screams of pain and death as figures crawl on their bellies into buildings or trenches, brandishing handguns, grenades, machine guns, and rifles. He introduces me to his friend, Carlos, a jut-jawed, thin-lipped, ropey-armed guy who gives me an unsettled feeling.

Guy Jr. tells me he's playing *Call of Duty II*, a "really hot game." He says there's a bunch of newer Iraq war games—one with an "awesome" aerial view of the Gulf War and cool smart bombs, but he prefers the WWII ones because "we were united against a real enemy—and the whole world didn't hate our guts—you could be a goddamn hero, you know?"

He averts his eyes from the screen for a second, gives me the once-over, and then turns back into the game. "Hey,

Cassie, you look great—just like a model. I mean it. I wouldn't recognize you."

"Well, thanks," I reply, taken aback. I can't possibly say the same thing about him. For one thing, he's thin and drawn, but with a lot more muscles than I remember—like a starving warrior. His skin looks ruddy, rough and red like a bad windburn. Shaved head with spiky hair growing in a little bit on top. His eyes are rimmed with bluish-black circles. The old, engaging, eagerness faded into what looks like hostile resignation.

Guy Jr. always struck me as the sort of kid who, given the right opportunity, might've starred in a daytime soap or something. He had that hulking, sweet-faced charm that always seemed to get him by—people tended to overlook his mistakes or let things slip. I used to imagine him traveling abroad, landing some exotic job—a footloose, glamorous future. Maybe he did too, and that's why he signed up for the reserves. That and the ROTC scholarships. Tiff said they promised him full tuition when he got out.

Christmas Eve dinner started out okay. But as the evening progressed, there was a kind of forced joy about everything—as if it weren't quite the homecoming everyone expected.

Aunt Ethel tries to act as if everything is like it used to be.

"Home is where the heart is, boys," she chirps, as she sets the big turkey bursting with fresh roasted chestnut stuffing on the table. Her face is all powdery and flushed.

"So, son," Uncle Guy says, "how is it over there?" The two boys give each other meaningful looks, and there is something unsettling about Carlos's smile. Almost feral. Guy Jr. ingests a big spoonful of stuffing and then licks the fork.

"The news is just terrible," Aunt Ethel joins in. "I'm so glad you boys are safe and sound."

"Mom, I don't think they want to talk about this," says Tiff.

"It's okay. You kind of get used to the violence. Not a big deal when we drop a mortar anymore," says Guy Jr. offhandedly, his eyes darting around the room like a pinball.

"Yeah. We used to sit around, have these surreal conversations. We'd hear a big *Boom!*"—Carlos laughs, as we jump—"and then make bets what size it was as the shit was still coming in."

Guy Jr. laughs, all nervous energy. His knee is banging against the table leg like a metronome.

"Yeah, was it a 60 or an 80? I got five bucks says it was a 120."

"Isn't there a safe zone? I mean, Jesus Christ," says Tiff.

"Doesn't matter where we go," says Carlos. "Death squads all over the place. Everyone's so paranoid. We sleep with nine-millimeters under our pillows."

"And no one in charge gives a shit," chimes in Guy Jr. "They fly in for an hour, get briefed, and then fly back out. Keep all their asses in a nice safe place. Fucking clueless."

The teapot whistles in the kitchen, and we all fall silent. At this, my mother taps my shoulder and whispers, "I'm not feeling so well, honey. Can you get me some ginger tea?"

My mother hardly ever complains when she doesn't feel well. She'll blame it on chlorinated tap water or Pluto's dwarf planet being killed off in the solar system. But in this case, I think she's just upset. We all thought this would be such a good change for Guy Jr., but sometimes changes are for the worse.

When Uncle Guy gets up to play the piano, Guy Jr. and his friend go back downstairs. My mother carefully lays her gifts under the tree for tomorrow. This year it's seed packages, exotic bulbs, and her own mixture of potpourri with apples and cinnamon sticks. Tiff's already given me my present, a vanilla-scented gift package with perfume, body lotion, and a candle.

"The lady at the makeup counter told me it's virtually impossible for a human being not to like vanilla," Tiff says, as if it's gospel.

The first present Tiff ever gave me, when I was nine years old, was Cutex Pink Chiffon candy pink lipstick with glitter. She was always on the cutting edge of fashion. I gave Tiff a very tasteful and sophisticated black sweater, which she'll wear when I'm around but probably no other time.

I volunteer to help her clean up but tell her that I have to leave right afterward because I need to get my mother home. We're both still reeling from the dinner conversation, and Tiff is unusually quiet.

"Do you think Guy is on something?" Tiff whispers, her face is deflated, almost stricken.

"I don't know, but his friend sure is weird," I say.

"No kidding. It's been so intense around here. They sleep all day, then they wander out in their underwear, and just sit around in the rec room drinking cases of Mountain Dew, smoking cigarettes, and playing video games."

"He's depressed, wouldn't you be?"

Tiff is quiet for a while. We robotically scrape the turkey and stuffing off the plates. She decides to change the subject. "So how are you doing? Feeling any better?"

"Not really."

"You know, I used to think if you just got rid of Frank, then you'd be happy. But you weren't. You keep feeling like you have to prove yourself, and for what?"

"I don't know," I say. "I just wanted a glimpse of the other side and I had it. It was there for me. And then I was exiled."

"I'm so sorry—" Tiff starts to say, but I interrupt.

"It's not about losing the job . . . Really, Tiff."

"Yes, it is."

"No, it isn't. It's about men, birds, life . . . Oh, forget it." I don't have the energy to go into my ivory-bills.

"I wish I could help," Tiff says, with frustration.

"I do too," I say.

My mother and I walk home in silence. The kind of silence that follows a jolt to the senses and can break your heart. It's one of those winter nights when you can see every star in the sky. Even Orion, the warrior, and his glowing belt.

CHAPTER 48

January is supposed to be the season of new beginnings, but I'm still wallowing in the season of regret. A drift of vapor hangs in the canyon air, and even when the sun does peek through, it's smothered by smoggy, discolored clouds. The trees are drooping with half-dead leaves, and the scrub grass that lines the road is brown and crusty.

I can't help thinking what might have been, what could have happened, if only I'd done things differently. After Tiff calmed down a bit about her role in my fall from grace, I brought up once again that I should have just told the truth.

"The thing about the truth is," she said, upon reflection, "you have to pick a version that works."

I answered, "There is no 'version' of the truth."

"Oh, yes there is," she said. "You're smart. You can fix this. Think of something that's believable."

"No, Tiff, there's nothing else I can say."

"Well, for instance, in *CSI* or *Law & Order*, there's always extenuating circumstances."

"Which in this case would be?"

"You wanted the job."

My mother keeps asking me how I'm doing. I'm not sure what to tell her. That I feel like I'm back at square one. That nothing ever changes. You are who you are whether you like it or not. She thinks I've lost my perspective. But I just can't see the possibilities anymore. Maybe you only get one moment in your life that changes everything. That's it. One to a customer.

❦ ❦ ❦

Sometimes to repent, you have to do the thing that frightens you the most. Take the difficult path. Run into the fire.

Just before I started back at the wildlife center, I made a decision. I called up Professor Pearce's private line, mid-morning, and asked if we could talk. There was a pause, which made the adrenaline shoot through my core, and then she said with that imposing British tone, "How about four?"

It's teatime, of course, when I walk into her office, punching that stupid door open for the thousandth time. Alison isn't in—a blessing—and Pearce even smiles as she sits at her desk, pours me a cup of tea in her see-through china, and motions for me to sit in the chair opposite her.

"This is such a shame, my dear," she says, flushing a bit from the rising steam off the cup. (No flask in sight for this little chat.) "I liked you right off the bat and I was so sad to hear—"

"I can't tell you how sorry I am about all this," I interrupt, hardly able to hear her words. "I obviously don't expect my job back, but I wanted you to know that I really didn't intend . . ." The phone drills through the air and Pearce grabs for it in a surprisingly urgent way.

"Have you found out anything?" she intones, looking right past me. There's a long silence as I see her shake her head with exasperation. Now she lets out a long sigh.

"All right, thank you. Yes . . . I'll ring you up later." She hangs up and looks across at me.

"Excuse me for taking that call, my dear, but I've just had such a frustrating conversation with the airlines. Marion and I went to a seminar in Florida last weekend, and I must say we had such a grand time."

I feel as if I've just barged into the wrong courtroom, but I sit at attention, trying to act interested, my stomach churning inside me, gauging the impending doom.

"Everything was so lovely," she goes on. "Interesting lectures, nice hotel, and then we get home and her suitcase arrives and mine doesn't. Of course, my favorite antique bracelet was in the bag. You hear about these things happening, but I always supposed I was different."

Come on already. I'm dying here.

"So, at any rate, I've been calling the lost-luggage department every day, reading them my code numbers, talking to this nice lady and that nice gentleman, and nothing happens. Nothing whatsoever!! How can this be? They keep assuring me it will arrive eventually, but it doesn't. So I ask them, where's the accountability here? It's so perplexing. We did everything right on our end, why can't they take responsibility and just admit they mucked everything up?"

I look at her blankly. I've completely lost my train of thought. I walked in like a schoolgirl, expecting to be expelled, and instead, all I hear about are the fucked-up airlines. Now her tone changes. I'm almost grateful. Ready for the execution. It's swift and efficient.

"If it was up to me," she says, "I'd keep you. But regretfully, I was told to hire a new, qualified applicant after the holidays. As unfair as it is, we require a BA, even for office staff." Thank God she wasn't holier than thou.

I answer that I understand, and if I had to do it over again, I'd tell the truth. There's really nothing more to say on either side. I think she really liked me, but that's beside the point. Or maybe she liked who she thought I was. But I am who she thought I was. Sort of. Stop!

I've known her five months. What did I expect? Maybe if I'd been here longer, she would have fought for me, but I suspect the verdict would've been the same. It's funny, though. Everybody, in the end, is caught up in their own stuff—and all the petty frustrations and aggravations that manage to seep into one's life, no matter how you plan against it. For Pearce, Alison, and the rest of the people in that office, I'm just a little blip in their universe. And now, I'm gone.

CHAPTER 49

I'm back working full-time at the wildlife center and spending less and less time at home.
Sometimes, I take Sam with me, but other
times, when there are a lot of sick birds in the in-
firmary, I worry he'll catch something, so I leave
him behind. I've taken to sneaking past him, but
he always knows.

"Hello, Cassie. Hello. Hello," he screeches.
And then a wolf whistle.

"Listen," I tell him, "don't have a hissy fit, but
I can't take you today. I'll only be gone for a few
hours."

No one who has ever lived with a parrot
doubts for a moment they have human emotions.
Sam lets out a mournful cry, then starts to mutter
to himself like an old man. Parrots are capable of
going into interminable sulks. They want what
they want when they want it, and sometimes it's
just so annoying.

This morning, when he catches me leaving, he
drops into his "last ditch" posture, flopping on

his back, feet up in the air, belly totally exposed. What a drama queen.

He gives me no choice. I casually walk back to the bedroom and open the jar where I keep his treats. My mother wraps them in little silver foils to look like Hershey's Kisses and I try to save them for emergencies. Sam's hearing is acute, and he knows what I'm doing. I hear him jump back onto his dowel and dance around, his foul mood suddenly lifted.

I toss in a few, then open the door to his cage and move it near his perch so he can climb on it during the day. As I walk to the door, I hear him unwrapping the crinkly silver foil with his long toes, and trilling with joy.

I tried not to think about Conner these past three weeks as I drove every morning up the unmarked, rocky trail leading to the wildlife center. Right now, the road is lined with hundred of kennels, crates, and wire cages in anticipation of the busy season, which begins in March. That's the month when mother birds start kicking out their babies from the nest.

The university must be back in session, and I imagine Zack and the rest of the kids who usually sit near me wondering what happened to that oddball lady who used to take classes with them. I'm like that woman who went on a cruise to Mexico and then vanished somewhere between Puerto Vallarta and Baja, and no one knows where. Gee, she was stuffing her face at the big buffet last night—I can't imagine what happened.

Seems everyone is disappearing these days. Tiff was over last night and told me some MPs came knocking on their door looking for Guy Jr. He never showed up back at the base. AWOL.

"I'm glad," Tiff says, with defiance. "No one wanted him to go back anyway."

"But can't he go to jail for this?"

"Only if they find him. Anyway, my dad's already called this lawyer and a shrink who's representing a bunch of other soldiers protesting the war."

"Oh my God."

"The man said we have a pretty good case. Guy has all these allergies, plus migraines and post-traumatic stress syndrome, and he can't sleep worth shit."

"Aren't you supposed to raise this stuff *before* someone goes AWOL?"

"Well, the lawyer did mention that. But they're never going to find him anyway," she says, and then hesitates.

"Cassie, I wanted to ask you a favor. Do you think you could leave your door unlocked for the next few days just in case, you know—would that be, like, a problem?" I can tell she's kind of embarrassed.

"I guess it's all right. I don't usually lock the door—just tell Guy to be careful of Sam and Black Dog."

"Thank you so much."

"Don't worry about it," I answer, and then I think, I'll just add "aiding and abetting" to the rest of my infractions.

CHAPTER 50

It is somewhat ironic that I work in a place that deliberately tries to keep people out. The wildlife center hides itself in an isolated patch of wood deep in the Santa Monica Mountains so people can't just drop off every wounded hawk, owl, possum, and coyote they find lying by the side of the road. We do the same thing with the phones. You can't just call this place and tell them there's a sick owl on your tennis court. The interns censor the calls. We discuss them at the end of the day, and decide who shall live and who shall die. Well, maybe it's not that cut and dried, but it's who we think we can save with our limited resources. Survival of the fittest is a big theme around here. Anyway, God can't be everywhere.

Conner called the wildlife center for the first time a few days ago. An intern took the call and put the message in the pile of nonemergencies. It wasn't until my mother went through the pile that I heard about it.

"Isn't this your professor?" she said to me.

I took the message and told myself I'd call him back when I got home. Then, when I got home, I told myself I'd call him after dinner. And then I fell asleep. The next morning I decided I couldn't do it. Not yet, anyway. Maybe in about ten years.

The second message he left was more specific.

"Cassie, we need to talk about your journals. Please call." He leaves me his cell number again.

So he just wants to send the journals back. I ignore a pang of disappointment. What was I expecting anyway? "Cassie, please come back"? I'll return the call tomorrow morning while he's in class and just leave my address.

I've been at work since six trying to rectify the dumb mistakes made by the interns, such as placing the bunny cages next to the hawks and putting holey towels in a baby bird's cage so it can get its head stuck and strangle itself to death. Now it's eight-twenty. I looked up Conner's schedule and his class should be in full swing. I walk down the road toward the highway, trying to find the spot where my cell works. It's usually right next to the mailbox. I imagine Conner onstage in the auditorium with Ahab, talking about Emerson or Thoreau or cow dung for fuel. I punch in his number.

"Hello?" he says, softly. Shit.

"Oh. Conner. I thought you'd be in class. I was just going to leave you a message."

"Don't hang up," he whispers. Then I hear him tell the class he'll be right back. Double shit. What professor actually answers their cell phone in class?

"Cassie. I need to see you. Why didn't you return my calls?"

"I'm sorry. Really. It's just that I haven't felt like talking."

"Can you meet me tomorrow night?"

"Oh. I don't know, Conner. What for?"

There's a long silence. It's that time of the morning when there's a vicious bite in the air and a raw breeze slams against my body. I look to the sky and wish there was a way to erase the sins of the past. "Okay. Where do you want to meet?"

We settle on a bar near Topanga at seven tomorrow night. I get small waves of trepidation, then focus on something else entirely—like what should I wear.

I race home early from work the next night and notice the door is ajar. My first thought is, maybe Guy's still here with his jittery, juiced-up friend. I don't have time for this. Not that I'm unsympathetic. I just want to shower.

My mind is consumed with playing and replaying the possible scenarios of my upcoming meeting with Conner. What I'll say. What he'll say. How he'll look at me.

I head for my bedroom, throw down my backpack, and start to take off my clothes. Black Dog ambles into the room and nuzzles up to me. I absently pet his neck and then it hits me. It's so quiet, it's frightening. Where's Sam? I run into the living room. My heart is pounding. He's not on his perch. Not in his cage. Not anywhere.

"Sam? Where are you?"

CHAPTER 51

"I heard a kill once, heard it before I saw it. There was a thump, and then a series of hoarse and rasping screams. A hawk had pinned a rabbit to the ground. It all happened so fast and was so close I could hear the beating of wings, like an Indian war drum. When I turned, I saw the rabbit flipped on its back and the hawk's talons piercing its stomach, its hooked beak aimed at the neck. For a moment they were face-to-face. Judas poised and waiting to give Jesus the kiss."

I look around at the group of assorted mourners listening to my story. They don't know where I'm going with this. But, for sure, they think it has something to do with my loved one who's passed. And they're right.

This is my first session with the Topanga Community Grief Counseling Service. I found the card in my bottom dresser drawer with a bunch of other papers related to Frank's demise, and decided it might help with my convalescence. My mother suggested pet grief counseling instead. She said I might offend the other mourners if they knew I was talking about a parrot. But I couldn't bear sitting there hearing someone weep over a kitten or a turtle. Sam was a human.

Last night, I pulled out the book *When God Doesn't Make Sense*. I slowly read it cover to cover. It seemed helpful at the time, but when I closed the book I felt the same way I did before.

So this is what it is. Grief. I am spinning upside down. My stomach in my mouth. My bones rattling around in my body. Everything shattering, dissolving into liquid. I fall asleep and dream he's still with me. I'll wake up and ruffle his soft little feathers, pour his bowl of Cheerios, and discuss the day's events.

They all ask me questions about Sam. How long we were together. They were surprised when I told them twenty years plus. How he died. They think the hawk story is just a symbol of a horrific death. I tell them I can't talk about it— not just yet. I don't say that I found a clump of bright green feathers smeared across the patio. That there were tiny red pinpricks of blood here and there, and it was obvious what happened. Guy Jr. left the door open. Sam flew out in a fright and a hawk got him. Or maybe a coyote, or one of the neighborhood cats. At this point it doesn't matter. I try not to think about these things, because when I do, I can still hear him calling my name.

"I miss him," I tell the group. I listen to the others talk about their grief and think about how strange it is when someone you've shared a life with is gone. Shortly after Frank died, my mother told me things about my father's death I never knew—that she manically sorted through his papers and clothes, turned his pockets inside out, looking for . . . what? Anything that would bring back the familiar— coins, keys, fragments of messages on torn pieces of paper.

But the familiar only deepened her despair, she said, stunting her life, and making everything around her seem sterile and drab. People's smiles lingered too long, flirty couples on the streets embarrassed her and forced her to turn away. She told me she felt gutted, like a fish, and that she had no idea how she would manage on her own. I was sorry that I was too young to help her or even notice.

Now it's my turn with Sam, dealing with the deadweight of disappointment every time I enter the kitchen and seeing that he's not there. There are scratches in the tile on the counter where his cage sat for years, and the wooden trim is gnawed with impressions of beak. I can't walk by the living room window where his new perch stood, and, worst of all, I can still feel the clasp of his long toes and the weight of his body on my shoulder.

I haven't felt like talking to anyone, although I did call up Guy Jr.'s cell phone and leave the message "Fuck you." Then I called back and said, "Fuck you to death." I don't care where he is, or whether he gets caught.

When Tiff heard about Sam, she called to say she talked to Guy Jr. and he told her he was only at my place for an hour, and "never even saw one bird." I didn't have the energy to beat her up about it, so I didn't argue. I guess there are some things in life you can never get to the bottom of, no matter what, and even when you do, the payoff isn't all that great.

My mother cleaned out Sam's cage and put it in the garage. But I didn't want it there. I laid it tenderly in the backseat of my car and took it to the wildlife center. She's been making noises about a hand-fed orphan parrot, and I didn't want her to get any ideas.

When Mom's friend Sylvia called to tell me she was sorry about the death of my pet, I shot back that he wasn't a pet. That he was a creature of superior intelligence. My childhood friend. I grew up with him, and we went through everything together.

It's funny. When Frank died, I was embarrassed because I couldn't grieve. And now I'm embarrassed because I can't stop.

About a week after this whole thing happened, my mother and I bought a free-form driftwood sculpture from an outdoor furniture sale on Pacific Coast Highway, along with a macramé rope hammock. We hooked up the hammock between two big old trees in the backyard and placed the sculpture beside it. That's Sam's Place now, and on a nice day, I fling my legs over the side of the hammock and swing away. A song keeps playing over and over in my head like an elegy.

> *"Pack up all my cares and woe,*
> *Here I go singing low,*
> *Bye Bye Blackbird."*

CHAPTER 52

The night Sam was taken, I was in such a state that I forgot to call Conner until it was too late. By the time I thought of it, it was almost nine, and he probably thought I stood him up. I left a message on his cell that there was a death in the family, and I'd call him when I felt better. He called right back and left a very nice message that he was sorry and to call him anytime.

I drag myself back to work a few days later, spending my first morning running errands, picking up supplies, and releasing an owl stuck in someone's fireplace during their Sunday brunch. As I pull up to the center, I see a familiar figure standing out front talking to my mother. What's Conner doing here? They're deep in conversation, and he's working on my mother the way he works on everybody, holding her gaze, using his hands for emphasis.

"You're here," I say, my eyes riveted on the stack of journals under his arm.

"You weren't easy to find," he says. My mother is looking at both of us, grinning like a fool.

"So sorry to hear about your loss," Conner says, giving me a kiss on the cheek.

"Cassie and that bird were just inseparable," Mom says. "It broke our hearts when we lost him," she adds. I wish she'd leave. Conner looks at me intently, trying to gauge the effect of his presence.

He stands out, as he always does—a figure who dominates any landscape. His whole demeanor seems to ask, "Aren't you impressed I'm here?"

Then Conner tells us about a close friend of his who lost his African gray on the day he left for college. The bird had been with him since he was born and was like a brother to him.

"To this day, my friend can't talk about that bird without tearing up—they were kind of kindred spirits." My mother is enthusiastically nodding yes! like she's at a revival meeting. I give her a look. She gets the hint, makes some excuse, and walks off.

"So how are you *really* doing?" Conner asks me. "Are you okay? Pearce told me you talked to her. I wish you'd come to me first."

"What could you have done?"

"Cassie, I understand why you made up the degree. It's a rigged system. Everyone knows that. It cuts people off before they have a chance. I could've convinced Pearce to fight for you."

"I don't think so. She was pretty firm about it. Anyway, I didn't want to put you or her in that position."

"You should have trusted me." I look at him skeptically. We both know I'm thinking about the ivory-bills.

"Anyway, I have to talk to you about these." He holds out my journals.

"What's there to talk about?" I answer darkly.

"I couldn't put them down." He opens one and begins to read.

" 'The male flies along at eye level only fifteen feet in front of me. When he finally perches on a stump, he holds his feet apart, and leans back on his tail like Black Dog, his wings outstretched. His garish feathers are so black they almost have a purple sheen in the sunlight. Now he's calling to his mate in a soft, intimate way. The otherworldly tone almost alters the state of the female's brain, like a drug.'

"You even quote Keats here, '. . . as though of hemlock I had drunk.' "

"One of my professors loved Keats," I interrupt.

"Well, it's perfect."

Conner puts down that journal and thumbs through another.

"Oh, this part—I liked this part." He begins to read again. " 'It flies with its head and neck outstretched like a wild goose going fast and straight, it doesn't wobble. Another flew along in front of me. I look up and see his bill— from this vantage point it looks the size of a small canoe. They're windblown vagrants, these birds . . .' Bottom line, Cassie, these are fantastic."

"I could have copied it from someone else. Remember?"

"I don't think so. It's your voice . . . your unique observations. I never for a minute thought you copied this."

"Maybe I was just looking at some other bird. Or a woodchuck. Or a ghost. Or nothing."

"Maybe. But when I did some research, reread the bird's history, I kept seeing the same thing over and over again. Everyone who's sighted the ivory-bills, even the ones who got them on film, would go back to the spot and the birds were gone. Poof. There was never any explanation. No one could figure it out. No signs of predators, no signs of mites or disease. The birds just took off. And then there were none."

I notice some of the interns looking at us as they carry a few of the cages into the back. Someone's car is idling noisily in the parking lot, and a few volunteers are driving up the road with some sort of sea rescue tethered to the back of their truck. I take his arm and lead him around back where the stacked-up pens create a wall of privacy.

"Oh, Conner, I don't know why I dragged you into all of this. I'm so sorry."

"Don't be. When you're a scientist, you come across this kind of thing every so often. And you have to make a choice. It's a leap of faith. It's Galileo telling people the earth revolved around the sun when no one could even imagine it, let alone see it. It's Leonardo da Vinci explaining how he could fly. It's Darwin. It's the black hole. It's anything in science that's new or invisible. You just have to choose to believe. And then live with your choice. By the way, nice work on the hawk paper."

"What? How'd you know that?"

"I know the way you talk. I know the offbeat way you describe things. That, and the fact that there was a Post-it stuck in between the pages that said, 'Hey, Zack, hope this helps. Cassie.' " I start to laugh.

"What a lazy slug. He didn't even bother to retype it, or for that matter, remove the Post-it. So you knew all this when you made that big announcement to the class?"

"Of course, that's why I asked you on the bird trip. I thought maybe one of you might come clean. I was thinking of saying something, but then it just didn't seem that important." He looks at me with quiet intensity.

"So you believe me?" I press.

"It's not important whether I believe you. Don't you get it?"

"So you don't believe me."

"I didn't say that."

"Well, what are you saying?"

"I'm saying it's possible."

"Okay. Got it," I snap.

"Cassie. Come on. Don't be so dramatic."

"I'm not being dramatic. No one has *ever* called me dramatic."

"Well, you aren't being reasonable. Who cares about the fucking birds! I just want to see you. Don't be stupid."

And then I simply walk away.

CHAPTER 53

Thoreau went to Walden because he wished to "live deliberately and face the essential facts of his life." And from all I've learned this past year, it gave him peace and soothed his soul. Okay, so it's a romantic notion, going to an isolated cabin in the woods, but right now, it's what appeals to me the most.

As luck would have it, my mom's friend Sylvia offered me her cabin for as long as I want. She won't use it until spring, when bird-watching season starts up again. The place is two hours north of LA on the far end of Lake Arrowhead, a couple miles from the nearest neighbor. You take the San Bernardino Freeway all the way to the end, stop at the 76 Station, put chains on your tires, and slowly snake your way up the two-lane US Forest Service road.

There's no electricity or phone up here, and cells don't work. A big fireplace provides the heat and the appliances run on propane. When it gets dark you have to light all the candles and keep flashlights by your bed. No noise, no neighbors to speak of, but you can hear dogs or coyotes barking in the distance and the occasional grinding motor of a snowmobile. It's just the kind of place I wanted, the kind of place you go to when you don't know what to do next.

I stock up on provisions—healthy foods my mother insisted would give me new energy and enthusiasm. At the last minute, as I'm actually getting into the car, I glance down at Black Dog moping in the corner. What the hell, I throw him in too. Every living creature can use a week in the wild.

I don't reach the cabin until almost ten. Sylvia had a guy from the diner leave the key under the mat and the place was stocked with fresh water, firewood, and a list of instructions on how to turn on the propane oven and open the fireplace flue. First thing I do is build a fire and wait for the place to warm up. I light a few candles, put them on the windowsill, and look around. There's an old bookcase loaded with yellowed paperbacks, box games, and several books on local hiking trails. A banged-up guitar leans against the wall. Good thing my mother isn't here or we'd be singing "Michael Row the Boat Ashore" and "Blowin' in the Wind" ad nauseam.

The warped wood-plank floor slants down slightly as if the cabin were built without a foundation. It feels a bit like a fun house in an amusement park, a little unsteady when you walk. Sylvia told me to only use the propane lantern for reading, so I set it carefully on the bench by the wall. Meanwhile Black Dog hasn't moved from the front door since we arrived, so I decide to take him out for a short walk before bed. It's pitch-black outside and he's shaking, nervous, and glued to my side. I don't get more than fifteen paces when he turns around, races to the car, and stands there barking.

"We're not going home!" I tell him out loud, and my voice echoes across the lake. I can't imagine what kind of life this dog must have led before he barged in on me that stormy night. I finally give up and go back in the cabin, Black Dog trotting in behind me. I'm dead tired. I decide to clean up and get in bed. I look around. Uh-oh. Where's the bathroom? I notice a toilet seat hanging on a hook near the fireplace. Not a good sign. Sylvia forgot to mention this tiny detail. I look outside and about fifty paces north is a three-sided shack. Shit. Literally.

I wash my face in the kitchen, brush my teeth, putting off the inevitable. Then I bundle up, put on my snow boots, steel myself, and grab the warm toilet seat. Here goes. The path to the outhouse hasn't been shoveled for months. I take one step on the crunchy surface of the snow, sink down to my knees, and plow through the snowdrifts until I reach the outhouse. The door is half open, seems to be frozen that way. I throw the toilet seat on the open pit and sit there staring at the shadowy mountain peaks. I notice an old magazine on the floor which I wouldn't touch for a million dollars.

When I finally get back to the cabin, Black Dog is beside himself. He greets me as if I've been gone for ten days. We end up side by side on the iron-framed cot, with Black Dog cowering under the comforter every time he hears an owl or coyote. Neither one of us gets that much sleep.

The next morning, I make a cup of coffee and look at some of the photos on the wall. There's an old group shot of Sylvia with her ex-husband hanging by the door, taken maybe twenty years ago or so. She looks like a retro version of a Scandinavian flight attendant—blonde, flippy hair, full makeup, some kind of red and white suit. Her ex looks like a lumberjack with full beard and flannel shirt. What an odd couple they must have been. Now she has long dark hair flecked with gray, like my mom, and I don't think I've ever seen her dressed in anything but jeans and a T-shirt.

I sit down on one of the wide wooden steps leading from the porch and warm my hands on the mug. The sky is overcast, smudge-gray, and Black Dog is still a bundle of nerves. He stands at attention, ears pinned flat back, then practically jumps in my arms when a garden snake pops its head out of the stuffing of an old armchair on the porch.

I'd planned to take a morning hike around the lake, make lunch, nap, and then drive to the diner around four to call my mother. But I don't really get myself going until after eleven and, by then, the weather has turned bleak. A nasty, icy snow fueled by an arctic wind gusts in my face when I stick my head out the door, so I decide I'd better just stay in. I put more wood in the fireplace, pull out my Bicycle deck, and deal a few games of solitaire.

I don't know why my mother likes this game. It's frustrating and boring. You can't win unless you cheat, and if you cheat it's no fun. Now I have to go to the bathroom again. I've stopped drinking water and coffee. I glance out at the storm. I'm holding out for as long as I can.

I pull out my nature books and start to read. Conner's hushed warm voice reverberates in my head. I can't stop thinking about him. Or about the fight. He called me stupid, but it *could* have been just an expression. The way Sam used to call me dumbfuck. Sam. Now I'm truly miserable. The snow is coming down in icy sheets. The temperature has plunged and the windchill factor must be below zero. I wonder if there's any booze in this place.

I find a bottle of vodka in the freezer, as if Sylvia needed a freezer. Black Dog's still restless, and now he's digging at something stuck in the corner of the planked wood floor, scratching the hell out of it. So I give him some kibble and pour myself a mountain-hearty shot. I'm thinking of switching it around. Mellow him out a bit. Okay. The time is now.

I grab the bottle of vodka, hitch the toilet seat over my shoulder like a designer bag, and head out into the storm. Not so bad, considering. When I get back, I pull off my wet clothes, crawl into bed, and listen to the ancient pines banging against the roof. Black Dog has finally relaxed enough to lie down in front of the fireplace. It's freezing cold, even with the fire, and the shadows of the flames are dancing like wood nymphs on the wall.

I take another swig of vodka and look around the room. The place is spare except for a row of coat hooks by the door and a mirror next to the cot, where I can see my reflection.

There's an old myth that the world was once divided into two kingdoms. The kingdom of mirrors and the kingdom of men. The inhabitants looked very different from each other but were at peace and could travel freely back and forth between the two worlds. However, at one point in history, the mirror people invaded the kingdom of men. After a fierce battle, they were beaten back, and their punishment was to become imprisoned in their world and turned into reflections. I remember the story ends with the hope that someday, the mirror people will break the curse and become individuals again.* Wouldn't that be something.

.

*Jorge Luis Borges, *The Book of Imaginary Beings*.

CHAPTER 54

I fall into a restless sleep, awakening several times during the night. The next morning I get up at dawn, add more wood to the fire, throw on my parka over my flannel nightgown, and go outside. The sky is blue glass, so clean and sharp it could slice right through you, and there's the sound of a million songbirds across the lake. The air is fragrant with the smell of spring, even though it's the middle of winter. It's a perfect morning. Even Black Dog is cheerful and frisky.

I decide to take a morning hike and head toward the steep hill behind the cabin. The snow looks like fluffy white bunny fur and there's an eddy of wind sweeping across the metallic sheen of the lake. The bright face of the water reflects the pines as Black Dog and I walk in silence for what seems like hours.

When we get back, the cabin is quiet and washed in a soft morning light. I shake the heavy snow off my boots and kick them off just inside the door. My face is damp with sweat and my leg muscles ache from the strain of my rapid descent.

I sit down on the couch and stare at nothing as Black Dog settles in the corner and falls asleep, his labored breathing growing steady as he sinks into a doggy trance. Now he's dreaming—you can actually see an animal dream. He lets out little yelps, his eyes roll under his eyelids, his nose twitches, and his paws move in a phantom chase. With Black Dog, he's probably running away from some imaginary confrontation. Or maybe not.

Maybe he's dreaming about a five-course feast. Wieners, whipped cream, steak bones. Maybe it's a full Kleenex box to tear apart. Now his tail is thumping. He's happy about something. Maybe his face is craned out the window of a car, his ears twirling like pinwheels in the breeze. He's contemplating a run on the beach, a roll in the sand. A belly rub. He loves celebrations. Tearing the wrapping paper off gifts. Maybe he's dreaming of birthdays, Christmas, and the Fourth of July. No. Forget that. The fireworks would scare him to death.

What I love about dogs is that it's all so simple. They know what makes them happy. The professor in my philosophy class said that this is what has driven Western civilization for thousands of years—figuring out what makes man happy. The ancient Greeks believed it was all about fate—whether the gods smiled on you or not. Aristotle and Plato considered it a state of perfection, almost impossible to achieve. The early Christians believed man could only be happy in heaven. The Enlightenment challenged that theory—man can be happy here on earth, as long as he is holy, artistic, brilliant, and a lot of other things most people aren't. The Romantics insisted it was all about your senses—being in love, getting high, drinking good wine. And then, along came Freud, the downer, who said man will *never* be happy. I don't believe that. Frank used to drive through a tollbooth, throw the smiling guy a couple bucks, and say, "What's he so fucking happy about?"

I have a recurring image of my mother in Joshua Tree telling me that on any given night you can look through our galaxy, see another galaxy, and then another one after that, on and on until infinity. It's the closest thing to happiness I've ever seen—at that moment, my mother was completely content, doing exactly what she wanted.

I can hear snowplows in the distance. If I wait another hour or so, I won't even need chains on my tires. I'm going home.

Just before I leave, I run back into the cabin and water down the vodka to keep the level the same. I'll send Sylvia a nice plant.

CHAPTER 55

When I get home, I sit down at my computer and sign up for two winter quarter night classes—English lit and Philosophy 240.

Then I decide to see Conner tomorrow afternoon. I leave the wildlife center early and get to school in time for his four o'clock lecture.

The afternoon sun is filtering through the length of the tall, narrow windows as I climb the stairs to Conner's class, and I can see my reflection through the glass—maybe one of the mirror people come to life. The deliberate walk, the boots, the scholarly-looking demeanor. To tell you the truth, I don't recognize her.

I look at the faces around me as the kids file in the auditorium and settle in their seats—the same assortment of goatees, cracked lips, fingernail biters, baggy pants, laceless sneakers, and blank expressions. A few shuffle around, looking for their friends, shifting from foot to foot as if waiting for a bus. Others, mostly a fresh new lot of eager, clean-cut coeds, are headed up front where Conner awaits and he doesn't disappoint. He offers them the facts with the same spellbinding digressions and effortless showmanship, drifting from subject to subject, and the class just drifts along with him. Myself included.

Conner's subject this afternoon is the effect of global warming on animal behavior, specifically, why bears have stopped hibernating in the winter. I find it hard to get a sense of how much time has passed as I sit there in the shadows in the highest row. It actually occurred to me at one point while he was speaking that, when I was in the cabin, I thought I saw a bear in the distance and what was he doing there? He was supposed to be curled up in a cave somewhere, burning through his layers of fat.

"This may be one of the strongest signals yet how climate change is affecting the animal kingdom. Bears are supposed to sleep through the winter, losing up to 40 percent of their body weight," Conner says as he starts to climb the stairs.

"Spain's bear population has completely stopped hibernating. We cannot prove this is caused by global warming, but this year was one—" He sees me and stops. The class is quiet.

"Excuse me," he says to the class. "I was momentarily distracted . . ."

He continues climbing the stairs toward me with an expression of deep concentration on his face. I notice he has a day's growth of beard and mussed-up hair. I also notice that his jacket is sitting awkwardly on his shoulders, the collar agape, but I resist a sudden and surprising urge to straighten it out and smooth down his hair.

"As I was saying, this year has proven to be one of the warmest on record . . . Okay. That's it for today."

Kids are looking at their watches, surprised. The class has twenty minutes left. A few of them feebly raise their hands but don't push it, as the majority stand up and trample past them. Conner smiles unapologetically and continues up the stairs until he reaches my row.

He clambers into the next seat, slumps down, and considers me for a long second. There's a slight cynical edge to his expression—a tilt of his chin. I feel exposed and control the urge to fly out of there and never come back.

"I called you," he says. "Twice."

"I know."

"You didn't call me back."

"My cell didn't work where I was and . . . I don't know. I just wanted to talk in person."

"Your mother told me you were up in some cabin. Like Thoreau, huh?"

"More along the lines of Sylvia Plath, except my stove was propane and not gas."

"Very funny, Cassie." There's an unexpected tenderness to his voice. Whatever emotions I anticipated—anger, impatience—are gone. He grins.

"Every time I see you I feel like I need a cigarette. Why is that?"

"I annoy you?" He puts his hand on my neck and starts playing with my hair.

"You make me crazy." He kisses me so gently it knocks the wind out of me. "Elusive, like your damn birds."

But we don't talk about them as we make our way across campus, between the ivy-covered buildings, down the grassy path to the red brick courtyard where I'd first seen him. Past the students lounging on their backpacks, reading novels in the shade of massive elms, the sunlight-speckled patios. I can feel the warmth of his body next to me, hear him talking in that tender and ironic tone, and, as I look around, all I can think is, well, here I am.

$\mathcal{E}$ p i l o g u e

Sometimes, when I'm driving home from the university, the sun reflected as a purple slash across the Pacific, the gulls crying out their sweet, plaintive calls, I look to the mountains and think about my birds. Every now and then, I wish there were a way I could go back in time and see them again, the quiet magic, the freedom, the endless mysteries. But then, I think about my life now, my future unfolding like heavenly grace, and I know that my destiny lies somewhere else.

One more semester and I'll have my degree. It's been a struggle with our schedules and moving to a new house in the canyon. Ahab and Black Dog sleep in the kitchen, side by side, like salt and pepper shakers. I guess you'd have to say we have an ordinary life, and I like it. It's comforting to know what comes next, day after day, lying in bed beside him at night, and listening to the familiar sounds of traffic way off in the distance. Knowing that he calls me when he gets there, or when he's on his way home, or if he's late or stuck in traffic and just wants to hear the sound of my voice, the way I want to hear his.

When we go out, which isn't that often, my mother comes over to take care of our daughter. They read myths, look at shooting stars, and she tells her stories of Philomela, who was turned into a nightingale, and the birds who were believed to be messengers of Zeus. I even caught Mom in the backyard one night showing her a footprint that looked "suspiciously like Bigfoot."

Once in a while, I still get those urges to get up at dawn, pull on my boots, and venture deep in the woods to my secret clearing. I'd settle down in my spot, pull out my journals, and visit with my little darlings. But somewhere, deep down inside me, a thought creeps into my head.

I hear it as a whisper. I hear it as a warning. Maybe the birds were never really there at all.